"What aren't you telling me, Grant?"

Beth asked warily.

Something in her voice caused him to turn around and stare at her for a long time. She flushed and shifted.

"What is it? Tell me."

"All right. The case against the guy I told you about is airtight. Not only did the Marshal's office recover the plates he was using to make the funny money, but we have an eyewitness who saw him operating the equipment."

"So what's the problem?" She pressed on.

"The problem is the big guys, the bozo's bosses, are really angry." Grant tried hard to make his tone light. "Consequently, there's been a contract put out on the eyewitness."

"Who's the eyewitness?" He could hear the edge in Beth's voice.

He shove his hands in the back pockets of his jeans, his jawline rigid. "Me."

Dear Reader,

The hits just keep on coming here at Intimate Moments, so why not curl up on a chilly winter's night with any one of the terrific novels we're publishing this month? American Hero Duke Winters, for example, will walk right off the pages of Doreen Roberts's *In a Stranger's Eyes* and into your heart. This is a man with secrets, with a dark past and a dangerous future. In short—this is a man to love.

The rest of the month is just as wonderful. In *Diamond Willow* one of your favorite authors, Kathleen Eagle, brings back one of your favorite characters. John Tiger first appeared in *To Each His Own* as a troubled teenager. Now he's back, a man this time, and still fighting the inner demons that only Teri Nordstrom, his first love, can tame. Terese Ramin's *Winter Beach* is also a sequel, in this case to her first book, *Water From the Moon*. Readers were moved by the power of that earlier novel, and I predict equal success for this one. Two more of your favorites, Sibylle Garrett and Marilyn Tracy, check in with, respectively, *Desperate Choices* and *The Fundamental Things Apply*. Sibylle's book is a compelling look at an all-too-common situation: a woman on the run from her abusive ex-husband seeks only safety. In this case, though, she is also lucky enough to find love. Marilyn's book is something altogether different. A merger of past and present when a scientific experiment goes wrong introduces two people who never should have met, then cruelly limits the time they will have together, unless . . . You'll have to read the book to see how this one turns out. Finally, welcome new author Elley Crain, whose *Deep in the Heart* is a roller-coaster ride of a story featuring a divorced couple who still have an emotional tie they would like to deny, but can't.

In coming months look for more great reading here at Silhouette Intimate Moments, with books by Paula Detmer Riggs, Rachel Lee (the next of her Conard County series), Marilyn Pappano and Ann Williams coming up in the next two months alone. When it comes to romance, it just doesn't get any better than this!

Leslie Wainger
Senior Editor and Editorial Coordinator

DEEP

IN

THE

HEART

Elley Crain

Silhouette® Intimate Moments®

Published by Silhouette Books New York

America's Publisher of Contemporary Romance

SILHOUETTE BOOKS
300 East 42nd St., New York, N.Y. 10017

DEEP IN THE HEART

ISBN: 0-373-07478-6

First Silhouette Books printing February 1993

Printed in the U.S.A.

ELLEY CRAIN

is the pseudonym used by the writing team of Carol Mendenhall and Elyse Allen. Elyse grew up one of six children on three hundred acres of South Texas brushland. When she isn't busy writing, she's busy teaching high school English and watching her two daughters at athletic events. Romance has always been a part of her life—from her honeymoon in Jamaica to candlelight dinners—and she views writing romances as a natural extension of the things she loves.

Carol is married, with two very active sons who think it's great that Mom has finally gotten one of her "love books" published. Outside of reading and writing romances, she enjoys scuba diving and confesses that she writes romances because "I fell in love on a blind date and still feel those special tingles when my husband looks at me."

To Emma: mentor, teacher and trusted friend. Thank you. And to Paul and Jobert for sharing her with us.

Chapter 1

"I'd rather be anywhere than here."

The thud of a beer bottle landing on the polished wooden bar accented Grant Stephens' remark. *Anywhere but Douglas, Texas, to hear Red Saunders' will read. Anywhere but here, where memories of her were as thick as fog billowing through a winter morning and as suffocating as heat scorching through a summer afternoon.*

Tom Wilson, sitting on the stool next to Grant, swiveled to survey the crowd that had gathered in the room. "Not me," he said. "I'm glad I'm right here. I guess in the ten years you've been gone, you've seen lots more excitement than this."

Grant grunted an incomprehensible reply. True, he had seen lots of things and been lots of places, but he wasn't sure he would describe any of what he had seen or experienced as exciting.

"Well, we haven't!" Tom exclaimed. "This is a pretty big shindig for us. This little ol' town has never seen a will

reading where the entire town was invited." Tom took a
swallow from the tall beer bottle and nodded his head.
"Yep, old buddy, this is a first for Douglas, Texas."

"I'm not sure about a historical moment," Grant
drawled, "but it sure looks like the townspeople took Red's
dying request serious. All of 'em are showing up."

Tom tapped Grant on the shoulder. "Let's go sit down
front. I want to hear every word out of Shorty's mouth."

Grant picked up his beer and followed Tom as he meandered from the bar to the front row of chairs that had been
set up especially for the reading of the will.

"Everyone thinks they're going to get a piece of his es-
tate." Tom flagged the bartender. "Besides, what else is
there to do around here on a Thursday afternoon?"

"Yeah, right." Grant also studied the crowd that had
gathered in expectation of cashing in on Red Saunders' departure. Red would have loved it. There were people in here
who hadn't spoken to him in years, probably since he'd built
the Longneck Palace five years ago.

Grant had only gotten sketchy reports from his sister
about all the pulpit banging that had gone on while the bar
was under construction. The Ladies' Circle had direly predicted that the opening of a bar in their fair city would fill
the town with loose women and alcoholics. Well, he didn't
know about the women, but he knew they didn't have an
AA chapter. That was too obvious, too open, for this town.
Secrets were the backbone of the community, gossip the
main channel of communication.

Red had played right into that with this will reading at the
bar. No one knew what the will said. Who would get all
Red's money? His land? Who would get this bar?

Tom waved to someone in the back of the bar and then
winked conspiratorially at Grant. "We're all particularly
interested in what he's leaving *her.*"

As Tom's words died, Grant turned his head to see the "her" who had just pushed open the door of the tavern, letting in a rush of cold air. The atmosphere in the wood-paneled room crackled with electricity. His body tensed.

Beth Channing Stephens walked in.

He watched as she nodded demurely to Shorty, the lawyer in charge, and mumbled something too low for Grant to hear. She turned to look for a seat in the crowded room. Her eyes glanced around, then collided with Grant's. She sucked in her breath and clutched her purse as if it were a security blanket.

"Come sit over here, Beth. We saved you a seat." Tom scooted over and made room for her between him and Grant. He patted the chair. "Come on. We want to get started."

Grant watched her look around the room. *She's trying to find another open seat,* he thought. He knew she'd come up empty when she took a deep breath and stepped toward them.

Her face is flushed, Grant mused. Ten years. After all that time, one look from her still made his blood boil. In his most honest moments, Grant could admit that one of the reasons he was here was about to sit down next to him. He'd said "no" when lawyer Shorty Bonds first contacted him about coming to these proceedings. His instinct for survival had kicked in. But when Shorty had spouted something about Beth's future being at stake, he'd packed his bag.

Not for her, he'd told himself. He'd done it for himself. He'd needed to prove she couldn't get to him, couldn't still make him tighten with want. So far, his experiment had failed. He still wanted her.

They'd been babies, really, when they'd married, and their physical attraction to each other had been so consuming that Grant thought he'd die without her. But her father, Martin Channing, had made it clear to him one day that he would never be able to take care of Beth in the manner to which she was accustomed or that she deserved. Channing had made him see that to really prove his love for Beth, Grant had to get out of her life forever.

He noticed many things about her as she reached Tom's side. The years had done little to diminish her elegant beauty, while accentuating her classic lines. Her high cheekbones were more pronounced than they had been ten years ago. The extra pounds of adolescence had disappeared, replaced by a mature sleekness. Her golden hair was shorter than when they had been together. It just grazed the top of her shoulders and hung in soft waves around her face. Her conservative, dove-gray suit looked out of place in this country bar with its neon beer signs but it did nothing to hide the alluring lines of her figure.

All of this Grant cataloged with a glance. When he felt her shoulder brush his as she finally sat down, his body reacted, remembering all the other times she had touched him. Damn, his entire life as a federal marshal had been spent hiding his feelings from people, and now, at just one grazing touch, he was about to lose it all. And over a woman he'd walked away from ten years ago. His ex-wife, Elizabeth Channing Stephens. He made himself look straight ahead, pretending to ignore her. But she made that impossible when she turned and said softly, "Grant."

He faced her and felt the full impact of those hypnotic blue eyes, cloudy now with sorrow.

"Beth."

One word, that was all? He'd practiced speech after speech, intending to deliver something stinging and memorable, and all that had come out was her name. Like an anthem, the anthem of a fool, he thought. He forced his attention back to the front.

He knew Tom and everyone else in this small Texas town would take notice of their both being here tonight and gossip about the meeting for weeks. After all, it had been ten years....

He could hear them clucking over coffee and saying, "She always was the classier of the two—never could see what she saw in him."

"Well, he was the best football player this town ever produced."

"Her daddy sure hated them being together."

"Like should stay with like. She was sorry she married a poor boy—ran right home to Daddy."

"We never did find out why he hightailed it out of town so quick after their divorce. And there's something strange about her leaving town just a year later."

"Well, they're both back now."

Just thinking about the gossip and small-town attitudes in this town made Grant antsy to get out. Beth had always been sensitive to what the townspeople were saying about him being from the wrong side of the tracks. He comforted himself with the fact that he was leaving town tomorrow. He still hadn't figured out why in hell Red had wanted him here. They hadn't been buddies in school. Classmates, yes— buddies, no. In fact, Red had always been a nuisance, panting after Beth.

Tom broke into Grant's reverie when he leaned in front of Beth and said, "Here it comes."

Grant's gaze followed Tom's, and he found himself looking at Shorty Bonds, who was in charge of this circus. Grant couldn't believe the three-piece-suit in front of the assemblage was the same Samuel "Shorty" Bonds who had cried if you looked cross-eyed at him while they were growing up. For Pete's sake, he'd reported Tom and Grant to the Douglas High principal when he saw them bring a Brahman heifer into the girls' locker room early one morning. Yes, times and people had changed, Grant decided. He snapped to attention when he heard Shorty say, "Red, as we all know, was not an ordinary guy."

Heads nodded, and Grant thought he even heard a few "amens" in the room. He felt Beth shift in her chair, and his eyes strayed to her profile. She was crying softly into a linen handkerchief. The elusive scent of the perfume she always wore played through his senses. He wanted to drill a hole into her mind and do a quick scan. Could she sense the tension in his body? Could she feel his interest in her? She'd always been able to when they were married. Had the years changed that?

He willed her to look up at him, but she had stopped crying and was staring at Shorty, who had moved to stand in front of Grant, forcing his attention back to the proceedings. "Red didn't want this to be just a run-of-the-mill will reading—"

Grant couldn't help but smile as he glanced around at the group of cowboys with their straw hats pushed back on their heads and their booted feet stretched out in front of their chairs. Many were leaning their seats against the wall under neon signs and sports posters. It was an odd choice of decor, but so like Red. A huge No Smoking sign hung down in back of the bar. This wasn't an ordinary bar, and Grant figured it made sense that the will reading would be no different.

"So, instead of me reading the will," Shorty announced, "we're all going to watch it."

The crowd gasped and then fell silent. Shorty motioned to Billy, and the young bartender went into the back room and rolled out a television with a built-in VCR.

"Got this special for tonight," Billy proudly announced.

After a long drag of beer, Tom asked, "What are you telling us, Shorty?"

"Red videotaped his will. He's going to tell you himself what he wants you to know."

Grant, forgetting the years between them, turned to Beth and said, "That's typical of Red. Remember, when he gave the graduation speech, how he pulled that black garter belt out of his robe, as an example of what would be part of our future?"

Beth looked at him as if surprised that he'd addressed her, then smiled wanly. "Yes, I remember. The principal almost fainted in front of the whole town."

His focus on Beth, Grant flashed back to graduation. He ignored the dozens of conversations that vibrated throughout the room and only saw her in her cap and gown, floating up to him after getting her diploma and kissing him on the lips in front of everyone. After startling those around them with her brazenness, she'd winked and gone back to her seat. Grant smiled at the recollection. She'd been so embarrassed after her brave show, and he was sure she'd caught hell from her father.

Suddenly he frowned. All show, that was what she'd always been. And he doubted if she'd changed. He blinked and found Beth staring at Shorty again, unmoving, oblivious to everyone and everything else.

"I'm not starting the tape until everyone is quiet," Shorty announced, wiping the sweat off his forehead with a blue checkered handkerchief, reminding Grant of that nerdy kid of years ago. "Now, calm down, y'all."

"Show some respect," Tom bellowed.

Silence eventually won. Everyone settled down, and Shorty pushed the Play button.

Before the picture focused, the song "All My Exes Live in Texas" blared through the speakers. The people in the room looked at each other and smiled. Grant's chuckle mingled with Beth's. Red was a character, even after the end. What a shame he'd died so young, denying the town the experience of Red as an old, crusty curmudgeon. A smile still touched Grant's lips when the face of the only real eccentric he'd ever known came on the screen.

Red Saunders lounged in an old rocker in his den, holding a glass filled with what looked like whiskey. Except for the fact that his features were thinner than Grant remembered, he looked the same. His Western outfit was right out of a John Wayne movie, leather vest and all. Red took a long swig of his drink before he started.

"Surprised you, didn't I? Thought you'd seen the last of me." He shook his head. "I tell you, modern technology is something, isn't it?"

Grant couldn't believe it. It was as if Red was looking right at him. This was too spooky, he thought, leaning forward.

"I'm glad you could make it." Red's green eyes looked straight at Grant before they shifted to where Beth was sitting. "And I knew you'd be here. You were always here when I needed you."

Beth's composure collapsed. "Oh, Red," she sobbed, her voice piercing through Grant with her special quality, that warm, bedroom-husky sound.

He heard the slight catch as she stifled another sob. What did Red mean? *She was always there when he needed her!* Needed her in what way? Grant knew the way *he* had always needed her, and it wasn't a platonic, glad-to-see-you way. He had needed her—*still* needed her—in the most elemental way a man could need a woman. Grant realized his body had coiled tensely again, and he compelled himself to relax and his eyes to focus on Red.

On-screen, Red's eyes left Beth, and he glanced around the room. Red smiled, and Grant knew he was having a big laugh on the group wherever he was now.

Silence shrouded the bar with an eerie heaviness. Expectancy clung to everyone's breath.

"It's like he's right here with us," a man whispered.

"This ain't normal." Billy shook his head and slid back behind the bar as if he were hiding.

Grant watched Red lean back in his rocker, and he heard him say, "I was going to do the routine of 'sound mind and body,' but I figure both parts are far from sound by this time," he said. "I never was right in the head, according to most of you folks out there."

Neighbor conferred with neighbor, agreeing with Red. Loud talking almost drowned out the video.

Beth stood up, causing the room to go quiet. "Will you people hush! Keep your childishness to yourselves for once." She sat back down and sighed.

Grant stared at her in surprise, grinned, then leaned toward her. "You tell 'em." He was going to add that it was refreshing to see she wasn't as meek as he remembered her, but she stopped that statement with a don't-press-me look.

Red started the bequests. "I'm giving my '57 Chevy to Delores—a beauty as well as a beautician. She deserves it. We had some great times in that old car."

Delores Ortiz, sitting with a cowboy at the back of the room, laughed lustily.

Grant glanced at the attractive but overly made-up woman and remembered how she and Red had maintained an on-again, off-again relationship that began in high school and continued until Red graduated and left for college. Delores had already been working in a local beauty shop back then. Today her dark hair was stylishly tousled, and her generously endowed figure was packed in a tight Western-style shirt and even tighter jeans.

"And to Tom Wilson—"

"Here it comes," Tom whispered loudly. "I only hope it won't embarrass me."

"—I bequeath all my guns and my truck."

"All right!" Tom whooped.

"I know you don't hunt, Tom. That's why you're getting the guns. I also know how much you appreciate a well-balanced firearm. Use them only on those beer cans of yours."

"Don't worry about that, I'm gonna shoot every tin can in the county with those guns," Tom vowed.

"And to Billy, I leave—"

Grant listened with only half his mind. He smiled when Red gave Billy the bar, making him promise to keep it the way it was, with an emphasis on it being a nonsmoking establishment. He chuckled along with everyone else when Red donated his Santa Claus suit to the church, for the children's Christmas Eve celebration. His senses sharpened when he heard Red say, "And now to the big stuff—all my land plus my house with everything in it."

Red scanned the room over the top of his drink as if he were actually surveying who was there. He took a sip, effectively heightening the dramatic tension in the bar.

Grant leaned forward, for some reason dreading what was to come. He glanced at Beth. She looked composed.

"There is one person in this world who has meant more to me than anyone else. But I can never think of her without thinking of someone with her, so I'm going to treat them as one and give everything else I own to Grant and Beth Stephens."

The room erupted in chaos. A chair crashed to the floor as its occupant leapt to his feet. A drink was overturned on one of the tables, and all those gathered around it had to scatter out of the way to keep the amber liquid from staining their britches. Shouts and cries and gasps punctuated the air.

"No," Beth whispered. "You can't do that."

"Hell." Grant stood up.

Shorty turned off the VCR. "Simmer down, folks. There's more on this tape—some conditions."

"I don't care what the conditions are." Grant spoke sharply to Shorty. "I don't want any of his land, and I damn sure don't want his house."

"You can't give it away," Shorty said, taking another swipe at his forehead.

"I just did."

"If you don't take it, Beth can't have it, and vice versa."

"What!" Grant's voice cracked like a whip through the tense atmosphere of the room.

"Just listen to the rest of the tape."

Shorty bent to start the machine again, but Beth's plea stopped him. "Do we have to finish this right now? Here?"

"I'm afraid so," Shorty answered. "Red wanted to avoid gossip. He wanted everyone to hear the terms, so they'd know."

"Know what?" Grant's stomach dropped. He had a feeling his world was going to spin out of control in the next few minutes. A world that he had spent the past ten years putting into careful order.

"I think I'd better let Red explain this." Shorty pushed the button. "Sit down, Grant."

Grant resumed his seat but sat ramrod stiff, on guard now.

Red's voice picked right up. "Well, I guess everybody's screaming and carrying on now." He smiled and hoisted his glass in a toast. "God, I hate to miss this."

"Get on with it, you sorry excuse for a human being," Grant muttered.

"Listen closely, Grant... Beth. Here are my conditions." Red dropped all pretense of the down-home cowboy and became serious. "If one of you doesn't want this bequest, both of you forfeit. You cannot sell out to each other unless you have both lived on the ranch for one year straight."

"Shorty, I don't want to hear any more." Beth stood abruptly, stepped over Grant's feet and walked briskly toward the door.

Grant watched, paralyzed for a second, before he grabbed his jacket and followed her out.

"Damn it! Wait, Beth!" he commanded her retreating back.

When she didn't turn to face him, he hurled after her, "You can't run from this, too."

She dug her heels in and spun around.

"What do you mean, 'run from this, too'? I'm not the one who ran out of town ten years ago. That's your style, not mine." She jabbed a slim finger against his chest.

Grant stepped back, propelled by her vehemence. Her blazing eyes and set mouth screamed her anger at him. He couldn't remember ever seeing her this upset, even when they had fought about the divorce.

"What's the matter?" Grant lowered his voice. "I'm sure we can get the will broken. Red must have been over the edge when he decided to do this. The cancer was messing up his brain cells."

"Don't malign Red." She spoke with tight control riding her voice.

She drew back and sighed. Her crossed arms and tapping foot told him she was furious over this entire conversation. But was she angry at herself as well as at him? And why?

"He thought he was doing the right thing, I'm sure," she said quietly.

"Yeah, well, I remember him when he was young, and he wasn't concerned about doing the right thing then."

"Well, some people grow up. They shouldn't be judged by what they did when they were teenagers." Beth's chin was set rigidly.

"Are we talking about Red now, or someone else we both know?" Grant folded his arms across his chest.

She studied Grant's features. His hair was longer than when she'd last seen him. There were hints of gray among the thick, black strands that curled against his collar rakishly. But some features remained the same. Those blue eyes were as glacial as she remembered, and that damn male arrogance still radiated from his tall frame.

She knew he was waiting for an answer. She switched her weight from one foot to the other and tilted her head as she considered her reply. She didn't rise to his bait, however, but asked a question of her own.

"What are you doing here?"

Grant's eyes widened in surprise at her question. "What do you mean? I'm here for the reading of the will, such as it was."

"You haven't been back in ten years." She looked him in the eye. "I, of all people, know you're not sentimental about paying your respects to the dead. So why come back now?"

His gaze flickered across her face. "I didn't plan on being here, but Shorty insisted I show up. Now we know why. But don't worry. I'm out of here tomorrow." He wouldn't tell her that he had been going through the motions of living for the last few years. Even though he lived hundreds of miles from her, hadn't spoken to her in years and had a job as a federal marshal, he thought of her every day and often wondered what she was doing now, if she had changed, if she was married.

"What about the will? If you leave, then the place goes up for sale. I can't let that happen. My work there is too important."

She searched Grant's face to judge his reaction. For some inexplicable reason, she wanted him to learn about what she was doing and see its value, to accept her work, to see that she was doing it for the sake of the animals. To understand that it had to go on, not just for the animals, but because of the depth it had added to her life. The fulfillment she derived from her work would be obvious if he toured New Start.

"Beth, you're talking to *me,* remember? I know your biggest worry is what designer outfit to wear next."

"What I do is important, Grant. I can't lose it."

"You won't. Who on earth would try to enforce something so ludicrous?" His lips lifted in a half smile.

"Shorty will."

"Nah." Grant shook his head. "Besides, why don't you just buy it yourself? We can forego this waiting-for-a-year stipulation."

"I can't. I don't have the money." Beth couldn't meet the fire that sprang to Grant's eyes. Money. It was still the same between them.

Ten years ago, he'd screamed at her about money. She'd been spoiled and naive then and asked her father to help her financially only a few months after her marriage. Knowing Grant was strapped, holding down a job and at the same time fighting to keep his football scholarship, she'd felt it was the right thing to do. When Grant found out, he'd hit the roof. But they'd talked out their problems and had just been getting their marriage back on an even keel again—or so she'd thought—when Grant had come home one day, silently packed his bags and left. She'd been served with divorce papers a few weeks later, and her world had never been right since.

Now they were discussing money again, only this time he *wanted* her to use it to get him out of a jam. Well, even if the situation had been the way it was before—and it wasn't—she wouldn't use money to save herself. She tossed her hair over one shoulder and looked squarely at him. "I need what I have to take care of my animals."

"Oh, yeah. Your little zoo out there." Grant rolled his eyes. "My sister mentioned something about you and Red trying to save the world's wildlife. That's a long way from managing Dallas's largest bookstore."

At Beth's raised eyebrows, he explained, "My sister kept me up-to-date on you before she moved away from Douglas."

Beth ignored his reference to her job in Dallas for one of the major bookstore chains. When Red had called her and urged her to return to Douglas, she'd jumped at the offer. Dallas was too glittery for her taste. Douglas was home. New Start was her life now.

"It's not a zoo. It's a rehabilitation center. I take mistreated animals, wild and domestic, restore their health and reintroduce them to the wild, or find them good homes. I've gotten quite a name around here for saving abused horses."

"Big business in that?" His voice crackled with sarcasm.

"Stop patronizing me." Beth wanted to slap the arrogant smirk off his face. "You haven't changed a bit. Still Mr. Macho."

He frowned, and his expression sobered. "All right. You have my undivided attention. Explain to me what you do on this wonderful piece of property that *we* now own."

Beth's mouth suddenly went dry, and she ran her tongue along her bottom lip. Grant was standing tall and strong in front of her. He had always had the power to dominate her with his commanding presence. Once upon a time she had enjoyed being cosseted and protected by such powerful masculinity, but she was older and wiser now. She wouldn't let him or any man control her again. Yet she had to fight the urge to snuggle into his warmth and let him keep the world at bay.

Taking a deep breath, she explained, "About three years ago Red and I decided to establish a refuge for neglected, hurt and abused animals. It started after I found a deer that had been hit by a car. I took it to the vet to be patched up. Then I asked Red if it could recuperate at his ranch. He was more than willing, so that's how the idea was born."

"So who bankrolled it? Red or your daddy?"

"My father has nothing to do with it." She seethed with indignation that he would bring her father into this conversation. "Red provided the capital to begin with, and I had a little money saved up that I invested."

"Sounds crazy to me." His tone was hard.

He listened to her, but he never heard a word she said, she thought in exasperation. Nothing ever changed.

"Look, I don't have to explain myself to you or anybody else." Her eyes sparkled with anger. "Since we seem to be partners now, why don't you come out and see New Start for yourself? Make your judgments after you see the operation."

His rugged features were unreadable. His eyes were not that icy blue now, but darker, like the sky after a blue norther.

Those feral eyes narrowed, assessing her, and finally he said, "If I stick around here long enough, you can give me the two-bit tour."

Mesmerized by his gaze, she forgot her animal refuge. Her thoughts were centered entirely on Grant. Who was he now? "What do you do, Grant? Where do you live?" Without meaning to, she voiced the questions she'd lain awake night after night asking herself.

Immediately a curtain of carefully controlled indifference dropped over Grant's face. He shrugged negligently. "I didn't come here to talk about me." His features were tense as he seemed to be fighting some inner battle. His voice was harsh, rigid. "Shorty told me I had to be here for this damn will thing, Beth. I'm not interested in catching up on old times or new ones. All I want is to leave again—soon. Can't you get your daddy to buy you out of trouble one more time?

She winced as if a fist had been driven hard into her heart. But she wouldn't let him see how much he'd hurt her.

"*Yes, I can, but no, I won't,*" she ground out.

Grant studied her for a minute. She met his stare without flinching, even when his eyes traveled over her body intimately, insultingly. She felt as if he were physically caressing her before his eyes clashed with hers again and locked.

"Let's set up a meeting with Shorty and see how ironclad this will is. I can wait 'til tomorrow afternoon to leave, so let's see if we can't unload this albatross in the morning."

"Fine," Beth said. "I'll go tell Shorty we'll meet him in his office at eight o'clock to figure this out."

She turned to go back into the Longneck Palace. Thinking out loud, she said, "I don't care how much I loved Red, I don't think I'll forgive him for this if I lose New Start."

"What do you mean, you loved Red?"

Grant grabbed her arm and swung her around hard against his chest. Beth instinctively put up her hands to stop the contact and was immediately sorry. Through the expensive fabric of his dress shirt she felt the firm ridges of muscle that crisscrossed his chest. She closed her eyes and remembered how she had loved to trace the intricate patterns that ribboned his broad torso. Inexplicably, the memory of that pleasure angered her.

"Let go of me," she lashed out. "You're always jumping to conclusions. You'll never change."

She pushed hard against him and was surprised when he released her. The brief contact with his body had robbed her of air. She gasped for breath, chest heaving.

Grant, too, seemed to be fighting for control. His face was flushed, and his square jaw looked rigid enough to shatter, but then she decided she must have been mistaken, because when she blinked and looked again, he seemed as arrogant and untouchable as ever.

He leaned toward her and smiled lazily. "You're right. One thing hasn't changed. We still burn each other with just a touch. I remember there were parts of me you didn't want to change. Don't pretend that's still not true." His voice sizzled with sexual innuendo.

"Go to hell," Beth ground out.

His eyes bore into hers before he answered, "No thanks. I've been there. It's taken me ten years to climb out."

Chapter 2

"I'm sorry, Beth, Grant, there's simply no way you can manipulate this will."

Shorty shuffled the papers on his desk as he faced them. They had arrived at his immaculate office at eight o'clock, demanding that he find a loophole. Now they stared at him, disbelief written across their faces.

"Why did Red do this?" Grant asked. "Hell, we weren't even particularly close friends." He glanced at Beth. "Why didn't he leave everything to you?" He shook his head. "This feels like one of his stupid practical jokes."

"It's not, believe me," Shorty answered. "Red didn't divulge his reasons for doing this, but I can assure you, he made sure it would stick."

"He did it for me," Beth said quietly. She had been silent through the entire meeting.

"For you!" Grant turned in his chair to face her. "Did you put him up to this?"

"Of course not." Beth tossed her hair back. "Red just...he just thought, well...never mind." She waved her hand and then addressed Shorty. "He was a dreamer, that's all."

Grant stared at her. "You really are something, you know that? Red, the lunatic, messes up our lives—"

"Your life—not mine."

Grant continued as if she hadn't interrupted him. "—And you write it off by saying he's a dreamer. He was no dreamer. He was just plain insane."

"Stop it," she demanded. "How could someone like you possibly understand?"

"What do you mean, 'someone like you'?" Grant fired back.

Shorty stepped in to defuse the potential explosion. "Look, I'm going to make copies of everything for you. I want you to wait here and calm down." He straightened his tie. "My secretary can hear all of this, and I don't want her to spread gossip about you two fighting again." With a warning glare at both of them, he left.

Silence stretched, laced with tension. Finally Beth sighed. "I wish we could handle this better. I don't want us to fight."

Grant's voice was low and his anger was subdued. "I don't, either. I just can't understand why Red would even think about me, much less leave me anything."

Beth studied her fingernails as though they were fascinating as she formed her reply. "He must have thought I would need help to carry on my business." She flashed her blue eyes at him for a minute. "Why he chose you as the lucky recipient, I don't know."

Grant stared at her before he stood and began pacing in the small office. "There's no way I can do this. I'm in the middle of a big operation at work. I can't just stop everything and sit around here for a year while you nurse sick animals.''

"Don't sound so condescending."

"I'm not." His eyes were icy as they focused on her. "I'm being honest—a trait you aren't all that familiar with."

She jerked to her feet. "That was uncalled for. I've been nothing but honest about this situation."

"As honest as you were when we were married?" He wished he could retrieve the question as soon as it shot out, but he couldn't. The anger that he'd kept harbored in his heart for ten years wouldn't allow him to call it back and apologize. He watched Beth's face pale and her hands clench.

"Beth, I—"

"Don't say another word." She picked up her purse and marched to the door. "Tell Shorty to mail me the copy of Red's will."

"Beth!" Grant called to her retreating figure, but she never even hesitated.

"There, there, baby. It's all right. Everything is all right." Beth's voice was a soothing caress as she tried to calm the big stallion she was moving to a different corral.

The crisp winter air and the horse's distrust of humans combined to make him skittish and dangerous. Clutching the lead rope tightly, Beth used all her skill to keep him from rearing and running. But the large gray jerked on his lead, pulling Beth with him.

Grant, who had just driven up, launched himself from his rented truck and sprinted to Beth's side. Snatching the leather line from her hand, he spoke in a soft yet firm voice to the animal. "Easy, boy, easy."

The stallion pawed the ground nervously and whinnied softly. Grant continued to croon to the horse, and his low tone finally settled the stallion.

It was then that he turned to Beth. "What are you doing with this animal?" His eyes were flashing, but he spoke quietly, to avoid upsetting the horse.

"Trying to get him into the corral," she answered, her words clipped, pointing a slim finger toward her destination.

"Well, you almost got trampled." Grant stroked the horse's neck and started to lead him gently to the fenced enclosure.

"I did not. I would have gotten him under control in a few more minutes." Beth walked on the other side of the gray.

Grant let the animal loose in the corral and turned to give Beth the lead rope and halter. "Here."

She studied him as he watched the stallion nuzzle the ears of a palomino mare. Grant was wearing navy slacks, a white shirt and striped tie and a blue tweed jacket. Even though his clothing looked out of place here at the ranch amid the dust and animals, *he* didn't. He looked as calm and confident as always. What was that old saying about fitting in with kings and paupers? The adage fit Grant perfectly.

He startled her when he suddenly turned and looked at her closely. "I thought this place was for sick or mistreated animals."

"It is." She looked toward the horse now racing around the corral. "Right now we have about twenty horses here, all abused by their previous owners."

"Abused? That stallion looks fine to me. In fact, you would have been the abused one if he was any stronger."

She tried to anchor a wisp of hair that had slipped from her ponytail. As soon as she thought she had it under control, a cool gust of wind sent it flying around her face again.

"You should have seen him when he came in. He stayed in his stall for two weeks and just ate and ate. He was almost starved to death." Beth looked at the horse and blinked back sudden tears. "Now he's quite the ladies' man."

"Turned him into a real stud, did you? Is that what you do out there? Take broken-down male animals and make them whole again?" Grant asked.

Beth studied him for a moment, trying to determine whether he was being teasing or patronizing.

She chose to ignore his comment. She didn't want to get into any veiled sexual repartee with him. She'd always lost those battles before, and she couldn't afford to lose this one now. Instead she explained about the horse.

"He was being used to sire foals for sale. That's all his owner wanted from him. It was horrible, from what the police told me. The horses were bags of bone, the place was filthy and many of the mares were diseased."

Her eyes pierced Grant's with a combination of sorrow and anger. "One of the problems in this state is that I can't take possession of an abused or neglected animal until a judge rules it's in danger of dying."

She could sense Grant's outrage as he stiffened beside her, and turned her back to the fence and leaned against it. Grant was studying her closely, as if he were having trouble digesting what she had said. Or maybe that *she* had said it.

She shifted under his close scrutiny. He studied her but didn't seem inclined to comment, so she asked, "What are you doing out here, Grant? I thought Shorty was pretty clear back in his office."

"It's a case of Muhammad coming to the mountain." Grant shrugged, and Beth tried not to think of the muscles rippling under his shirt. "I felt we still needed to discuss a few details. Privately. You obviously disagreed, given the way you rushed out this morning."

Beth pushed the hair off her forehead. "I didn't see any reason to stay, since you were in such an obstinate mood."

"Really?" Grant took the stubborn strand of hair and smoothed it behind her ear. He was standing so close to her that she thought she could feel his heart beating, strong and vital against her breast. "I think you were afraid to be there with me."

Beth jerked away from him. "Why on earth...? I've *never* been afraid of you. Especially not now."

"Why not now?" Grant tilted his head. "I've got your future in my hands. At least, that's what Shorty led me to understand."

Beth whirled away and stalked toward one of the barns. She called back over her shoulder, "Grant, I don't have time to spar with you."

"You may not have time to spar, but you'd better have time to hear me out."

She was almost to the door of the barn when he took her arm and turned her around.

"Grant, I—"

"I'm not staying here for a year."

His voice was like a razor as the words sliced through her heart. But she wouldn't allow him to see how much he hurt her. "You've as much as told me that already."

Goaded by her cool attitude, he flung at her, "You're not so complicated. You've always been easy to read. Life's always handed you everything, but not this time—this time is different."

Beth stared at him. His eyes were hard, like blue agates—polished, but lifeless. This wasn't the Grant she remembered. She'd never seen his eyes this unreadable, except for the day he'd found out about the money she had secretly asked for and accepted from her father.

"How dare you pretend to know what I think? You've *never* had that ability."

She tossed her head, unwilling to think about her foolish teenage blunders. Had she ever felt this helpless before? Even when she realized her marriage was not going to survive? After her talk with Shorty, the fear that had been planted as she watched the video at the saloon yesterday had blossomed into full-scale panic. She knew the will couldn't be broken. *Damn you, Red,* she thought, *you've really messed things up for me.* Knowing Grant's rock-hard determination, she knew he wouldn't stay in Douglas willingly. But she couldn't lose her dream. There was only one way to save it. She *had* to convince Grant.

"Hey, guys, what do you think of this?" Delores Ortiz interrupted them with several quick toots on a car horn and a jaunty wave. They'd been so preoccupied with their disagreement that they hadn't noticed the brunette driving up in a turquoise convertible. "Still drives like a dream."

Beth smiled as she watched her friend park the car and give it a loving pat. "I wondered where you were."

"Sorry I'm late." Delores joined them, her pillowy breasts swaying under the sweatshirt she wore. "I had to pick up the car." She motioned to the convertible. "And then I had to take it out for a spin."

"Naturally," Beth said, shaking her head and chuckling. "It's okay. I've just been feeding the animals."

"Really?" Delores looked up at Grant. "Hi, Grant. Good to see you again. You here checking out your inheritance?"

"No," Grant said emphatically. "I came out to get everything settled with Beth."

"Oh." Delores eyed the two speculatively before she turned to Beth. "Did you get Studmuffin taken care of?"

Grant suppressed a choking sound.

"Yes, he's in the corral, trying to live up to his name."
Beth laughed. "I think you had better check on the goats. I
haven't seen them this morning."

"Okay, but let me say hello to my fella first." Delores
walked over to the fence of the corral and whistled. The gray
stallion trotted over to her. Delores wrapped her arms
around his neck, and the horse shook his mane in a preen-
ing way. Then Delores headed into the woods to look for the
errant goats.

"Studmuffin?" Grant's eyebrows were raised, and his
sinfully long eyelashes framed the surprise in his eyes. The
ghost of a smile twitched around his full lips. "Is that really his name?"

Beth forced herself to look away from those lips she remembered all too well. They could give such pleasure.
"Delores named him. Said he reminded her of someone."

"Did you ask who?" Grant's voice was low, insinuating.

Beth shook her head. "There are some things I'm happier not knowing."

"What's she doing here, anyway?" Grant nodded toward Delores's retreating back. "Is that her horse?"

"No, she's my assistant. We really run this place together, with the help of some volunteers and sponsors. And,
of course, Red used to help out some until he became too
weak from the cancer."

That left them both without anything to say for a minute.

Finally Grant broke the silence. "Beth, we need to settle
this thing once and for all. I can tell we can't talk here without interruptions. Where do you want to finish this discus-
sion?"

Beth thought for a minute, then nodded. "You're right, we do need to settle some things. Let me check on one of our ponies, and then we can go up to the house and talk."

Just then a beeper sounded.

"What the hell?" Grant demanded.

"That's mine." Beth couldn't help but smile at the astounded look on Grant's face. "I'll be right back. I need to use my car phone."

She headed toward her truck, chuckling out loud at Grant's expression.

Returning in only minutes to find him standing where she had left him, she said, "I have to go out to a ranch on the other side of town. Wanna come along?"

"Send someone else. We haven't finished talking."

"No, Grant, there isn't anyone else."

He looked in the direction where Delores had disappeared and then back at her. "Since I'm determined to settle this, I've got no choice. Lead the way."

"You can always wait here."

"I'll go with you. I want to see the abusebuster in action."

Twenty minutes later they pulled up to a ramshackle building that fit the term *barn* in name only. The wood was rotting, and boards were missing from the walls. The tin roof looked as if half of it had been peeled away by a giant can opener. In back of the barn was a large corral, where six pitiful-looking horses stood.

A tall young man in a deputy sheriff's uniform greeted her, then looked with curiosity at Grant.

"Joe Clay, this is Grant Stephens, an old friend." She wondered if Joe Clay had picked up on the fact that she and Grant shared the same last name. "Grant, this is Joe Clay Phillips. Joe Clay calls me when my services are needed."

"Nice to meet you, Grant. Beth here is an angel in my book." He beamed an ear-to-ear grin down at her. "If she didn't take in these creatures when we called, they'd probably die. Without her, the law says abused animals seized by the county have to be housed at the stockyards. You can imagine what would happen to them there."

Grant looked at Beth, a spark of interest growing in his eyes. The Beth he'd known would have run from the harsh reality of these animals' lives. But from what he could tell, she faced it head-on and in the process had gained the respect of most of the citizens of Douglas. He wondered how long she could fool the good citizens with this holier-than-thou routine. Could she really have changed, grown up from that spoiled girl he remembered?

"What have we got here, Joe Clay?" she questioned the deputy.

"We were tipped by an anonymous caller that this guy, Dewey Smith, had some horses stuck off back here in the brush. Seems he buys retired racehorses at auction and breeds them to sell foals."

"Look at them." Beth's voice was deep with anger and sorrow.

They looked over the rotten timbers of the corral at the horses. The animals' skeletons showed through their sagging skin, and some had festering wounds. They stood quietly, heads bowed.

"What happens to this guy, Smith?" Grant wanted to see him tarred and feathered—or worse. As a federal marshal, he'd seen plenty of innocent victims, but he'd never gotten used to it. Maybe he and Beth had something in common after all.

"He's been taken into the sheriff's office for questioning." Joe Clay shook his head sadly. "An animal cruelty investigator has already been out here."

"And now what?" Grant demanded.

"She'll probably file an animal cruelty case, which is a Class A misdemeanor." Joe Clay gave Grant a level look.

"A misdemeanor?"

"The maximum penalty is a year in jail or a two-thousand-dollar fine or both, but nobody ever gets that."

"This is so much like how we found Studmuffin," Beth announced as she pushed a curl away from her face.

"There's something else, too." Two pairs of eyes sought out Joe Clay's. He pointed west, where a stand of mesquite trees flourished. "We found a pit out there where horse carcasses have been burned. There're a lot of bodies."

"It's so sad." Beth looked up at Grant. "Usually there's a lot of ignorance involved in these starvation cases rather than direct cruelty. Someone buys a horse thinking that one acre of land will support it. But this guy…" She left her ugly thoughts hanging in the air.

"Well, let's get the horses loaded," Joe Clay said solemnly.

Beth got in her pickup and expertly backed the long horse trailer up to the narrow gate. Grant did a double take, surprised by her ease in handling the trailer.

He had seen her wheel around town in a sports car, but never in a truck with a load of half-dead horses. This was a side of Beth that had either been deeply buried or completely nonexistent when he'd known her before.

The three of them easily put halters on the starving beasts and led them into the long-bed trailer. In their emaciated condition, the horses didn't raise a ruckus. Immediately they began to munch on the fresh hay Beth had waiting for them.

Slamming the tailgate closed, Joe Clay turned to Beth. "How's it going out there now that Red's gone?"

"Okay. I'm numb right now."

"You call me if you need anything." His brown eyes searched her face. "Do you mind if I come out and check on these horses soon?"

Grant, who'd been watching the exchange, narrowed his eyes. This young pup had a giant-size crush on Beth. He remembered the feeling—always wanting just to be around her, no matter what the reason. He could almost feel sorry for him. Almost.

"That'll be fine, Joe Clay. Come out anytime you want." Her eyes darted to Grant before she gave her attention back to Joe Clay. "I can always use an extra hand at New Start."

The deputy waved to Beth and wished Grant well.

"Hope all the horses make it," he called as they drove slowly down the dirt road.

When Grant and Beth got back to New Start, he helped her unload the horses into one of the corrals and shovel more hay for them. Beth retrieved a jar of dark blue ointment from a cabinet located under the overhang of the barn and patiently slathered the smelly antiseptic on the horse's wounds. Grant shook his head in disbelief.

Glancing up at him, Beth said, "Think of some names. You get the honor of naming these."

"I'm only going to be here a few days. That's not long enough for me to think of good ones. You do it," he told her. Then he frowned. "Do you think any of them will make it?"

Beth frowned, too. "I don't know, but I'm going to do everything in my power to see that they do." She didn't realize her jaw was set in a determined line. She meant to do her damnedest to help these horses live. It gave her life a focus—a purpose that working in a bookstore had never done. "Come on. Let's go check on the pony I wanted to see an hour ago."

They were in one of the barns now, and Beth stopped at a stall to inspect a skinny palomino Shetland pony.

"This one's name is Twinkle Toes." Beth smiled as she looked back over her shoulder at Grant. "She's pretty old. The vet estimated she's near twenty."

The pony had stopped its munching at the sound of Beth's voice and now turned to nuzzle her jeans for a moment. Beth affectionately rubbed Twinkle Toes's back and then scratched behind her ears. Glancing up at Grant, she smiled at the look of genuine interest she read on his face. Crouching beside the pony, she inspected each small hoof.

"Why the name Twinkle Toes?"

She swept her gaze up Grant's tall frame and was shocked when a frisson of desire skittered through her body. Why did he have the capacity to make her feel giddy and out of control? As if he could read her thoughts and intended to take advantage of them, he moved to stand right beside her.

She lowered her eyes and answered, "Twinkle Toes was found along with eleven other horses and ponies in a dark barn. Maybe because of that, she's blind."

She looked up from her inspection of the pony's hooves and saw that the look of controlled fury had returned to Grant's eyes. Instinctively she knew that he would fight physical abuse with physical abuse. It reminded her of how he'd looked after a particularly physical football game.

"It was terrible," she continued. "She was standing past her knees in manure." Beth shook her head. "And she's permanently crippled, because her previous owner had let her hooves grow too long. We check her feet every day for signs of infection. That's why we call her Twinkle Toes."

She stood up and brushed off her jeans before walking out of the stall. Grant stared mutely at the pony, then turned toward Beth, but she couldn't meet the intensity of his gaze and turned her back on him to close the stall gate. She pretended to fumble with the latch for a few moments to give herself time to sort out her riotous emotions.

Grant was behind her, waiting. Would he hang around this time until they had settled their differences? She didn't remember him ever staying around so they could *really* talk, *really* communicate, to solve a problem. She remembered him slamming doors as he left or the cold silences if he stayed. What she didn't remember was this seeming patience. What she did remember about their disagreements was the making up. That was how he'd always solved everything, with his persuasive lips and hands.

Their love had always been communicated through their bodies. Maybe, if they'd just allowed themselves the luxury of really listening . . . Beth forced herself to stop that train of thought. She'd learned years ago to focus on what you could do, not what you should have done.

She stepped back slightly, and their bodies brushed together. Instantly, as if her mind wasn't attached to her body, she felt her breasts grow heavy and a familiar throbbing begin at the apex of her womanhood. She must be crazy, but she wanted more of Grant.

As if he'd been reading her mind, his hands closed over her shoulders and he leaned into her until she felt his breath, hot and sweet, against her ear. "Beth, I never would have placed you in a barn looking after half-starved animals, but you look good here. You look right."

She closed her eyes and let herself absorb his touch. Her body responded to him as a freezing person would to a fire—it reached for him, unconsciously flowing toward him, allowing him to invade.

His hands tightened on her shoulders, and she felt his thighs against the backs of her legs. His solid warmth felt so good. She wanted to stay this way forever—absorbing Grant's power and strength.

She pulled away from him and sighed. She had to stop this craziness. She didn't like the way her body was responding. Her senses were filled with him: his clean, soapy smell; his hard, muscular touch; his even, steady breathing. Would his lips taste the same as they had so long ago? Would they be as warm and demanding as she remembered?

She turned and was immediately flush against his body. His hooded eyes told her nothing, so she watched the pulse point in his neck as his breathing quickened. When she raised her eyes to his again, she gasped. Gone was the cold, lifeless gaze. It had been replaced by blazing fires, burning with a need she recognized. She feared he would see it mirrored in her eyes, so she quickly looked away.

She moved a few steps back before she said anything. "Okay, I'm finished here. Let me check on Studmuffin and make sure he's settling into his new surroundings all right. Then I'll tell Delores where I'll be."

Grant stood fixed to the spot and watched her walk away from him, his eyes lingering on the sway of her hips in the snug jeans she wore. What the hell had just happened? He'd come out here determined to get rid of an unwanted complication. Now he was ready to follow her like an adoring puppy.

It was his fault. He never should have touched her, felt her softness through the material of her blouse. He definitely shouldn't have leaned close enough to get a whiff of her perfume. His knees had almost given way as the memories of her sweetness had engulfed him. Lord, when she had turned and her breasts had brushed against his arm, he had almost backed her up against the stall gate and begged her forgiveness—promised her anything—just for a little taste of paradise.

He shook his head in disgust. Nothing had changed. She still had the power to bring him to his knees. It just took a sigh and one look from those blue, seductive eyes. She was right. They had to get this over with before he did something he really regretted. He wanted to talk with her about the past, explain how he'd felt, but he knew that was foolish. After all, her father had convinced him that he wasn't good enough for Beth, couldn't make enough money to satisfy her. Now he just had to keep telling his body and brain that over and over again. He followed her into the late-winter sunlight.

She gestured toward her truck. "Jump in. I'll drive you up to the house."

"No, thanks." Grant shook his head. "I don't want to come back down here when we're finished ironing out our problems. I'll drive myself."

"Suit yourself. Just follow that road east." She pointed toward a dirt road leading through a grove of oak trees. "It's Red's place. That's where I live."

Red's place? The same uneasy feeling he'd had when she proclaimed her love for Red at the reading of the will got to him again. Damn, why couldn't he beat this streak of caveman possessiveness? He had no claim on her. So what if she'd been Red's lover and that was why she nursed him through his cancer? Grant's jaw tightened and he refused to think more about it.

After all, what could he expect? Beth was a single woman. She could do whatever she wanted. During the past ten long years, he had certainly tried to find a woman who could spend her life with a cop. Actually, when he analyzed his feelings, he was jealous of the time Beth and Red had spent together. Time spent on building and pursuing something worthwhile and gratifying, whether they'd been lovers or not.

He drove slowly down the narrow dirt road to Red's house so he could acquaint himself with New Start. He was surprised at how well tended the place looked. There were a total of five barns, each with its own corral. In addition, there were several large, zoo-style cages. He saw what looked like a jaguar prowling in one.

When he got to the ranch house, he parked and got out of the truck, eyeing the large, native stone two-story structure. It was a handsome place that fit this rugged countryside well.

Just as the chilly air was starting to seep into his bones, Beth arrived and parked her pickup beside him. She swung her long, denim-clad legs out and hurried up the walk to the front door with its oval glass window.

After fiddling with the key for a few seconds, she finally pushed the door open. "Come in." She led him down a wide hallway and turned left into Red's study. "Have a seat. Can I get you some coffee?" She threw the keys on the desk.

"Yeah, sure."

Beth slipped out of the room, leaving Grant to look around. He recognized the room where Red had videotaped his will. The whole room shouted Red's eccentricities. The walls were covered with photographs of cars, animals and women. Statues of the same crowded every available surface. The only corner of the room that attempted some sort of normalcy was where the desk and computers stood. But even here there was a lamp with a naked lady as the base and a tasseled shade. Red had never changed. Grant smiled.

Beth swept back into the room with two coffee mugs in her hands. "Here." She offered one to Grant. "I don't remember you using sugar, so it's unsweetened." She blushed at her obvious reference to how close they had been and added, "I can get you some—"

"I still don't use sugar," Grant broke in. He nodded to indicate the room. "This place sure does shout 'Red,' doesn't it?"

Beth laughed and agreed then sat down on the leather sofa. "He was never conservative in anything he did, and this room is testimony to that."

The pleasantries had been exchanged, and now they were left with the bald fact of why they were in a room—alone— for the first time in ten years. Grant was the one to bring them to the point. "Beth, I don't know why Red did this, but I'm not staying here for any damned year. Not now, not ever."

"I know," she said quietly. "You made that very clear this morning. After I got home, I called Shorty and begged him to give me an alternative. He said that you could establish a residency here, at least on paper, by just sticking around for sixty days—it wasn't what Red wanted, but it might solve our problem."

Grant sat down behind the desk in Red's massive leather chair. He stared coldly at her. "Beth, I'm not living in this town for a year *or* for sixty days, not even one more day. Don't you get it? I'm involved in a serious operation at work right now. Besides, this town never thought I was good enough for it, so I'm out of here. Why don't you just buy me out and we can all be happy?"

"I told you before, I don't have the money to buy you out. I'm leveraged, and I can't get any money from the banks." She sighed. "Why don't you give the people of Douglas a break? I never heard anything awful said about you. In fact, most people were damn nice about how hard you worked and what a marvelous athlete you were."

Grant looked at her. It was the first time he'd ever heard her curse. "People were always asking how my mother and sister were, how did I keep up with a job and sports. What they were really saying was 'you're poor and you're trash.'"

"Listen to yourself, Grant. You're reading something bad into typical small-town concern. Can't you get past that schoolboy pride?"

"I've been working on it the last few years." He studied her flushed face. Why was she insisting on this charade of not having money? Who was she fooling? Her father had enough money to buy this place a dozen times over. "Just get the money from your old man. Don't you always go to him when you need extra change? Isn't this as important as all the clothes and the car you went to him for when we were married?"

Beth tossed her head and stiffened her spine. She had known he would try this. "Yes, I could go to my father, but I won't. I promised myself never to do that again."

"Don't get ethical on me now, Beth. This is not the time."

She stood up. "This is exactly the time. All my life I've depended on someone else to do things for me. This is the first time I've built something on my own. I'm standing alone on this."

Grant was taken aback by the determination that shot from her defiant stance and snapping eyes.

"I'm desperate, Grant. Tell me what it would take to make you stay here."

"What are you offering?" Grant murmured, deliberately lowering his voice.

She looked him squarely in the face and after a long pause said, "Me."

Chapter 3

"I've already had you." Grant's voice dropped to a whisper and he leaned toward Beth. "What's so special about this time?"

Lord, she thought, can I go through with this? It was the only thing she could think of that might save New Start.

She steeled herself not to take a step backward as he came from behind the desk and moved closer. She knew he was testing her, purposefully insulting her because he didn't believe she was serious about her proposition. She could feel the heat of his body, powerful and potent, and she decided she had to do something to prove she wasn't joking. Reaching up, she slowly wound her arms around Grant's neck and pulled him seductively toward her.

His forehead furrowed in surprise at Beth's actions. She kept her eyes homed in on the blue of his as she said in a voice full of promise, "You tell me what's special this time."

She rubbed her lips back and forth against his as if to acclimate them to the feel of each other. She drew back to judge his reaction and was rewarded by the look of pleasure that had replaced the doubt on his face. Smiling inwardly, she parted her lips and again sought the warmth of his.

His lips didn't respond for a moment, so she laved his bottom lip with her tongue before pressing a hot and demanding kiss against his mouth. He relaxed and allowed her tongue to delve between his lips, then deeper. She pulled back and smiled at him, not knowing how sexy her kiss-reddened lips looked. She nipped soft kisses down his throat and ran her hands up and down his arms. Finally she brought her lips back to his. She didn't know if it was Grant or she who groaned with a mixture of longing and desire, but the wanton sound acted as a stimulus to her already-raging emotions.

Grant enveloped her in a hard embrace, pulling her closer still. Beth was almost overwhelmed by the fervency of his reaction. His lips had taken charge of the kiss, and his tongue now pillaged her mouth in a fierce, steady rhythm that intimated the lovemaking ritual. She wound her fingers through the hair that fell over his collar, holding on as her world reeled out of control.

Somewhere in the fog, where feelings were all that mattered, Beth drifted. She enjoyed the sensations Grant's lips worked—but suddenly reason reared its head and screamed. She had kissed him to lure him into staying in her world to save her dream, but it had become more than that. It was an odyssey of rediscovery. She had lost herself in the feel of him, in the smell of him, in the taste of him.

She had to pull away now. She had to take back control of the situation.

When Beth had been much younger, she had given up her mind, her body, her very soul, to become an extension of this man. In the intervening years she had convinced her-

self that her shameless responses to Grant had resulted from
her father's forbidding her to have anything to do with him.
Of course Grant had become irresistible to her. But she
wasn't about to let herself become ensnared by his mascu-
line charm again.

Another thought hit her with somber clarity—she
couldn't prostitute herself, not even for New Start.

Breaking the kiss, she pulled away and shrugged out of his
embrace, lowering her eyes from his piercing stare.

She racked her brain for some clever comment to throw
at him, but her capacity for speech seemed to have been in-
cinerated in the fire of their kiss. It was Grant who broke the
silence between them.

"That was quite a show." He raked a hand through his
hair when she looked up at him. "What was that, a little
memory jogger?"

Beth, her composure back in place, answered slowly, "I
wanted to prove to you that I'm serious about my offer."
She turned away from him and walked over to run her finger lightly over the keys of the computer. She looked back
at Grant. "But now I'm sorry."

"Oh, I'm not. It was a great incentive." He jutted his jaw
out in his infuriatingly cynical way as he walked over to
stand by her. "Just how far are you planning on taking this
little demonstration?" He brushed a stray lock of hair from
her face. "Should I ask you to slip into something more
comfortable, so we can negotiate this whole setup in the
bedroom? Or are you just a tease, Elizabeth Stephens?"

Beth slapped his hand away. "Can't you understand how
important this is to me? I'm not a tease." Her voice trembled with emotion. "I thought I could do whatever was
necessary to keep New Start, but I can't. I thought I could
offer myself to you and go through with it without a qualm,
but I was wrong."

"Not quite the martyr you thought you were, then." Grant's words were cold.

She studied the rigid set of his features before throwing up her hands in a helpless gesture. "I wish I'd never touched you, never even known you."

Grant laughed mirthlessly. "A little too late for that." He raked his eyes over her. "And your body wasn't singing that tune a few minutes ago."

"You don't get it, do you, Grant?" Beth straightened her shoulders. "This isn't a silly high school game. I'm not the naive girl you married. I know what I want out of life now, and it's New Start. Since I don't have the money to buy you out, I was offering the only thing I do have." Her eyes met his levelly. "I'm dead serious about keeping Red's place. I just have to find another way."

His eyes searched hers, and she sucked in her breath as a fierce light sparked in his eyes and grew in intensity. She recognized it as desire. The mix of emotions flowing between them—longing, mistrust, anger, lust—was a palpable thing.

Before either of them could act on the moment, the phone sounded, like an air-raid warning.

She answered, then turned with a look of surprise and extended the receiver to Grant. "It's for you. I'll be in the kitchen."

"Thanks," Grant said as he took the phone from her hand. "I gave my office several places where I could be reached. I guess Shorty gave them your number."

Beth nodded and walked out of the room. She went into the kitchen and stood at the back door, looking sightlessly out at the backyard as she tried to get her skyrocketing emotions under control.

What was happening to her? Grant had been back in her world for less than twenty-four hours and already she was

losing her carefully tended grip on her feelings. Was she
making the biggest mistake of her life by inviting him back
into it? How could she ever have considered offering her bed
in exchange for the animal refuge? Because she was desperate, she admitted to herself. The refuge gave her a chance to
right some of the wrongs in this world. Instead of reading
about life in the books in the store in Dallas, she was living
life. It was gritty, it was sad, it was wonderful, and *she* was
helping to make a small difference.

She'd been hoping he would soften toward her if she explained how important New Start was, that he would want
to stay and help her with her dream. But he still had the chip
on his shoulder that she'd helped put there. And what did
she really want? Was she more terrified that he would leave
and she would lose New Start, or of what would happen if
he decided to stay?

"Beth?"

She started at the sound of her name and whirled around
to face Grant. Her eyebrows rose at the sober expression on
his face.

She stood very still as he studied her for long moments.
Instinctively she knew he was trying to make up his mind
about something, and she knew her future was at stake. Finally he gave a quick nod, as if he had made a decision.

"That call was from my boss," he said, his voice shattering the tense silence. "I've got a little vacation time coming, and he said I should take it now."

Beth's heart began to pound. She was almost afraid to
hear his next words.

"I guess I'm all yours for at least four weeks." He
wouldn't tell her that it wasn't really a vacation, that the
brass thought he should lie low in Douglas before the case
he was working on came to trial. It might be unhealthy for
him to return to St. Louis right now.

"Oh, Grant." She took a deep breath. Maybe everything was going to work out after all. She started toward him but pulled up short. "But four weeks. That's not long enough. The will says—"

Grant threw up his hands to silence her. "Beth, a month is all I can promise. Then we'll see what happens next."

She inclined her head and pondered the man in front of her. His eyes had lost their frostiness, and the tension in his tall frame seemed to have disappeared. She knew he was making quite a sacrifice in giving her this small amount of time. He had always liked to call the shots. His stubborn male ego was on the line, and she had to tread lightly so as not to have the whole arrangement blow up in her face.

"You're right," she assured him. "We'll play it one day at a time."

They smiled at each other, and an arc of electricity sparked between them. Galvanized by the reaction of her body to a simple smile, she hurried past him, then turned to gesture with one hand. "Come on," she invited. "Let's go sit down in the living room and talk about the next month."

She led him into the large, airy living room, filled with overstuffed couches and ottomans and small occasional tables. Indicating one of the sofas, Beth was surprised when Grant grabbed her hands and pulled her down beside him.

"This is a nice house," he said, letting his eyes rove around the room. "When did Red build it?"

She let her eyes feast on the room, too. She loved this house and especially this room, because Red had asked her to decorate it. "It took over a year to build and longer to decorate. He moved in about six years ago."

"And when did you move in?"

Beth was shocked at the harsh tone of Grant's voice. Was it jealousy that she heard coloring his words?

"I moved in three years ago. I was already working for Red, doing bookkeeping for his various enterprises, when he had found out he had the terminal cancer. When he first asked me to move in, I said no, but the sicker he got, it seemed cruel not to be close to him and try to help." She shrugged and looked down at her hands folded in her lap. "So here I am."

"Yes, here you are," Grant agreed. "And now I'm here, too." He looked around, then pinned her with a penetrating look. "Well, where do I sleep?"

"What?"

"If I'm going to stay here, I've got to have a place to sleep. And I should warn you, I don't cotton to couches or bathtubs."

Beth was relieved that he hadn't insisted on sharing her bed. She still wasn't sure where all this was heading, but at least for the time being he wasn't pressing her to carry out the proposition she had withdrawn.

"There are three empty guest rooms upstairs. You can have your pick."

"Which bedroom is yours?" His eyes pierced hers, holding her captive.

Her breath caught in her throat. "I'm in the one at the far end of the hall."

"Then I'll take the one at the other end. Don't want to be tempted, do we?" He grinned at her, and she knew he was teasing.

"No, we don't," she answered.

Silence stretched between them until Beth said, "If we're going to be staying together, at least I should know what you do now. You wouldn't answer my question yesterday. Did you become a policeman?"

"I went past that. Your daddy was wrong—I didn't wind up as a broken-down cop," he said. "Disappointed?"

Beth blushed as she remembered the arguments her father had had with Grant about his majoring in criminology. When her father had finally accepted the fact that she and Grant were married, he had offered to set Grant up in any one of the businesses he was involved in. Of course, Grant would have none of it, saying he would make it on his own. He'd always been a lone wolf.

She met his eyes squarely. "I don't think being a policeman is a disgrace. I think it's a very honorable profession."

"Great." He smiled grimly. "Then you'll think being a federal marshal is close to sainthood."

"A federal marshal?"

"Yeah, I moved from the police force to become a deputy marshal. And last year I was promoted to federal marshal." His voice was full of pride.

"Isn't that dangerous?" All she could think about were the many TV shows featuring gun-wielding maniacs and pyscho killers out to get anyone connected with the law.

As if reading her thoughts, he said, "It's not like the movies. We usually bring people in without a fight."

She sighed. "I'm glad you're not in much danger, then."

The call from his boss came to mind. This current case was the exception, but he wasn't about to tell her that. And, he had to admit, in some ways the call had been timed perfectly. He could use this break from his job to see the day-to-day operations of New Start and find out why a sparkle of pride and pleasure came to Beth's eyes whenever she talked about it. Even if his boss had forced him to take this vacation, he would make the best of it. Besides, he had plenty of vacation time, since he never used any of it. He had learned long ago that to get anywhere in this world you had to give yourself one hundred percent to the effort. And it had paid off, since he had risen through the ranks faster than anyone before him.

Despite all his efforts, though, the case he was on now was at a stalemate. He had spent hundreds of hours logging evidence against a big-time counterfeiter named Terence Anderson. Anderson did his dirty work for some very influential people. Grant hoped that eventually, under the pressure of his upcoming trial, Anderson would break down and implicate his bosses. It was just a matter of time. Perhaps it was better for Grant to be here than back at his office. Maybe the time would go more quickly.

Beth got up from the sofa and ran her hands down the front of her workshirt, smoothing the material over her firm breasts.

Grant inhaled sharply.

"Make yourself at home. I'm going to call Delores down at the barns and tell her lunch will be ready soon. Does stew sound okay to you?"

Grant gazed into the clear blue of Beth's eyes. He'd always thought that her dark eyelashes were the longest he'd ever seen and sexy as hell. He could remember waking up early during their marriage just to watch her fragile features as she slept. Those eyelashes had lain like mink against her creamy cheeks.

He could remember tracing the line of her full lips as she slept, too. She had often said she thought her mouth was too big, too pouty, but he had assured her that it was her most sensuous feature. Often, as he ran his thumb lightly over those rounded lips, she would awaken, and a glorious session of lovemaking would ensue until both were sated and fell back to sleep again.

"Grant?" Beth's husky voice cut into his delicious memory.

"Huh? Oh, yeah, stew sounds great."

"It won't take me long. I just have to warm it up," she said as she left him alone.

He heaved himself off the plump couch and wandered over to the bookshelf that covered one whole wall of the room. He picked through the books, finally selecting several volumes and thumbing through them.

Even though he was having trouble getting past this jealous streak toward Red, Grant smiled. Red must have loved mysteries. The shelves were full of them. He set the book back on the shelf and continued scanning it until he spied a tall blue-and-gold-bound book. He shook his head.

"My God," he said out loud as he pulled out the Douglas High School yearbook, *Bear Tracks.* He sat back down on the couch to take a look at his life when it had been simple.

He opened the book in the middle, and there was a picture of Beth holding a tennis racket in one hand and a trophy in the other. She had just won the district singles title. Her smile was bright and winsome, and Grant's mind strayed back to a time years before, to another tennis match, one between himself and Beth. . . .

The moon provided the light they needed as he and Beth tiptoed onto the Douglas Country Club courts, giggling and shushing each other every time they bumped into a net or linesman's chair.

"I'll beat you at this country club game," Grant touted, unzipping the borrowed racket and taking it out of its case. Even though he never got to play tennis, he was supremely sure of his athletic prowess.

Beth rocked back and forth on her feet as she bounced a ball. "We'll see."

"Let's at least make this interesting." Grant gazed at Beth's breasts stretching the front of her designer tennis dress. "Every time one of us scores a point, the other has to take off a piece of clothing." Grant's eyes glowed with mischievous aquamarine highlights.

"Are you crazy, Grant Stephens? Strip tennis?"

Even in the dim glow of the moon he could see her cheeks pinken and her lashes dip in embarrassment. They hadn't been dating long, and he knew she was half fascinated, half frightened of him. He had learned quickly that she was innocent, not at all like the picture he had conjured up in his mind of a spoiled, experienced rich girl.

His reputation as a rakehell preceded him, but many of the rumors about him were just that. He was a good athlete and loved a good time, but he also had to work long hours to help support his mother and sister. He didn't mind that the stories about his escapades got blown out of proportion, though. Every guy liked to be thought of as being bigger than life, he reasoned.

Grant knew that part of the reason Beth was dating him was because she was drawn to something she found dangerously exciting. He could tell, when she fiddled with the buttons at the throat of her expensive outfit, that the idea of strip tennis titillated her imagination.

"Yeah, strip tennis." Grant's eyes caressed and dared her at the same time. "You don't have anything to worry about, anyway. You've had ten years of lessons, and I've never touched a racket."

Grant saw Beth suddenly wipe her palms on the side of her white dress and knew that he had unnerved her. She had trouble getting words out of her mouth. "I . . . I d-don't think—"

"Beth, it's just a game. Besides, I've seen you in a bikini before."

She nodded as if making a sudden decision. "If jewelry can count—and shoes and socks—I'll play."

"It's a deal." Grant turned to hide his smile and walked to the baseline.

Before he had time to set up, Beth yelled, "I'll serve first." She smashed the ball across the net and the game began.

After fifteen minutes they had both lost their shoes and socks, and Beth had forfeited her jewelry, and the next loser was going to have to give up a major piece of clothing. She served and rushed the net too early; his return sailed past her and bounced dramatically on the line. Grant thanked the god of high fashion that she'd worn a dress instead of a two-piece outfit.

"My point, sweetheart. You lose," he said, doing an awful Humphrey Bogart imitation.

"Grant, I don't have anything left except my dress and shorts."

"I know. I'll take the dress." He grinned, wiping his brow with the back of his hand. He liked seeing her squirm, but he had never been serious about her really taking off anything substantial. He let her off the hook. "Or, if you want to keep your clothes on, I'll take a kiss instead."

Beth looked visibly relieved. "A kiss?"

"Yeah." Grant lowered his voice. "But more than those little pecks you give me at the front door that you think pass for kisses."

With his last words he jumped the net, sending Beth stumbling backward a few steps.

"I've been wanting to kiss you, really kiss you, for weeks." He stalked her, then gathered her in his arms. Suddenly a harsh light flooded the court, effectively blinding them. They broke apart guiltily.

"Who's out there? What are you doing on this court?" boomed a voice from beyond the light.

Momentarily frozen, they gaped at the club pro as he advanced toward them angrily.

"It's just me, Rick. It's Beth Channing. I was giving Grant some lessons," Beth squeaked.

"In the dark?" Rick looked at both of them and apparently surmised that tennis was not the only lesson being learned by this pair. Still, he'd probably seen plenty of crazy things happen on these luxurious courts, because he didn't appear too surprised by their antics. Grant thought Rick smiled before he said in a gruff voice, "Well, now is not the time for lessons. Get out of here."

"Okay, we're going." Grant grabbed Beth's elbow and started off the court.

Rick's command halted them. "You might want to take those shoes and things with you." He pointed to their discarded valuables.

"Oh, sure, thanks." They both dove for the losers' pile and ran out, holding their sides to keep from laughing.

Grant was in the middle of a loud laugh when Beth wandered back into the room. "What's so funny?"

He looked up with a twinkle in his eyes. "You." He motioned for her to come over and take a look.

She giggled when she saw the picture he was pointing to. She was wearing a cheerleading outfit, caught in midcrash as she lost her balance.

"I never realized how bowlegged you could look. Had you been riding for a month straight before this picture was taken?"

Beth jabbed him in the arm. "You're the reason I look like that and you know it." She smiled and playfully stuck her nose in the air. "You and Tom were throwing something disgusting at me, and I was trying to avoid being hit."

"Oh, yeah, I forgot." Grant grinned. "By the way, it was just wadded-up paper."

"Now how could you remember that after all these years?"

"I remember everything about those days," Grant said, his voice dropping to a warm whisper.

Beth stared into his rapier-sharp gaze before laughing abashedly and replying, "Right."

He patted the cushion beside him. "Sit down a minute and look at some of these pictures. I can't believe the hairstyles."

Beth sat down and laughed with Grant as he turned the pages.

"Oh, look, there's your sister." She pointed to a beautiful female version of Grant. "Where is she now?"

Everyone knew everything about everybody else in a small town, and Beth knew that Lydia had moved with her mother to Lubbock after she graduated from high school. She also knew that Lydia returned occasionally to visit friends, but their paths hadn't crossed since she and Grant had divorced.

"She's still in Lubbock. I financed her education at Texas Tech."

She could see the chip on his shoulder coming back as he imparted this bit of information.

Since his father had abandoned his family when Grant was twelve and his sister was eight, he had worked odd jobs to help support his mother and sister. He was fiercely protective of his mother and defended the fact that she was uneducated and had worked as a waitress at one of the few restaurants in Douglas. She often had worked a double shift to bring in extra money. His sister had worked, too. Grant had always seemed embarrassed that he didn't make enough to totally support them. He had never believed that Beth had liked and admired Lydia. "What's she doing now?"

"She's a dietitian." His lips thinned. "She doesn't work anywhere anymore. She's married and has three children and stays home with them."

Beth was surprised by the disgust coloring his words. "I think it's great that she's married to a man who can afford for her to stay home and raise her children."

"Yeah, it's just terrific." Sarcasm was rife in Grant's voice. "Sorry *I* didn't measure up during our marriage. I couldn't even afford your gas bill, much less a fancy car."

"Grant, I wasn't making a veiled reference to us." Why did he have to misinterpret everything she said? "I'm happy for your sister, that's all."

"I wanted her to get her education and use it to be independent, not to slave after a man and children."

"Grant Stephens," Beth shook with anger, "you have the most perverted view of the world. Didn't it ever occur to you that Lydia may be doing exactly what she wants to and therefore she *is* independent?"

"Oh, sure, and after she gives him her heart and soul, he'll run out on her."

Beth stared down at the book. So that was it. He thought that in every relationship someone ran out—first his father had deserted his mother, and then he felt that, at least emotionally, she had run out on him. She looked back up at him and saw a lonely, insecure boy. She wanted to take him in her arms and soothe away his loneliness.

But she couldn't. *Her* emotions were just barely under control after a lifetime of dependence on others. She wasn't ready to sacrifice that.

She allowed herself a moment of grief over their ill-fated marriage. If only their young love could have been nurtured beyond the physical explosion their lust produced.

She cleared her throat and asked, "What does your mother think about all this?"

"Mother died four years ago," he stated flatly.

"Oh, Grant, I'm so sorry. You know how much I loved and respected Maryann."

It was the truth. Grant's mother had had an air about her that was hard to define and impossible to dislike. She was down-to-earth in her dealings with life and people, always pleasant and fun to be around. If there was such a thing as a romantic realist, then that was Maryann Stephens. Beth knew her death must have caused tremendous grief for Grant. He had adored his mother.

"She didn't suffer. She died instantly in a car accident." Grant fingered the stiff cover of *Bear Tracks*.

Not knowing how to ease his pain, Beth turned the conversation away from his mother. "I miss seeing your sister. I'm sure she kept you filled in on all the gossip."

He made a sound that sounded like a growl deep in his throat. "I couldn't care less about what went on in Douglas."

"Nothing much ever happens that's newsworthy, anyway."

"Oh, I don't know. Red kept things happening. Why do you think he stayed in this town?" Grant searched her face for an answer.

"It was home," she said simply. "It's where everyone accepted him no matter how crazy he seemed."

"Is that why you came back?"

"In a way."

"Or did you come back because you loved Red?" At her surprised expression, Grant spoke slowly, almost menacingly. "That's it, isn't it, Beth? You loved the guy and came back to be with him. You probably always loved him. He had money just like you. That's what you really wanted in a man, wasn't it?''

Beth paled visibly, a haunted look rising to her eyes. Her voice was reedy. "You're blind, Grant. I'm mourning the loss of a good friend who died too young and too painfully. I was never attracted to Red in the way you're suggesting, and you know it."

"I *don't* know it." Grant struggled to keep his voice under control. "I don't really know you at all, Beth. I was married to you for eighteen months, and I don't know you at all."

Beth had been eighteen when they'd gotten married. He'd been a senior in college, but no more knowledgeable about life and love than she had been. What if he had taken his time to discover all the facets of her personality? Would he have loved her enough that her father couldn't have driven him off with his persuasive speech about Beth needing the finer things in life?

"Maybe that's because you were so busy being Mr. Football Star, Mr. Basketball Star, Mr. Everything. You didn't take the time to know me."

She had thrown his thoughts into his face. To cover his chagrin, he flung at her, "And I suppose you tried hard to get to know the real me?" He couldn't control the bitterness that seeped into his tone. "Did it ever occur to you that the reason I worked extra hard at doing well in football was so I wouldn't lose my scholarship? I also worked full time."

"Yes, it occurred to me, and I understood, but it was hard going from being together all the time to suddenly never seeing each other." She had sorted and cataloged what had gone wrong with their marriage a million times in her mind, but words seemed to reduce the complexity of it. "And then..." Her voice dropped off.

"What?" Grant needed to know what she was reluctant to tell him.

She took a deep breath. "Then it dawned on me that I was living in your shadow, that I didn't have a separate identity. I had to find out who I was, and you wouldn't let me do that."

Grant studied her as her words filtered through his brain. Their relationship had been a roller-coaster ride from beautiful couple to admired newlyweds to bitter divorcees. He had always believed she was in the wrong for going to her father for financial help, but maybe he could have given her more credit than he had for being a person in her own right. Hell, he'd just been trying to make life easier for her.

Her blue eyes were filled with that innocent earnestness that he always found fascinating. Despite being such a pampered girl, she possessed an innocent charm. It never failed to touch some inner corner of his heart that no other woman had ever been able to penetrate.

He looked down at the book in his hands and flipped another page. There was a picture of the two of them standing under a large oak tree. They had been dubbed "Cutest Couple."

"You were so beautiful, Beth." He turned to her, unmindful of the yearbook as it slid to the floor. "You're still beautiful."

He reached up and cradled her head in his hands before gliding his thumbs across the pouty surface of her mouth. He watched in fascination as her lips parted slightly, and he needed no more urging before settling his mouth over hers.

It was a deep, soul-searching kiss that sent his senses whirling. Beth's arms crept around him to clutch at the material of his shirt. Her lips were warm and tasted of promises and pleasure and poignancy.

Grant lifted his head and stared at the dewy surface of her lips. Suddenly he saw her melting expression as a trap, the same soft, seductive steel-jawed trap she had sprung ten years ago. He let his hands fall away from her face.

He bent to pick up the book. "I guess I got carried away with this nostalgia thing." His voice hardened as he continued, "You can't sucker me this time. So save those sweet kisses for innocents like Joe Clay."

Chapter 4

"It's hot in here," Delores muttered from the doorway of the living room as Beth hurried from the room.

"What?"

"Nothing." Delores flopped down on the couch and picked up the book that Grant had dropped there. *"Bear Tracks,"* she read from the cover. "So that's what you two were doing, reminiscing?"

Grant, still looking at the doorway where Beth had disappeared, answered distractedly, "What?" He turned his attention to Delores, looking at her speculatively. "Yes, we were talking about old times. About Red."

"Don't look at me that way." Delores shook her already tousled hairdo. "Men only want two things when they look at a woman like that. And you ain't getting neither."

Grant eyed her closely and grinned. "Oh yeah? What do they want?"

"Information and sex, and not necessarily in that order."

Delores fluffed her hair as she relaxed on the couch. "Which is it with you?"

Grant's laughter rolled up from deep in his chest. "You always did get right to the point, didn't you, Delores? I like honesty in a woman." He plowed his fingers through his hair. "But you're wrong this time. I don't want either one."

"Just my luck. A strikeout." Delores gave her hair a last pat before surveying Grant's face. "But I think you're either fooling yourself or you're lying, Mr. Football."

Grant stood up and paced restlessly about the room. Finally he stopped and planted himself in front of Delores. "You and Red were close during school. Were you ever jealous of Red and Beth?"

"Sorry, Grant," Delores said firmly. "I don't know if any of the rumors are true or not, but even if I did, I wouldn't tell." She smiled in a contented feline way. "All I can tell you is that I've never been jealous of Beth."

She eased herself off the couch and stood face-to-face with him. "You were, and probably still are, the biggest charmer this county ever produced. Come on, let's see if you can use it on the cook."

Just then the doorbell chimed a pathetic version of the refrain from "Home on the Range."

Grant looked down at Delores's smiling face. "Red's idea of a novel doorbell?"

Delores nodded and yelled in the direction of the kitchen, "I'll get it."

She swung open the door, and Grant was surprised to see Shorty Bonds standing there, three-piece suit and all.

"Hiya, big guy," Delores purred.

Grant looked sharply at the twosome in the doorway and was surprised to observe Delores's metamorphosis from trusted friend into sexy siren in the presence of the short, nervous attorney. They were opposites, but as he watched

Delores coo and rub her body suggestively against the sputtering man, he knew stranger things could happen than for these two to fall in love.

"We were just about to have something hot for lunch. Do you want to join us, sugar?"

The way Delores pronounced the word *hot* made Shorty run his finger around the collar of his stiffly starched shirt.

"Hello, Grant," he croaked in greeting. Then he turned his attention back to Delores. "That sounds great, Delores." He formally took her elbow and escorted her primly past Grant, but not before Delores winked at Grant.

Beth greeted Shorty with a hug and hurried to set another bowl on the table. Shorty held Delores's chair while she seated herself, and Grant held Beth's. She whispered her thanks, and then the four old high school classmates sat down to their meal.

"What brings you out here today, Shorty?" Beth held her breath, fearing he might add some new and even more difficult stipulation to Red's will.

"It's about that jaguar. I may have located an avenue for returning him to the wild."

"That would be terrific, Shorty." Beth's relief was twofold.

"How did you get that jaguar, anyway?"

All eyes turned to Grant. It was apparent to him that the three people facing him often discussed the day's events at the refuge and had forgotten that he was there—a novel experience for him.

"It was a cruelty situation. We got him from a roadside show. One of those small, sleazy outfits that set up in small towns."

Delores took over the account. "It's hard for us to care for a big cat. He's healthy now, and more dangerous than we can deal with."

"And—" Beth smiled at him, her sudden action making him as hot as one of Delores's wild suggestions "—we can't release him into the wilds around here, even though jaguars were once indigenous to South Texas."

Shorty turned to her. "I've been in contact with a jaguar release program in Central America. We've just about nailed down an agreement."

Delores leaned toward Shorty, ran her hand up and down his arm, and gushed, "Oh, sugar, you are so smart. Did I ever tell you how much I love a man with a big...brain?"

Shorty blushed beet red to the tips of his ears. Beth laughed and glanced at Grant. She seemed accustomed to Delores's outrageous behavior and obviously enjoyed her silliness. Grant joined in the laughter and clapped Shorty on the back.

The lawyer regained his composure and swallowed. "Oh, I almost forgot. New Start received another healthy check from our anonymous donor."

Beth raised her eyebrow and nodded at Shorty. "We can sure use it."

As the meal progressed, Grant asked Beth, "When did you learn to cook?" He was busily soaking up gravy with a biscuit. "This is delicious."

There was no trace of sarcasm in his voice to dim her pleasure. "I conquered the range over the years. Nothing fancy, though. I'm glad you like it. Do you want another helping?"

"Sure." Grant motioned with his hand as Beth started to rise. "I'll get it."

She studied him while he ladled the steaming stew into his bowl. He seemed totally relaxed here; he fit in perfectly. The chip on his shoulder had disappeared for the time being. *This is how it will be while he's living here*, she thought. Having him this close, playing house, was going to take more out of her than she had thought. She couldn't seem *not* to pay attention to him. His presence dominated the room. His voice, his laughter, his gentle teasing, made her aware of how much she had missed him all these years.

Delores spoke up. "Well, while you two are playing happy homemakers—" her eyes sought out Grant's and Beth's "—I'm going back to work."

It was Beth's turn to blush, but Delores went right on as though she hadn't noticed the other woman's discomfort.

"Some of us still have chores to do." She pushed her chair away from the table and carried her dishes to the sink. "Whose turn is it to do the dishes?"

"I'll get them." Beth rushed to get Delores out of the kitchen before she could say something else to embarrass her. "Just stack them in the sink. I'll wash them later."

Grant jumped in. "I'll do them."

All heads turned to observe the once-mighty football hero volunteering to do dishes.

He smiled at them. "In fact, put me to work. I intend to do my share. I can't just sit around here for four weeks doing nothing."

Delores's eyebrows shot up. "Staying for four weeks? When did this happen?" She held up her hand to ward off the answer. "Never mind. Don't tell me the cold reality, let me fantasize."

"It's not like that." Beth hurried to explain, hoping her defensiveness wasn't evident in her voice. "Grant had some vacation time, and he decided to stay and see if we can get this mess with the will straightened out."

"I told you, let me fantasize." She eyed Grant and then Beth for several seconds. "You two are something. I know Red loved a challenge, but this may be too much even for him."

"What are you talking about?" Grant's eyebrows drew together.

Delores picked up Beth's keys. "I'm outa here. Beth, I'm going to take your truck to get the feed, okay?"

Beth nodded.

Delores rushed to the back door, only pausing long enough to hurl over her shoulder to Shorty, "Later, sugar." Then she was gone.

"Hey, come back here and explain!" Grant yelled after her.

Beth laughed nervously. "Forget it. Delores is always making cryptic remarks like that. You'll go crazy if you try to figure them out. Isn't that right, Shorty?"

Shorty had regained his composure. "That's for sure. She thinks she knows all about the world. I've tried to get her to go to college, where she could really learn some things, but she insists she knows all about people without a formal education." He shook his head wearily. "I'll never figure her out."

Beth laughed and put an arm around Shorty's shoulders. "Don't even try. She's way ahead of all of us in the people department."

"You're right, of course." He folded his paper napkin fastidiously and glanced up at Beth. "I need to discuss some new sponsors who've sent in pledge cards." His eyes swept meaningfully toward Grant, who was industriously rinsing out their bowls. "Do you want to retire to Red's—er, your study?"

Beth followed his look and nodded. Grant swung around to face them.

"I'd like you to talk this out in front of me. After all," he added, "I have an interest in this place now."

Beth watched him carefully. "Grant, you really don't have to get involved."

"I know I don't have to, but I want to understand all the workings of New Start."

Beth searched his eyes for a reason. "Why?"

"I want to see why it's so important to you. I want to investigate the place that made you offer—" Beth knew he had been about to say "your body," but he stopped in deference to Shorty's presence. Instead he turned to Shorty with a question. "Are you Beth's legal adviser?"

"Yes. I've been Red's lawyer since the day I passed the bar exam, and Beth took me on when she and Red began working together. I thought they were crazy when they began tending these abused animals." He smiled warmly at Beth. "But they were both adamant and totally dedicated, so I help as much as I can."

"And to show that he's not entirely a stuffed shirt," Beth giggled and looked at Shorty with affection, "he's adopted one of the goats."

"What does that mean, 'he's adopted one of the goats'? And what did you mean about sponsors?"

Shorty was in his element explaining legalese. "New Start is a nonprofit organization. Private donations, sponsorships and adoptions help offset operating costs."

"Feed and veterinary bills can run as high as seventeen-hundred dollars a month," Beth broke in.

"And people pay to sponsor an animal?" Grant stashed the silverware in the dishdrainer.

"Yes. We try to find homes for most of the animals, but several of our permanent residents have sponsors who pay a small monthly fee to help maintain them." Beth put a plastic container of leftover stew in the huge refrigerator. "Sponsors and adopters receive a picture of their animal and a certificate of adoption.

"And what they really like," she added, "is that they can come out to visit their pet."

"Not bad." Grant nodded. "What about the physical work of the place—keeping it clean, feeding the animals and so forth. Do you and Delores do it all?"

"Oh, no. We have volunteers to help with the chores, and sometimes people are sentenced to work here. You know, community service. We also have two veterinary students working for us every other afternoon right now. Working with these animals is great experience for them."

"Interesting," Grant said. "I'm impressed. You seem to have the nuts and bolts clearly in place."

Beth blushed with pleasure. Never had Grant given her a compliment about something she had done. He had often told her she looked beautiful or her hair was pretty, but he had never told her that her actions were worthwhile. If she was honest with herself, though, during their marriage she had been focused on making herself beautiful, so he'd only noticed what she'd wanted him to. To cover her uneasiness, she turned to Shorty. "Let's see a list of those new sponsors."

"Oh my gosh." Beth jumped up from the winking electronic eye of the computer, where she had been logging donations. "What time is it?"

"One-thirty." Grant had been looking over the New Start brochures that were mailed to various clubs, organizations and church groups soliciting contributions. "Why?"

"I've got to go into town for a Cornyval meeting at two." She was already exiting the spreadsheet and shutting down the computer.

"A what?"

"An organizational meeting for this year's Cornyval."

"Cornyval?" Grant raised his eyebrows.

"Yes, you remember the Spring Festival that Douglas has every year? A few years ago it was renamed Cornyval. I'm on the planning committee." She marched past him, heading for the door. "I need to run upstairs and change clothes. And I'll call the student vets and see if they can look after the horses we picked up earlier. If I hurry, I can just make it."

"How do you intend to get there?"

Beth stopped in her tracks and glanced back at Grant.

He turned to her curiously. "Delores borrowed your truck to get feed. She said she didn't want to get her convertible full of hay and grain. It's parked out back."

Beth groaned in frustration. "I don't have the keys for it. I'll call Tom Wilson and see if he can pick me up on his way—"

Grant cut her off. "I'll take you."

"You don't have to do that."

He took her by the elbow and guided her to the foot of the stairs. "Hurry now. If I'm going to be here for a month, I might as well start getting into the local culture."

"Glad to see you could make it, Beth." Mildred, the minister's wife, buzzed around Beth and Grant as they entered the recreation hall of the church. "And, Grant, I'm surprised to see you still here. I was so overcome by Red's ideas about children and Christmas at his will reading that I didn't really get to talk with you."

She left her greeting hanging in the air, waiting for one of them to clue her in to Grant's presence, but she was disappointed, as neither felt inclined to give an explanation.

Only slightly perturbed, Mildred rushed on, "We haven't started yet. Come and sit over by the coffeepot."

"I'm here strictly as an observer." Grant smiled his most charming, disarming smile for the spritely woman and backed away. "I'll sit over here, out of the way."

"Glad to see you again, Grant." Tom Wilson shook his hand. "Hope this kind of thing doesn't bore you."

"Oh, no. Just carry on as if I wasn't here." Grant eased himself down onto a hand-me-down couch in the corner of the room and leaned his head against the wall.

Beth studied him briefly before following Mildred over to the two card tables and chairs set up for the meeting. One of the tables held a coffeepot and a bundt cake with white frosting oozing down the sides.

"Have some cake. I made it last night," said Mildred. She cut herself a hefty slice.

"No, thanks. I just ate a little while ago."

"I'll take a piece." Tom grinned with anticipation. "And make it a big one."

Beth watched as her two partners on the committee settled down with their cake and coffee. "Okay, let's get started."

Mildred brushed some crumbs off her lips. "What's our theme going to be this year?"

"What it is every year—spring," Tom mumbled between bites.

"I think we should change it this year." Mildred sat up straighter. "I think we should have a Hawaiian theme."

"What?" Tom shook his head. "Mildred, every year you want to wear your grass skirt, and every year we say no."

Beth jumped in. "Let's not start this argument again."

Grant laughed inwardly. Somehow he had grown accustomed to dealing with life on the edge. Escorting federal prisoners, tracking down Mafia hit men, developing an intimate knowledge of weaponry and narrowly escaping death in a drug kingpin bloodbath. Hell, he'd even been in on nabbing Noriega in Panama. Now here he was in a church recreation room listening to a heated debate about a luau versus a barbecue. He must be losing his grip. No one would believe this at the office. His boss, Bill Johnson, would have a real belly laugh.

In fact, he didn't believe it himself. What had gotten him here? No, not what, but who. Beth. Always Beth. He looked at her trying to mediate between Tom and Mildred.

Her calming fingers touched Tom's arm, and Grant thought about how they felt when she caressed him or just smoothed away the worry from his brow. She laughed at something Mildred proposed, and the sound reminded him of sunlight and music. Yeah, only one person could get him to stay in this hole of a town. This town that had treated his sister, his mother and him like poor white trash. Only one person. His Beth.

But Beth had defended the town, had said he was listening to his pride and not the townspeople. Certainly Tom and Mildred were treating him kindly. So did Delores and Shorty. Could he have been too young and hotheaded to see the difference between neighborly concern and caustic putdowns? Was Beth right about this place?

He was jogged back to the rec hall when he heard Tom calling him.

"Hey, Grant? Are you going to be here for my party this weekend?" His old friend looked over at him expectantly.

"I don't know. What kind of party is it?"

"A sighting in. I'm trying out my new guns."

"Tom Wilson, you can't shoot anything with those guns. Red said so in his will." Mildred puffed up with indignation.

"I know it, damn it. Er...excuse me." Tom reddened. "Didn't mean to say that in a church. You know I don't believe in killing wildlife. We're just going to be shooting at cans." His eyes danced with anticipation. "I can't wait to show off those firearms. They're beauts."

Grant grinned from the couch. "I'll bet I can outshoot anybody in this town."

Beth's eyes widened in surprise. "Grant—"

"You're on," Tom interjected. "I'm going to spread the word."

Beth got up from the hard metal chair and walked over to Grant. "We're finished here."

He stood up and stretched. "Since I've been so patient, I deserve a reward." He looked at her from under dark lashes. "Come on, I could use a drink."

Ignoring his hot look, she said, "Okay, but I pick the place."

"This isn't exactly what I had in mind when I said I wanted a drink." Grant looked around at the old soda fountain in the Douglas Drugstore.

"I know." Beth smiled as she slipped into one of the red vinyl booths. "You'd probably rather be at the Longneck Palace, but I love this place."

"Scoot over." He slid in beside her, forcing her to move next to the wall.

"Grant, there's a whole seat across from me." She looked pointedly at the empty place.

"Yeah, I know, but this is how I remember us always sitting when we came in here." He slid a little closer, pressing his thighs against hers. "These seats do seem a little smaller than I remember, though." He glanced around. "Everything else looks exactly the same."

Time hadn't changed this place, he noted. The worn wooden floor, the big mirror running the length of the fountain, the old jukebox that lifted out records and spun them on a turntable. He wondered briefly what would happen now that companies were no longer producing records. He smiled to himself. The Douglas Drugstore probably hadn't bought new records in years, so it didn't matter. No, nothing had changed.

He turned to share his thoughts with Beth, but then bit back the words. *This* Beth, he knew, wouldn't agree with him. For her, things *had* changed. She was no longer Daddy's little darling. She was a woman who took in abused animals and sheltered them with her compassion.

Startled by the yearning his tender musings unleashed in him, he reined them in before he was forced to admit his need for the new Beth. With a conscious effort, he replaced them with the comfortable contempt he had nurtured for the old Beth.

"What'll you have?" The teenage waitress chewed gum and rocked impatiently on the balls of her feet.

"A cherry Coke," Beth answered without thinking.

Grant looked at her and raised his eyebrows. Turning back to the girl, he added, "I'll have a plain Coke."

"That's all?" The young waitress cracked her gum.

"Yes," Beth and Grant answered simultaneously.

Grant waited for the girl to leave before he turned to Beth and asked, "You come here often?"

"Every once in a while. It brings back fond memories."

"I bet. Being the rich girl in town, driving the latest car, wearing the best clothes. I think I can see why you like coming here. Me, I have different memories of this place."

She was surprised by the anger in his voice and stung by his words. Her own anger surfaced. "I can't help that I was born to a family with money. You can't help that you weren't. Can't you just accept those facts?"

They stared at each other, tempers simmering. Finally she took a deep breath. "What *are* your memories of this place?"

"I remember having to sneak around your father and meet you here on the sly. I remember never being good enough, always having to worry whether I could afford to buy you one of those damn cherry Cokes.'' He looked around the cozy drugstore and shook his head. "Hell, I didn't fit in then and I don't fit in now. Only this time it's different. Before, I wanted to fit in. Now, I don't.''

Beth took his hand and squeezed it. "Grant—"

He yanked it away from her. "Forget it."

Their drinks arrived, and Beth sipped at hers. They were sitting so close that Grant could feel every movement she made. She had slipped into a long, large sweater and skirt for the meeting, and her legs pressed intimately against him under the table. It was torture to be this close to her again and have the same old inadequacies assail him. Had it been wise for him to agree to stay on for four weeks? He didn't think so. He should get out of this town just as soon as he could. He didn't want Beth to see how she could still affect him.

Forcing a lightness into his tone that he didn't feel, he asked, "What's it going to be?"

"What?"

"Mildred in her grass skirt or Mildred in a hat with flowers all over it?"

Beth smoothed the tension out of her face and smiled. "Probably both, we're going to have a Spring Luau."

Grant chuckled. "Figures. Only in Douglas, a town where no one has ever been to Hawaii and most probably doesn't really believe it's a part of the United States, would there be such a thing as a Texas Luau."

He threw two dollars down on the table. "Let's go." He grabbed her hand and pulled her from the booth. "I've got to go by the hotel, check out and get my clothes. We might as well do it now while we're in town."

Beth rode in silence with Grant to the Faraday Hotel. Years ago it had been an elegant hotel that boasted velvet curtains and cut-glass chandeliers in the lobby. Time and the economy had replaced the refined with mediocrity, and the hotel was now clean but shabby. It was the only hotel in town, however.

Grant paid his bill and then turned to take Beth's elbow to lead her up the stairs to room 212. As he fumbled with the key, they could hear the telephone ringing in his room. Swinging the door wide, he hurried to answer it.

Beth closed the door and stood self-consciously, watching him on the phone. She didn't know why she hadn't waited for him in the car, but she hadn't wanted to leave him alone. He had been broodingly silent on the short drive here. Now, as she watched him yank at the tie around his neck, she wished herself safely back at her ranch.

"What did the snitch say?" Grant's voice was professional and deadly. He shook his head.

"That's not good enough. We need to know when and where. I don't give a damn what Johnson says. Turn the screws."

Beth rubbed her arms as a sudden chill iced her veins at the coldness in Grant's tone.

"Yeah. Oh, and Timmons—" his Nordic eyes sliced towards Beth "—after today, you can reach me at this number." He repeated the ranch phone number and hung up. He continued to stare at her for so long that she shifted nervously. In a quick movement he turned from her, jerked open the closet door and grabbed his suitcase, then set it on the bed.

"Was that about your job?" Beth wanted to defrost the atmosphere in the room. "Is something wrong?"

"Yeah, we've gotten word that one of our prisoners is about to be sprung."

"'Sprung' as in let go?"

"'Sprung' as in forcibly snatched back to his fold." At her look of uncertainty, he explained. "We're holding a big-time counterfeiter who is extremely valuable to his operation because he's very good. His people want him back. They'll do anything to get him, and it could get messy."

"Oh." Beth's voice was small and reedy. "It sounds so dangerous."

"Naw." Grant shrugged. "My people can handle it without anyone getting hurt."

He turned back to the closet to gather the few shirts he'd brought with him, and Beth noticed the way the muscles bunched and rippled across his shoulders as he moved. She still found the play of visible power fascinating. And exciting. And dangerous.

Trying to keep her thoughts from drifting down that sensual path, she glanced around the room. On the floor in front of a freestanding cheval glass she spotted a pair of socks, rolled neatly together. Memories assaulted her.

He still rolled up his dirty socks. That used to drive her crazy. The only way she could tell clean socks from dirty was that the dirty ones were always on the floor. She always tripped on them. Unconsciously she walked over and picked up the socks. When she stood up with them in her hand, she looked in the mirror and saw Grant staring at her with a puzzled expression on his face. Slowly his eyes traveled the length of her body and back up again. Mesmerized, like a rabbit watching the approach of a fox, she stood rooted to the spot.

Silently he came up behind her and reached around to take the socks from her. His hand, warm and gentle, closed around hers as his eyes locked with hers in the mirror. His message was telegraphed to her body by the tips of his fingers and the seductive pull of his eyes.

Beth, wanting to run from his touch, found all reason drained from her body when he bent his head and planted wet, shimmering kisses around the back of her neck. A moan—was it of pleasure or pain?—escaped her lips, and she swayed back into the solid wall of his body.

He wrapped his arms tightly around her, after leaving a path of love bites along her neck, his lips and teeth sought and found an ear. Leisurely he performed exquisite torture as he took turns nipping at the delicate lobe and laving his tongue in the tender shell.

It was a potent combination that sent erotic pulses skittering through her body to finally pool in the center of her femininity. Her eyes drifted closed, and her head fell back against his warmth. Her senses were filled with him. The woodsy after-shave he wore teased her nostrils as his quickened breath feathered her cheek. And her whole body felt the pounding of his heart as she pressed into him.

"Beth, open your eyes." His voice, deep and husky, permeated her euphoria.

She opened her eyes to meet his hungry gaze in the mirror. His eyes were dark, promising sensuous secrets in their depths. Hypnotized, she watched him slide his hands across the nubby knit of her sweater to cup the undersides of her breasts. He cursed softly.

At her raised eyebrows, he chuckled, "You're wearing a bra."

She smiled and felt her breasts grow heavy with yearning. His fingers kneaded and shaped, and when he ran his thumbs over her nipples, even through the bra and sweater, they both could feel the tight beading of those tiny peaks.

"Grant," she whispered, about to turn in his arms when she moved her hand and felt the wadded socks in it. Reason washed over her, dulling the point of her desire. Oh, God, what was she doing? She wouldn't fall victim to this man's charm and dominance again!

Sliding Grant's arms away from her, she pulled from his embrace and turned to face him.

His eyes widened and then narrowed as he studied her. His voice was dark. "What happened?"

She looked him directly in the eyes, but her voice was not quite steady. "Grant, you've just witnessed how my breasts react to you. But that's all you'll get. We can't get involved like that again. I won't let us."

As he studied her, his eyes lost their warm lights and returned to icy blue. "Don't challenge me, Beth. I've been challenged by better women than you. And I've never lost." He leaned toward her, and his voice dropped. "Think about it."

Chapter 5

"Here, let me help you." Beth reached for the grooming comb the little girl held in her hand. Beth worked it cautiously through the horse's tail, showing the girl how to avoid hurting the horse. "There. Just remember to be gentle. Brush it the way you would want your mother to brush your hair." She ruffled the blonde's long ponytail before bidding her and her mother, who was standing close by, goodbye. She then headed into one of the barns, passing other volunteers who were busily grooming other horses.

Grant was leaning against the fence. He had watched the entire scene from this vantage point. The skies were overcast, but Beth was a ray of golden light. In work boots, standing in mud, she had been helping a little girl groom a horse. He never would have believed it. He couldn't remember her ever being sweaty or grimy. She had always been fresh, "just out of a band box," his mother used to say. And just as fragile. She couldn't deal with the reality of not having enough money, of having to wear the same thing

more than once a week. Well, it looked as if she had gotten
over that little quirk.

Not that she didn't still look appealing, even in her di-
sheveled state. She did. He found this grown-up Beth who
wasn't afraid to show her blemishes incredibly desirable. His
body had been doing a slow burn ever since he'd seen her at
the reading of the will a week ago. In the past few days,
every time she turned those clear blue eyes his way or sashayed past him, his body tightened and he thought he was
going to go crazy from wanting her. They had both been
pretending that the scene in the Faraday Hotel hadn't happened, but he knew they were both very much aware that it
had. Her hands-off demand had heightened his ache for her.
They took turns being scrupulously polite to each other or
snarling like bears. The situation was like living on a razor's edge.

What if they were to go to bed together? Then what?
Would this constant ache be soothed? He doubted it. Besides wanting Beth in his arms, he found he liked watching
her putter in the kitchen. She took such delight in cooking,
and he was a welcome guinea pig for her concoctions. He
was growing accustomed to building a fire at night in the
great stone fireplace in the study and then working quietly
with Beth on the masses of paperwork that went along with
running New Start. He knew he would miss those peaceful
times when he left.

Drawn by some invisible magnetism, Grant pushed himself away from the roughly hewn fence and followed her into
the barn. He squinted to make out her form. She was
standing on the rails of one of the stalls, talking quietly to
Twinkle Toes. He came up behind her, appreciating how her
jeans fit as snugly as a second skin, showing off the soft
roundness of her derriere and the long length of her legs. He
remembered how, as a high school cheerleader, she'd teased

him with a show of her bloomer-clad bottom. But back then he'd been a boy; now he was a man.

If he were ever to free himself of her magnetism, he had to keep their relationship on a business level. "How's ol' Twinkle Toes today?" he called.

Beth straightened and whirled. "You startled me."

"Sorry." He thought the color staining her cheeks made her even more attractive. "I was just wondering how the pony is."

"Oh, she's fine." She turned back to study the little animal. "I was just checking up on her. I think what she needs is more sunshine, though." She managed a quick glance at Grant. "So I think I'll get one of the vet students to fix that broken place in the yard fence and move her up to the house. What do you think?"

She cocked her head innocently at him. He was lost for a moment in the swirling blue of Beth's eyes. As he watched, her tongue came out to moisten her dry lips, and he fell deeper into the whirlpool.

"You treat these animals better than people," he groused.

"That's because they deserve it. They've all been mistreated or ignored. They need a little attention." She looked away and sighed wistfully. "Red used to say we all need kindnesses in our lives—big and little ones, every day."

After a moment she went on. "Why are you here? I thought you were going out into the woods to help Delores find the goats?"

"I did. We found one of them, so I brought him back. Delores is out there searching for the other two. What's the deal with these goats, anyway? Can't they take care of themselves?" He unbuttoned the sleeves of his shirt and proceeded to turn back the cuffs. Even though the afternoon was blustery and cool and hinted of rain, the search for the goats and the closeness in the barn had heated his blood. So did the woman in front of him.

"Goats are strange creatures—very mischievous. It doesn't help that Delores babies them. She wants to pen them in, and they keep getting out to roam in the woods. They're very stubborn."

"Wouldn't it be best to let them roam?" He couldn't understand all this concern over goats.

"It would be okay, except that every now and then we lose one to a coyote, and they can get themselves into some pretty hairy situations that we don't have the time to handle."

He pulled on his leather work gloves. "Well, I've got to get back to the search. I'm just having a hard time calling out, 'Here, Rhett, here, Scarlett.'"

Beth laughed. "I guess you brought in Ashley."

"Yeah." Grant's eyebrows lowered. "What is Delores, some *Gone With the Wind* nutcase?"

"No, she just names the animals after characters they remind her of."

"Right. I can hardly wait until one reminds her of Rambo or the Terminator."

"You'll get used to it."

Before Grant could come up with a quick comeback, Delores came tearing into the barn, screaming, "Come quick! They're caught. I need help pulling them out."

"My God, Delores, what happened to you? You're bleeding." Beth rushed to her friend's side to examine a long cut on the inside of Delores's forearm.

"I tangled with a barbed-wire fence." She winced as Beth turned her arm to look for other wounds. "The fence won," she added.

"You go into town right now and let Dr. Simons look at that." Beth's voice was stern. "You'll probably need a tetanus shot."

"But the goats—"

"We'll get them." Beth cut her off. "You go on now."

"All right," Delores agreed reluctantly. "They're in that grove of trees near the old windmill."

"Here, wrap this bandage around your arm so you don't bleed all over the upholstery of that convertible." Beth had produced some white gauze from a first-aid kit in the barn. "Now *go*. She hurried Delores into the convertible and waved as she drove away.

"After you." Grant motioned for Beth to lead the way. "I have no idea where the old windmill is."

He slung a rope over his shoulder, and the two of them set off across the pasture at a fast clip. He yelled at her above the rising wind, "How do you think they got themselves caught?"

She glanced at him before shaking her head. "I don't know. We'll find out soon enough."

They slowed down as the open pasture gave way to a brushy area filled with oak and sycamore trees.

"They must be somewhere around here," Beth informed him. "The windmill's broken-down now, but it used to be near here."

Just then they heard a small cry coming from off to their left.

"This area was hit by a small twister during the spring rainy season last year," she observed as they surveyed the damaged and uprooted trees all around them.

The two goats were trapped under a fallen log on the side of a shallow ravine. They lay on their sides, bleating and trying to wriggle free, but they were solidly caught.

Beth put her hands on her hips and stood over them, clucking like a mother hen. "I told you not to come out here. But would you listen? No. Now I have to haul this tree off you and hope that nothing is broken."

"Let's see if we can figure out how to get those two rascals out of there." Grant had to raise his voice to be heard as the wind picked up and whipped his words away.

He walked around the tree, trying to see how the goats had gotten trapped, crouching down occasionally and examining the damage, hoping simple leverage would get them out. No such luck. They would have to lift the entire log off.

"Let's try to lift it first," he instructed.

Just as he and Beth tried to hoist the log off, a crack of thunder shattered the air. "Oh, damn. It's going to rain." Grant raked his hair back from where it had fallen across his forehead. "Let's hurry before we're all caught in the downpour."

Even with both of them straining to boost the log up, they were barely able to move it. "These oak trees are like iron. Let's tie the rope to the log and then throw the other end over that tree branch and hoist the thing off." Beth motioned with her hands to demonstrate what she meant.

Grant looked at her and gave a "might as well" shrug. He tied the rope to the fallen log and then tried pitching it over the branch. It didn't work.

"I'm going to shinny up there and drape the rope over that big branch," he shouted over the rising wind.

"Grant, be careful," she admonished.

"Beth, for Pete's sake, I'm a federal marshal. I've handled gang members and drug cartels. I should be able to handle two goats. When I get up there, I'll pull the rope and you push the log. Okay?"

"Okay." In spite of the situation, she smiled at his boasting. Her experience told her that two goats could put a crime boss to shame for mischievousness.

He shinnied and worked his way up the tree until he was able to pitch the rope over the branch. As he positioned himself solidly in the tree, it started to rain. Big, heavy drops announced a quick, hard, cold rain.

"Grab it and hold on tight," he yelled as he took the rope. "When I count to three, push. One, two, three!"

They tugged. They pulled. They pushed. Harder and harder, until the log began to move. Grant held the rope and then leveraged himself so that his weight was holding the log.

"One more time," he hollered at the struggling Beth. They yanked. The log came up. The goats had enough room to slide out.

"Thank goodness," Beth sighed.

The two animals, wobbly and wide-eyed, looked at the humans and began to bah like crying children before they scampered away.

"Okay," Grant yelled, "let's let the log down nice and easy."

Even as the words died on his lips, Beth lost her footing on the muddy, slippery surface and teetered precariously.

"Hold on, Beth!" Grant's muscles bulged as he strained to hold the dangling log. "Knock the log away from you and roll. I'm going to count—"

Too late!

Beth toppled, her legs scissoring directly under the oak limb. Grant could see the fear and pain in her face, but she determinedly kicked the log, then rolled out from under it. Grant dropped the rope and scrambled down out of the tree.

"Beth! Are you okay?"

She struggled to a sitting position, and he gathered her close in his arms.

"Beth, Beth, are you all right? Are you hurt?" Spears of concern and fear pricked his chest painfully.

"I think I'm okay." She could hardly form the words.

"Let's get you out of this rain." He looked around for the goats and saw a flash of white as they hightailed it back in the direction of the barn. He figured they were fine.

"See if you can stand up." He put his arm around her shoulders to help her.

"Ouch." She moaned and would have fallen without Grant's support. "I think I may have sprained an ankle."

Grant didn't hesitate a second before scooping her up in his arms and hurrying toward the barn.

"Put me down, Grant. You'll hurt yourself carrying me."

"Hardly." His eyes flicked down at her. "You don't weigh any more than you did when we were married."

That reference to their brief, ill-fated marriage hushed her.

By the time the bedraggled couple reached the barn area, the rain was coming down in a steady cadence, chilling them to the bone. The sponsors and volunteers had all packed up and left, as had the veterinary trainees.

Grant carried Beth into the barn and stood her against the wall. He opened his mouth to speak, but the words never came. His eyes traveled down her body. She was shivering uncontrollably, and when his gaze stopped at her chest, she was afraid to look down.

Folding her arms across herself, she shouted above the clatter the downpour made on the tin roof, "I'm sure Jack and Marcus took care of all the feeding. If you could just get something to steady me, I'll make a last check of the barns."

Grant shook his head. Catching her up in his embrace again, he carried her out into the rain. He tried to shield her

body with his against the cold droplets that felt like pin-
pricks even through his workshirt. He sprinted to the truck,
dodging mud puddles along the way. Opening the passenger side, he shoved her in.

"Wrap my jacket around you. I'll be right back."

She felt miffed by his high-handed behavior and grateful
for his intervention all at the same time. A most unsettling
feeling. As she draped the corduroy jacket around her, she
looked down and groaned. The soaked material of her
blouse and bra had become almost transparent. Grant had
had a clear view of her breasts. The dusky centers were hard
against the cold cotton cloth.

Mortified, she shook her head. Of course, he'd seen her
with nothing on more times than she could remember, but
this put her at a disadvantage in their present relationship.

The door flew open, and Grant landed in the driver's seat.
Rain water ran in rivulets down his face and arms, and his
hair shone with blue highlights. Beth thought he had never
looked more appealing.

"I think I checked everything," he said.

"It'll be okay. The animals should be able to take care of
themselves."

Suddenly realizing that he must be freezing, she whipped
off the jacket and offered it to him.

"You keep it," he said. "I'll be fine as soon as we get
home."

The word *home* hung in the air like a signal flare. Both
silently agreed to ignore it as Grant started the engine and
ground the gears to set the truck in motion. Neither spoke
in the few minutes it took to navigate the slippery road to the
house.

After he parked the pickup, they sat staring out the window. The rain was relentless, driving hard and rocking the
truck.

"Think we ought to wait a few minutes for this to let up a bit?"

At Beth's nod of agreement, Grant settled back in the seat. A second later he sat up abruptly, moving from under the steering wheel in the roomy cab of the truck.

"Let me see your ankle," he demanded.

"It's all right, really," she insisted, but he was already picking up her foot and swinging her leg across the seat.

"I'll just ease this boot off, but it may hurt a little," he said quietly. He worked quickly and efficiently to pull the work boot off without causing Beth undue discomfort. Even so, she drew in her breath sharply as her foot finally slid free.

After removing her cotton sock, Grant gently examined her ankle. "God, your foot is cold," he chuckled. "I remember when you used to put your feet against my back to warm them and I..." His voice trailed off, and he continued to busily inspect her damaged ankle.

He looked as though he could have kicked himself for bringing up their marriage. His brow was furrowed, and a frown marred his features.

Beth tried to ignore his comment, but ignoring Grant's warm, gentle touch was something else. He had always been able to excite her with the merest glance, and the soothing massage he was giving her foot was playing havoc with her already taut nerves. She wanted him to leave, yet she longed for him to stay. What was the matter with her?

"I think it's only a slight sprain," he was saying. "You'll be okay if you stay off your foot for a few days."

"Yes, thanks for the diagnosis." She tried to pull her foot out of his grasp but he held it firmly.

"Let me see if I can't warm it up. Turn and lean your back against the door."

He tugged on her calf. Before she could stop him, he had tucked her foot between his thighs, where it nestled cozily against his sex. Heat, desire. They all ran riotously through her bloodstream.

"We really need to be getting inside." Her voice was weak, even to her own ears. She tried to struggle away from him. Against her foot, she felt his manhood harden. Her eyes were huge, like saucers, as she grew still and stared at him.

He smiled at her, totally disarming her with the captivating sexiness of the look on his face.

"Interesting that you have this effect on me after all these years, isn't it?"

Terrified of the hot languor that stole through her body, Beth bit out her words. "You just like to play games with me, Grant. You know that you've always had this power over my body. You saw it in the hotel room. This is just another part of your game."

The words poured out. "Sometimes I think I was only attracted to you because you were the forbidden fruit. My father didn't want me near you, so that made you even more desirable."

She cleared her throat as he pinned her with his frozen eyes. Her voice dropped to a whisper. "I was too young to understand it all then. But now I know I've got to have everything in a relationship, Grant. It can't be just physical."

It was quiet in the small enclosure until his next words made her tremble inside. "I'm surprised you still have my last name. I've wondered if there was another husband."

Knowing she couldn't avoid his questions, had to face this head-on, she explained, "No, I never married again. I was confused for a long time after we split up." She paused and ran her fingers through her hair. A few strands were beginning to dry, and wispy curls were forming around her face.

"Did you see other men?" Grant seemed intent on elic-iting every detail of her love life in the past ten years.

She sighed. "I saw a few men off and on, but there were no serious relationships. I finally figured out that what I need and want out of life is to be needed and wanted." She smiled at Grant's frown. "The animals," she said simply. "They need me. No one in my life had ever before asked anything *of* me." Her voice dropped to a whisper. "You and my father wanted to do everything *for* me."

"I grew up with the idea that that's what a husband is supposed to do—take care of his wife." There was a note of hurt in Grant's voice.

Beth reached out and covered his large hand with her own, then ran her thumb back and forth across his thumb. "I grew up with the same idea, but it didn't work for me, for us. I needed to take care of you occasionally."

Grant's eyes had turned a darker, liquid blue, and Beth held her breath for several seconds before she broke the spell by pulling her hand back from his.

She had wondered for ten years about *his* life. Was there a wife? Children?

"Tell me about you, Grant. Have you married again?"

His eyes lost their luminosity and began to freeze again. Dear God, maybe he had a wife and children living some-where right now, and here he was, sitting, cozy as could be, with her. After all, she didn't really know him anymore.

"Grant Stephens—" she sat up straight and glared at him "—do you have a wife and five children hidden some-where?"

The shadow of a smile crossed his lips but was immedi-ately replaced by that sad line she had noticed earlier. His words reassured her. "No, my little gossip columnist. I'm not one of those men with a different wife and family in every city. Is that what you think of me?"

She studied the planes and angles of his face, from his broad forehead to the slightly crooked nose to his well-formed mouth. No, she knew he was a man of honor with perhaps a dash of rascal thrown in. But he wouldn't leave a wife and children behind and set up housekeeping with another woman.

"Of course not, Grant. But you still haven't answered my question."

He sighed. "Okay, okay, I haven't exactly lived the life of a monk for ten years." He looked back at the rivers of water pouring down the windshield. "I had one serious affair. We came close to marriage." His eyes flicked over her. "She was different from you. She was beautiful like you, but more worldly. She didn't have your innocence."

He stopped, and she knew he wasn't going to explain further. But she needed to know. She didn't know why, but it was important to her. "What happened? Why didn't you marry her?"

"Leave it alone, Beth. I've already told you enough."

"No, you haven't, damn it." Her eyes snapped with fury. "You waltz in here and ask all sorts of insinuating questions about Red and me, but it's not okay for me to ask questions? Now, you tell me why you didn't marry this woman."

"We just decided we weren't right for each other after all."

"Grant." She grabbed his arm, trying to force him to look at her. "Why?"

"Because she wasn't you, damn it." He bit the words out, all the pain of the past ten years pouring through his tone. "She didn't have hair like honey, skin like warm apricots and eyes like cornflowers. That's why. She didn't have a little catch in her voice when she was making love. That's why." At Beth's startled look, he added, "Are you satis-

fied? You've ruined every other woman for me. I can't be
happy with anyone else. It's like a curse."

"Grant." Her voice was hoarse with emotion.

She leaned toward him, and he gathered her into his shel-
tering arms. Moving her injured foot out of the way, she sat
in his lap like a young child seeking solace. Laying her head
against his chest, she could hear his heart beating, strong
and powerful, through his shirt. He combed his fingers time
and time again through the silky curtain of her hair.

They nestled against each other for a long time, enjoying
the warmth and feel of each other. Beth wondered at how
right it felt to be here in Grant's arms after all these years.
They fit together perfectly.

A sudden thought struck her. Had she been fooling herself into thinking that she was only physically attracted to
Grant? Could it be that she still loved him, as she had loved
him ten years ago, not only because he was the dashing hero
of her girlish dreams, but also because he was a kind, good
and decent person?

The idea panicked her. She couldn't—no, wouldn't—
share that with him. If he knew she loved him, he would try
to control her life again. She had to find her own way in the
world now, without the help of this man. But it was so good
to be in his arms again, so right.

They held each other for a long time without talking. It
was a tender embrace, not at all like the passionate caresses
that had typified their marriage. They seemed to want to
give comfort and reassurance to each other simply with the
closeness of their bodies.

Finally Beth broke the sweet silence. "Have you ever
heard the folk song that says, 'Life is a bittersweet song'?"
She felt Grant shake his head in the negative. "Well, sometimes, like now, I think that's true."

They sat cuddled together for a few more minutes. Finally Grant kissed the top of her head and pushed her back into the passenger seat. "Even though this feels wonderful, I think the rain is letting up, and I need to get you inside." His eyes appraised the still-wet blouse visible where his jacket hung open in the front. "You need to get out of those clothes."

He reached down to hand her her boot. "You carry this and I'll carry you."

"But, Grant—" Before she could finish her protest, he was out of the cab and hurrying around to open her door and swoop her up.

He dashed through the gate, pausing only long enough for Beth to unlock the front door before he stumbled into the foyer. They laughed like schoolchildren. Grant pretended to drop her several times, so Beth entwined her arms even more tightly around his neck.

He swung around and deposited her in a chair in the living room. He looked long and hard into her eyes, and then whispered in her ear, "I know exactly what you need."

Chapter 6

Grant turned away to start a fire in the massive stone fireplace. Beth's brows drew together in confusion. Oh, dear Lord, she thought. This looked like a seduction scene—the blazing fire, the wet, clinging clothes—and the man.

She stared at his silhouette and mused that he was much like the fire he was nursing to life. Volatile, hypnotic and hot. She shivered with anticipation, and Grant caught the movement out of the corner of his eye.

"Move closer to the fire," he said. "I'll be right back."

Beth scooted down to sit on an overstuffed pillow closer to the fire. Her blouse and jeans were beginning to dry. She took off Grant's jacket and held it for several seconds, breathing in the scent of him. He still used the same aftershave he had used ten years ago.

"Here."

She hadn't heard his approach. He was standing behind her, and he handed her a kitchen towel, which she immediately used to fluff her drying hair. He sat on another pillow and reached for her sprained ankle.

"Looks like it'll be tender tomorrow, but the swelling isn't bad." He had brought some ice in a plastic bag and was binding another towel around the injured area to secure the ice in place. "This should take care of it." He looked up at her and smiled. "You see, I did know exactly what you needed."

Beth almost groaned out loud. She had overestimated her feminine charms, because Grant obviously had no intention of seducing her. Why did she feel so disappointed? Did she really want it to happen?

She managed a wan smile. "Thanks. This fire is great. My hair and clothes are starting to dry."

Grant studied her for a moment. The firelight cast glittering highlights in her hair so that it looked like molten gold. She smoothed his jacket and set it aside. She wouldn't meet his gaze. Why had her eyes been closed as she held his jacket close to her face when he walked back in the room? Was she dreaming of what could be between them? Or was she lost in what had been?

"I know one more thing that will make this scene complete." He stood and walked out of the room.

Beth settled comfortably on the pillow and combed her fingers through her hair. A few minutes later, Grant returned, carrying two steaming mugs.

She looked up in wonder. "What's this?"

"Hot chocolate." He grinned and handed her a cup. "I even found some marshmallows. I remember how much you love them."

"Oh, yes. They're great when they're melted and gooey. Lots of sticky stuff is best."

She grinned back at him. His eyes were dark and mysterious in the firelight.

He settled down on a fluffy cushion, and they sipped the delicious cocoa for several seconds in companionable silence.

Finally Beth asked, "When did you learn to cook?"

He chuckled ruefully. "This is not exactly gourmet fare, but living alone for years makes learning to cook the mother of all necessities."

"Well, this is delicious. The marshmallows are just the right touch."

She gazed at Grant and smiled, and he felt his heart slam into his ribs. She had no idea how beautiful and wild and sexy she looked with her hair so artlessly mussed and her damp clothes still clinging to the curves of her body.

He set his mug on the hearth and reached over to remove hers from her suddenly stiff fingers. Then he moved toward her and leaned close.

Her eyes were huge pools of blue satin before her thick fringe of lashes swept down in anticipation of his kiss. A shaft of desire as hot as the flames in the fireplace shot through him as he ran his tongue gently across her upper lip. Then he drew back, and she opened her eyes. As she watched, he drew his index finger slowly across her lip where only moments before his tongue had been. Then he put the marshmallow-smudged digit in his mouth and savored the taste.

He smiled. "Delicious."

A mixture of a moan and an exclamation escaped from deep in Beth's chest as Grant locked his hand around her neck and drew her swiftly to him. Their lips met in a kiss that seared their brains, their hearts, their souls. The emotions that had been held in check since that day in the Faraday Hotel were unleashed and raging. The kiss went deeper as their tongues danced and mated in the most primitive way.

"Sweet, sweet," Grant murmured as he slid his lips along one of Beth's flushed cheeks before returning to claim her mouth again.

Slowly he lowered her so that she was reclining against the pillow. Carefully, he spread out her hair in a golden mantle across the plush cushion.

He placed a gentle kiss on her lips and whispered, "Delicious and just right."

Beth sighed—a sound he thought sounded like a kitten's purr when it had had its fill of cream. As he bent and rained languid kisses down her blouse, she restlessly moved her head from side to side. When he lightly grazed the tips of her breasts, she arched her back in helpless reaction.

Grant looked up at her and smiled while he ran the pad of his thumb across the stiff peak that showed clearly through the material. "You always were so sensitive here. It used to drive me crazy that all I had to do was look at you and your breasts would pout."

She breathed his name as she reached for him and brought him once again to claim her lips. This was real. This was good. This was Grant, she told herself. Grant. Her mind began to clear the sensuous web that his kisses and caresses had spun. Should she let this happen? Did she know Grant any better now than she had ten years ago?

Suddenly she stiffened and drew back.

Grant studied her. "What's the matter?"

"I really want to make love with you, Grant, maybe even more than I did ten years ago." She smiled sadly. "But I want more than sex."

How could she make him understand? She didn't want to make the same mistake again. She was ten years older and fifty years wiser than before. She wanted to go beyond the physical with him. Sky-blue eyes met frosty ones. "Now we need to learn about each other."

He had been watching the play of emotions across her face, but now he looked at her sharply. "What is this—a new course entitled Beth 101?"

She sat up and sifted his hair through her fingers. "Don't you understand what I'm saying?" she asked.

He took a deep breath and let it out slowly. "Okay, we'll play it your way. But you know where I stand—I want you, Beth Stephens." He frowned. "Just one more sip." Gently he rubbed his lips back and forth across hers. Then he drew back and handed her the mug of lukewarm chocolate. "Maybe soon we can finish things while they're hot."

The mellow aroma of fresh-brewed coffee met Beth's nostrils as she came down the stairs the next morning. Her ankle was sore, but not enough to keep her from her daily schedule. Clutching her white terry-cloth robe around her body, she smiled as she recalled the events of the previous evening. Grant had been the perfect gentleman, depositing her at her bedroom door. She knew he was unhappy with the condition she had set, but he had agreed nonetheless. They would both be happier, she reasoned, if they really got to know what made each other tick before they reestablished a physical relationship. It was sweet of him to have the coffee started this morning.

Entering the kitchen, she halted abruptly. A tall man with silver hair and an impeccably tailored business suit turned from pouring a cup of coffee.

"Daddy!" Beth expelled the word on a ragged puff of air. "What are you doing here? How did you get in?"

Martin Channing, as tall as Grant, as imposing as Mount Rushmore, walked over to give his daughter a fatherly peck on the forehead. "That's not a very nice greeting for a man who's been out of the country for weeks. And don't you remember? I insisted you have a key made for me so I could check on things."

Beth nodded. "I'm glad you're back, Daddy." She poured herself a cup of coffee. "I have something I need to tell you."

"Beth, I—"

Father's and daughter's eyes swung to the kitchen doorway to see Grant, dressed only in a pair of jeans, hair rakishly uncombed, staring with half-closed eyes back at them.

Martin Channing was the first to speak. He turned to his daughter and ran a hand through his perfectly styled hair as he shook his head. "Beth?"

"Grant is helping me with New Start for a while." She desperately wanted her father to accept Grant.

"Help?" Mr. Channing snorted in disgust. "When are you going to learn you don't need his help? You've never needed his help." His blue gaze was ominous as his silver brows drew together. "He's just using you again."

Grant didn't reply, but his rigidly controlled stance told Beth that he was fighting himself to keep from reacting.

"Stop it!" Beth exclaimed. "Let's just sit down and have a civilized conversation."

Grant eyed Martin Channing speculatively. "Like Beth said, I think we should talk, but I want to finish getting dressed first."

He wheeled and left the kitchen but stopped at the bottom of the stairs when Channing grabbed his arm. "Get dressed and get out. Out of this house and out of Beth's life."

Grant wrenched his arm away.

"Get out, Stephens!" Channing yelled. "I won't let you mess up her life again."

Controlling his temper with a supreme effort, Grant said, "Don't push me, Channing. I'm not the same 'boy' I was the last time we met. If I get out of Beth's life this time, it'll be up to her, not you." He pivoted and stalked up the stairs.

Why had he said that? He wasn't really *in* Beth's life, and he didn't want to be. Just seeing her domineering father made him flash back to their marriage, to their fights about money, about Beth taking her father's help. He had believed in her, only to find out from her father that she had been going behind his back for money from Channing the whole time they were married. She often pretended it was nothing, but Channing had told him the whole story: Beth had asked for lots of money plenty of times.

He didn't want to remember that, especially after what had happened in the truck and then by the fireplace yesterday. It had been so sweet, so right. She was still the only woman who could make him feel the world was his if only she was there with him.

Damn, he was going crazy. He didn't want to start anything with her again. It hurt too much. He needed to get out of this town that was full of memories and broken dreams and get back where he belonged, fighting other people's demons.

Less than five minutes later, Grant, fully dressed and hair combed, halted in the doorway of the kitchen. Beth and her father were glaring at each other. Neither noticed his presence.

"Dear God, Beth. It was bad enough when you moved in here with that crazy Saunders, but I could explain that, since he was sick. But Grant . . . ! How am I supposed to explain that to the town?"

"You don't have to explain anything to anyone, Dad."

Martin raised his eyebrows when she referred to him as "Dad," not the little-girl "Daddy" she usually called him.

"I'm an adult now, a fact you can't seem to accept. If an explanation is needed, I'm the one to give it. This is my life."

Hot damn! Grant couldn't believe his ears. Beth was standing up to the old bastard.

"I might be able to accept you as an adult if you acted like one."

Grant walked over to the kitchen counter to pour himself a cup of coffee. When Beth and her father paused to look at him, he said, "Don't let me interrupt."

Beth shifted on her bare feet, but her voice was calm. "I explained the will to my father."

Channing fumed, "I'm not interested in what that fool Red did." He gestured toward Grant. "I want him out of here."

"As I said, Dad, what *I* want is important here, not what *you* want."

Grant leaned back against the counter, his legs crossed at the ankle. "Sorry, Channing, I promised Beth I'd stay."

"Promised Beth you'd stay. I've heard that before," her father said with a sneer. "If that's all, it shouldn't take much to drive you off." He looked directly at Grant. "It didn't the last time."

Grant set his cup on the counter.

Beth whirled toward her father. "Dad, I think it's time you left."

"You don't need him, Beth." Martin moved closer to Beth and attempted to put an arm around her shoulders.

"Goodbye, Dad." She marched across the room and flung open the door.

Martin glanced at the open door, at Grant, then at Beth. Then he looked at his watch. "When you've had time to think this over, after Grant is long gone, Beth, I'll be here for you." He gave her another kiss on the forehead, ignored Grant and stalked out the door.

Several moments of silence followed Martin Channing's departure. Grant eyed Beth with a new respect. "I've never seen you stand up to your father." He smiled. "It was quite impressive."

She blushed. "What do you want for breakfast?"

He fought to control the smile trying to turn up the corners of his mouth. "Not a thing. I've got work to do."

Beth pounded the bread dough, her thoughts wandering to this morning's encounter between her father and Grant. Although her father still harbored hostile feelings for Grant, Grant had leashed his anger. A smile teased her lips. Maybe Grant had returned to Douglas a changed man.

A full week had passed since he had moved into this big house. She was used to his teasing banter in the morning, his creative problem-solving ideas during the day and his steady presence in the long evenings spent working in the study.

She gave the dough a final slap, then covered it with a dish towel and set it in the oven to rise. Delores had come by earlier, and Beth had told her that she was going to do some chores around the house this morning and nurse her tender ankle. No questions asked, Delores had left to see to the animals.

Beth stood at the kitchen window looking out at the crisp, clear morning. This was her favorite time of year—late winter/early spring—when the weather was totally unpredictable. The storm had washed the air clean, and now everything sparkled. Water droplets looked like diamond dust in the bright sunlight. The temperature would probably get into the high seventies by afternoon.

The large barnlike structure beyond the yard fence caught her eye. It wasn't a real barn, but Red had thought every farm in Texas ought to have a red building that held surprises for visitors. And his certainly did hold surprises. Inside was a small museum dedicated to the pioneer spirit of Texas. He had collected farm artifacts, Civil War memorabilia, spurs, barbed wire and other reminders of the range wars that were part of the state's history. It was one of her favorite places.

Before she realized it, she was out the door and limping toward the museum. She hadn't gotten out of the yard before she heard the *thunk, thunk* of someone hammering. She rounded the east corner of the house and pulled up short.

Grant was leaning over a section of the wooden fence, nailing a plank in place. Even though the morning was cool, he had his shirt off, and his back glistened with a fine sheen of sweat.

She couldn't resist the temptation to admire the play of muscles and ridges across his back. Solid and strong. Each stroke of the hammer sent sinew and muscle racing in an exciting network of bulges and ripples across his physique. Watching him made her forget the chilly weather, and her body was suddenly flushed with heat. She swallowed quickly several times as her mouth watered at the powerful sight.

She took a step toward him, but stopped as something warm and wet nuzzled her hand.

"Twinkle Toes." She bent down to wrap one arm around the pony's neck and used the other to scratch behind an ear.

Grant swung around at the sound of her voice, and Beth enjoyed the sight of the soft, springy hair that grew like a dark carpet across his chest. She let her eyes follow the path it took, bisecting the lower half of his torso to disappear into his jeans. He put on his shirt, and abruptly her view of his body was cut off.

She smiled up at him, timid as she suddenly remembered what had happened that morning.

"What's Twinkle Toes doing up here?" she asked.

He finished buttoning his shirt and came to stand beside her. "You said you thought she'd make a good yard dog, so I thought I'd fix this fence myself and bring her up from the barn."

What a thoughtful gesture, she mused. Her smile grew wider, and Grant smiled back.

"What a nice thing to do, Mr. Stephens." She studied the pony for a moment. "And I think Twinkle Toes will definitely benefit from some TLC."

"Wouldn't we all," he muttered under his breath.

She leaned back her head and laughed. "Grant Stephens, are you a pathetic puppy or what?"

He laughed, too. "Well, I *do* need some tender loving care," he said in his rascally, little-boy voice. "A kiss would do for starters."

Beth surprised them both when she transferred her arms from Twinkle Toes's neck to Grant's. In less than a heartbeat, she had sealed her lips to his.

He reacted like a starving man receiving sustenance. His mouth parted, and his tongue plundered the sweetness of hers. She leaned into him farther and opened her lips more fully as a sigh escaped them. Finally she pulled back, and they stared at each other for a moment. Now why had she done that?

Grant made a show of turning back to fixing the fence.

"Here, let me help you," Beth offered. Her cheeks were pink and glowing. If he could send up the white flag, then so could she.

He hesitated only a second before he showed her how to position the plank correctly. "You hold the boards while I hammer them." He put several nails between his lips and proceeded with his task.

"Grant, I'm sorry about what my father said."

The hammer paused in midair, and he looked sharply at her. Something else stood between Grant and her father that she couldn't put her finger on. The undercurrent of secrets had crackled this morning. What was it?

Grant's eyelashes swept down, and he continued with his job. She was afraid he wasn't going to acknowledge her apology when, finally, he spoke around the nails protruding from his mouth. "I'm sorry, too. Your father and I bring out the worst in each other. I'm proud of the way you stood up to him."

Beth wondered if she could trust her hearing. Grant had just apologized. People did change, she marveled. The sunshine took on a new brilliance.

She was afraid of destroying this tentative understanding between them, but she was desperate to know more. Her palms felt sweaty and she could hear her own heartbeat. But she *had* to know what had alienated Grant and her father. "There always seems to be something unspoken between the two of you."

He arched his back, straightening out the kinks. "It's no mystery. You went to your father for money during our marriage. That's all." He threw up a hand to halt her instant reply. "I know you didn't want to hurt or humiliate me. We went over this a hundred times before the divorce. But I can't forget it. It made me feel like less of a man because I couldn't provide for you."

Relief flooded her. The bitterness and anger that usually colored his voice when they discussed this issue was missing today. She was sure he was making a great effort to be unemotional.

"I've said I was sorry so many times that I can't say it again." She watched Twinkle Toes munch the yellowed grass in the yard. "I can't go back and change what I did, but I'm sorry I hurt you. You were already holding down two jobs. It didn't seem right to burden you with what I needed. So I screwed up. I did what I'd always done—I went to Daddy."

The solemn look on Grant's face didn't quite ring true. Was he telling her everything? Why didn't it feel right? What was missing in this puzzling picture of human emotions?

He put down the hammer. "I've worked through some of my anger, and someday I'll get it all out. Seeing your dad this morning made me regress, I guess. Come on." He took her elbow. "Let's get a drink of water."

"Let's go sit in there and enjoy our drink." Beth pointed toward the red building. "I was headed that way when I heard you hammering."

"Good idea. I've been wanting to explore some more of Red's domain."

"There's an old refrigerator out there that he always kept stocked with soft drinks and beer."

They entered the cool interior of the building, and Beth turned on the lights. Grant let out a low whistle.

"That Red was a crazy devil." He wandered down the rows of knives, plows, arrowheads and other reminders of the history of the state.

"Here." She handed him a bottle of cola. "Yeah, he wasn't happy unless he was collecting something. That reminds me, we don't want to forget Tom's party tomorrow. He can't wait to actually shoot some of Red's guns."

"Well, I'll be." Grant had roamed over to the far side of the building.

"What is it?" Beth hurried over to see what prize Grant was holding in his hands.

"This card says this is the football I threw to Tom when we won against Wolverton in the last fifteen seconds of the game to clinch the district title." His eyes were bright with excitement when he looked up at Beth. "How did Red get this ball?"

"Knowing Red, he probably bribed the team manager to give it to him."

"My gosh, look at this."

Beth looked and couldn't suppress a giggle. It was a faded, slightly moth-eaten bear costume that Red had worn as mascot of the school.

"He loved being outrageous," Beth explained. "When we were young, before you moved to Douglas, Red and I used to play a game we made up called I Wonder. He would wonder what it would be like to hear a crowd cheering for him. Since he wasn't very athletic, I guess this is how he got the crowds to cheer for him."

" 'I wonder,' huh?"

"Mm-hm. We used to play it by the hour."

They sat down on the floor and leaned against the wall. Grant stretched his long legs out in front of him. He seemed lost in thought. Beth drew her knees to her chest, dangling her soft drink from her hands.

"Let's play I Wonder." He tilted his head to study her. "I wonder what would have happened if my family had never moved here?"

"I'm sure I would have married Jimmy Martindale or Frank Bainbridge or somebody else my father considered appropriate. I wonder who my mother would have wanted me to marry? I was so young when she died that I don't have any idea of her tastes."

"I think I would have married a little mouse of a woman who did everything I asked her to do, waited on me hand and foot and produced twelve children who all looked exactly like me." He scooted down to sprawl on the floor. He rolled over on his stomach and looked up at her with impish lights glowing in his eyes.

"Twelve children, huh? All looking like you." She shook her head in mock-dismay. "Poor things. I wonder what would have happened if we'd had children?"

Grant grew still, and the roguish light died in his eyes. It was replaced by a dark and electrified spark that smoked with desire. "I wonder, too. I think they would've been beautiful, since they would all have looked like their mother."

Beth wanted to give in to the seductive images and hypnotic tone of Grant's voice, but she couldn't. She had to keep this conversation light. Even if she still loved him, he didn't feel the same toward her. Yes, he definitely wanted to take her to bed. She couldn't mistake that gleam in his eyes, but what then? He would leave her with a broken heart again, and this time she knew it would never heal.

"Oh, I think half of them would have to look like their father. Six little blackguards and six fairy princesses." She hoped the frivolous tone she forced into her voice fooled him. If she was lucky, he wouldn't find out that she was serious about wanting his children. "Sounds like a well-rounded family."

"A well-rounded family. That's about the only thing I've ever wanted and not been able to get." His voice was low and melancholy.

She reached out and smoothed a lock of his hair that had fallen across his forehead. He caught her hand and brought it to his mouth, then kissed the upturned palm. Suddenly he frowned, then smiled up at her with a tender expression as he sat up, breaking the wistful spell.

"What is it, Mr. Stephens?" She narrowed her eyes.

"You," he said, and his voice was husky.

At Beth's confused look, he turned her palm toward her face and explained. "I thought I'd be kissing this soft, dainty hand, and I find out yours are as rough as a field hand's." He shook his head. "It's going to take me a while to get used to the new you. It's amazing what you do for those animals."

She struggled up from the floor and held out her hand to help him up. "Well, this field hand has bread rising in the oven. Come into the kitchen while I check on it, and then we'll get some feed for Twinkle Toes."

Back in the kitchen, Beth leaned into the oven to check the progress of the bread. Just then the telephone rang.

"I'll get it," Grant said and picked up the receiver. "New Start," he announced crisply into the phone, and she smiled. "Yeah, what have you got, Timmons?"

He turned away from Beth, shutting her out as he talked to one of his home office subordinates, Timmons. He kept his voice low, giving only monosyllabic answers. Finally he spoke clearly, "Okay, keep in touch. Yes, I will." The last was said quickly and with exasperation.

"Something wrong?" Beth asked.

"Nothing out of the ordinary for my profession. The friends of the counterfeiter we locked up are upset that we headed off their attempt to spring him. They've been sending some nasty messages to the men in my office."

"Why?" she asked. "He'll be brought to trial and found guilty and put away for life, right?"

"Right." He stared out the big window. His mind seemed miles away.

"Grant, what aren't you telling me?"

Something in her voice caused him to turn around and stare at her for a long time. She flushed and shifted.

"What is it? Tell me."

"All right. Our case against this guy is airtight. Not only did we recover the plates he was using to make the funny money, but we have an eyewitness who saw him operating the equipment."

"So what's the problem?" She pressed on.

"The problem is the big guys, the bozo's bosses, are really angry." Grant tried hard to make his tone light. "Consequently, there's been a contract put out on the eyewitness."

"Who's the eyewitness?" He could hear the edge in Beth's voice.

He shoved his hands in the back pockets of his jeans, his jawline rigid. "Me."

Chapter 7

Beth stood watching the waters of White Creek as it made its way slowly through Tom and Jenny Wilson's pasture, but she didn't see the beauty of the scene. Instead, her mind was centered on what Grant had told her. There was a hired assassin looking for him.

Her heart ached and her stomach churned at the thought of such hatred and violence directed toward Grant. How could he carry on his life with such nonchalance, knowing he was a marked man? His life was so different from hers. He was used to this sort of thing, he had told her, then assured her that the U.S. Marshal Service in St. Louis was doing everything in its power to track down the killer, which he felt sure they would do before the shooter found his target.

But what if they didn't?

He'd told her not to worry, that the men and women of the service were professionals and would handle everything. She had to trust them, too, or she would go crazy with worry, so she turned her back on the small stream and slowly wandered back to the others. When she arrived, they were getting ready for the sighting-in.

"If Red could see the way you shoot, Tom, he'd let you shoot at animals," Shorty said, grinning. "You haven't hit a single can all afternoon."

Tom turned around, holding the heavy gun across his chest, barrel pointed skyward. "Shouldn't you be frying more fish?"

"No. It's my turn to shoot." Shorty stepped up and lifted the gun out of Tom's hands. "Step back and pay attention to how I stand."

"Oh, shut up." Tom gave Shorty a playful jab in the shoulder. "Don't rub it in."

Trusting the Marshal Service to protect Grant, trusting Grant to take care of himself, Beth forced her concerns aside and joined the fun. She laughed as she watched the men try to kill all the cans stacked on the hay bales.

She thought about Red holding and examining the firearms lovingly. Many people had thought it was odd that Red owned so many guns, but Beth knew that he loved them for their quality workmanship and sleek lines rather than as instruments of destruction. Red never used them to hunt. They were just one more part of his vast collection.

"Did you notice the hand-carved ivory handle on this piece?" Tom stroked the antique gun gently.

"I never thought I'd get to shoot a gun crafted in 1899," Shorty said.

Beth smiled at the pleasure Red's gift had brought to these men.

Tom and Jenny Wilson's spacious ranch was the perfect setting for this sighting-in. Long tables were loaded with covered dishes and big deep fryers with fish fillets, courtesy of the fishermen in the group. Children laughed and shouted and seemed to be everywhere at once, except in the shooting area. A hundred yards away, lazy White Creek meandered through oak and pecan trees, and some of the children splashed in the gentle rapids under the watchful eyes of older children and several mothers.

"Beth, come and join us." Mildred waved her over to a cluster of women sitting in lawn chairs under a huge oak tree. "We're talking about the Cornyval."

No doubt they were more interested in the latest scandalous gossip about Grant and her living under the same roof, she thought dryly. They undoubtedly assumed they were sharing the same bed, too. Funny how their speculations didn't bother her at all.

She strolled over to join the group and informed Mildred, "Since you're discussing the Cornyval, I may as well tell you now, I'm not wearing a grass skirt, no matter what—even if we have a Hawaiian theme."

"Why not?"

To hide her smile, Beth turned around and pretended to watch Shorty set up the cans for the next round.

"I've got to keep an eye on the shooting. I'm supposed to be the official scorekeeper." She pushed a stray curl back behind her ear. She was wearing her hair loose today, enjoying the feel of the gentle breezes as they played with the long strands. The erratic Texas weather made it warm enough for shorts.

Mildred, known for her tenaciousness, pressed the point. "Why not? You'd look great in a grass skirt. And I've waited years for this."

Beth, knowing she would eventually give in but aware of how much Mildred liked and needed to railroad the Cornyval, kept up her halfhearted protests. "I'm not sure we ought to do the luau thing. I talked to Tom..." She shrugged.

"Don't you dare back down now because of something Tom said." Mildred puffed up, preparing to do battle.

"Well, he said folks around here want a more traditional festival—like it's always been."

"Tom Wilson doesn't know what people around here want. Just look around you." She gestured to take in the whole scene: men shooting at targets set up on haystacks, kids sneaking up to the dessert table and running with their treats down to the river and women shooing after them. "He thinks people want to shoot at cans stacked on hay. You want to trust his word?" She finished with a flourish, proud of herself for making such a dramatic point.

"Well—"

"'Well' nothing. You're in that grass skirt, and that's the end of it."

"I'm in agreement," Grant said as he walked up from behind Beth to join the group. His eyes glowed as he appraised her. "I'd pay good money to see you in a grass skirt, swaying and moving to the music."

The group of women tittered, and Beth felt herself blush.

"See." Mildred put her hands on her ample hips and gave her head a nod, officially ending the conversation.

Beth turned to Grant and told him saucily, "You don't have a thing to say about what I wear and don't wear."

His eyes traveled the length of her from head to foot and back up again. What did he think he was doing, looking at her that way with everyone watching?

"I know. But I think you owe it to the town."

"For what?"

"For putting up with you all these years."

The women all laughed and murmured in agreement, and the awkward moment was past.

Beth shook her head at his little-boy antics. "What are you doing over here eavesdropping, anyway?"

"I'm on a mission from our leader." Grant performed a mock salute. "It's time for the doubles' match. And you're my partner, remember?"

Beth sighed. She'd forgotten. She'd promised to be Grant's shooting partner for this contest. Each team had ten shots, five per partner. The team that finished second had to set the cans up for the rest of the evening. The team that won got bragging rights.

"You're going to regret asking me. I haven't shot a gun in years. I doubt I even remember how."

"Don't worry, I'll steady you and give you some pointers. Besides, I'm so good, you just have to hit a couple and we'll win."

His boyish boast warmed Beth's heart. "Are you always so confident?" she asked.

"When I know what I've got, yeah." His voice dropped to a low whisper, daring her to pick up the challenge. She refused, pushing past him to lead the rest of the way. Grant didn't mind at all, because he enjoyed watching the gentle sway of Beth's hips. The soft material of her shorts hugged her derriere tightly enough to make his heart beat faster, and the long expanse of her silky legs made his blood pound in a heavy cadence through his body.

"Who's our competition?" Beth asked as they arrived at the shooting area.

"Shorty and Delores, Steve and Sarah, and—"

Grant was interrupted by Mildred screeching, "I'm coming, Tom Wilson. You don't have to drag me."

"I do, too, woman. You promised me if I'd let that luau idea through, you'd be my partner in the shoot, and you're not backing out now."

Beth stared at Grant, suppressed amusement adding sparkling lights to her eyes. "*Mildred* is Tom's partner? Why?"

"You don't remember Deadeye Millie, the woman who won the ROTC Turkey Shoot every year in high school?" Grant chuckled at the memory.

Beth's eyes glowed with remembrance. "I'd forgotten! Tom must really want to win this thing. I understand now why he went along with the luau idea for Cornyval."

"Yeah, he wants to beat me. And the word is out that Mildred has been practicing every day for a week." His grin told Beth just what he thought of the great plot to win the shoot off. "And I think Jenny is too busy with the food and the kids to help Tom out."

The other contestants joined Beth and Grant.

Shorty shook a coffee can filled with slips of paper. "Come on, Beth, draw for your team's place."

She drew out a slip of paper, read the number and groaned. "Number one."

"All right. We'll know exactly how many we need to hit after they finish." Tom rubbed his hands together with glee.

"Hey, don't count us out." Delores sashayed up to take a number from the can. "You might find yourself eating crow. Me and Shorty are a pretty powerful pair. Aren't we, sugar?" She winked at Shorty, who blushed and shuffled his feet. "Besides, we've got a secret weapon."

"Number three." Delores waved the paper as she sauntered slowly back to Shorty and hooked her arm through his, causing his blush to skyrocket from bright red to deep crimson.

"Right. Shorty's gonna sue us if he doesn't win," Tom teased as he reached into the can.

Tom opened the paper, slowly peeking at the number. "All right. Number four. We're last." He looked over at Steve. "I guess you go after Beth and Grant, buddy."

"Let's get started," said Reverend Hanson, Mildred's husband. He was acting as the judge for this contest. Even sore losers found it hard to challenge the minister of the biggest church in town. "Grant, who's shooting first, you or Beth?"

"Beth," Grant answered. He pulled her over to the table where the guns were and gave her some shooting tips. "Listen to me. Just relax, stand with your legs apart—" his voice dropped so low that only she could hear "—and take the gun into your hands like a lover."

Beth's equilibrium slipped, and she swayed against Grant. He stood behind her and put his arms around her to guide the butt of the shotgun to her shoulder.

Days had passed since her declaration that they needed to learn all about each other. He had been charming and the time had been enjoyable for both of them as they learned what made each other tick.

She had found out that he was now into jazz and collected Fats Waller and Dizzy Gillespie albums. They were planning a trip into Houston soon to scope out some used-record stores. She had told him about her passion for Russian literature and ballet. He had surprised her when he suggested that while they'd be in Houston, they take in the ballet. Both of them played chess, and almost every night they sat for an hour or two hunched over an onyx board and pieces that had belonged to Red.

Not once in that time had he touched her intimately, but often his eyes reflected undisguised need when she caught him watching her. She sensed that his hunger for her was tightly leashed, ready to spring forth with just a sign from her. Daily, her grip on her own longing for him slipped. He was different now. He was a whole person, changed from the one-sided jock she had married.

Her thoughts pulled up abruptly. Maybe *she* was different. Had she grown up in the past ten years, leaving behind that self-centered only child of Martin Channing that she'd been?

Grant caressed her hands as she clutched the gun and leaned his head in close to hers. Lord, how could she concentrate when she could feel heat and man the entire length of her back? His enveloping arms overwhelmed her, and she fought to steady her breathing.

Grant's soothing whisper did little to calm her as the warmth of his minty breath tickled her ear. "Careful, darlin'. You're in control."

Control, she thought as her knees began to tremble. Far from it.

"Look down the barrel to the front bead," he continued in a throaty baritone. "When you've lined up the bead with the first can, gently squeeze the trigger. You won't miss." He gave her a small hug before releasing her and stepping back. "I have complete confidence in you."

Beth tried to plant her feet firmly and follow all of Grant's suggestions, everything except the lover part. If she did that, she would never manage to fire a round. Her hands were shaking as it was. The image of Grant caressing her in the hotel room rose in her mind, but she firmly tamped it down. Instead, she thought of gentling a newborn foal or calf. She fired and missed. Without dropping the sight, she squeezed off another shot and hit the next target.

She turned in triumph to her partner and found Grant grinning at her. "That's it. Only three more."

Beth smiled back, then concentrated on the next can. She fired and missed, but hit the next two. She set the gun down just in time to get swept up into Grant's twirling hug. "You did it. That should be enough."

Tom tapped him on the shoulder. "Don't you think you're celebrating a little early? You still have to shoot, and so do all of us." His gesture indicated the rest of the competitors. "So please, put her down and shoot the gun."

Grant settled his body into a shooting stance before he picked up the gun. When he did, he and the weapon seemed one unit. He flexed his shoulders and rested the butt of the gun against his right shoulder. His eyes squinted on the target, and he fired off the five rounds rapidly, in staccato-style, hitting all five cans.

"Shoot!" yelled Tom.

"I just did," Grant joked as he put down the gun. He turned to Beth and grabbed her hand. "Now, how about a victory kiss?"

Beth, astonished and frightened by the display she had just seen, shook her head. The shotgun had been an extension of Grant's body. The realization that he used guns with deadly intent in his work suddenly hit her with the accuracy of his shots. She'd never given any thought to what his job might entail, but his prowess with the gun had given her some insight. This was a part of Grant that she hadn't learned about yet, and she doubted she would like it at all. Her life was centered around saving lives, not taking them. The thought of him using a gun against another human being, even a criminal, made her wince. Could she ever get used to his cops-and-robbers life-style, with real guns shooting at real people?

"You sure about that kiss?" he was asking her now.

"Let's wait 'til the end." She smiled in an effort to shake her sense of foreboding. "We don't want to jinx it."

"Yeah, give us a break," Tom teased.

Steve and Sarah got five points total. Then Shorty stepped up to the mark. He fired off his rounds, hitting four out of five.

"Sugar, you sure know how to shoot that thing," Delores crooned. "Everything you got shoots good, don't it?"

Tom shouted with laughter, and Steve chuckled helplessly.

Shorty gave Delores a pleading "please be quiet" look.

"Okay, let me get the feel of this." Delores massaged the gun barrel, caressing Shorty with her eyes the whole time. "Yeah, feels just right."

Delores closed her eyes and fired, missing every can. Peeking through her blue mascaraed eyelashes, she asked, "How many did I hit?"

Doubled over with laughter, Tom told her, "None. That was a hell of a secret weapon, Delores. You wanted us to laugh ourselves silly so we couldn't see the target?"

"Hush, Tom Wilson, and do your thing."

Tom turned to Mildred. "You first."

Mildred, sighing, picked up the gun and settled it on her shoulder. She developed her "deadeye" gaze and knocked five cans into the next county.

"There." She turned to Tom with a smirk on her face. "That's for the luau. The rest is up to you."

Tom chuckled. "I knew you could do it." He looked over at Grant. "Go ahead and get ready to start stacking up cans, Grant."

"I'll wait."

Tom took a deep breath, then let it out. Methodically he aimed for each shot and hit four cans. He let out a whoop that startled two small boys into dropping the cookies they had just swiped off the table.

"We did it. We beat him. We actually beat him." Tom raised his clenched fists above his head in a sign of victory.

Grant smiled good-naturedly and shook Tom's hand. "Congratulations." He turned to Mildred. "You did a great job."

"Yeah." She preened. "I just did it for the luau. No hard feelings?"

"None." Grant held out his hand to Beth. "Come on, we've got set-up duty."

"Sorry my poor shooting cost you the match." Ten years ago his male pride would have been stung, she thought, but he accepted the defeat amiably today.

"I'll try to think of some way you can make it up to me." He smiled down at her, and the warmth she had experienced when he showed her how to sight the gun was nothing compared to the rush of heat that swirled from neck to knees now.

They walked the one hundred yards to the bales of hay. Even though the bales were three deep, the stacker stayed down the slope near the river, out of harm's way. When more cans were needed, a cow bell rigged up on a long string signaled the work crew to begin.

Beth and Grant put out about fifty cans and slipped down the grassy embankment, shielded from view by overhanging grapevines. The river was strung with paper lanterns, which lit the area with shades of blue and yellow and red and looked like a romantic twilight scene in a movie about the South. They settled onto a blanket that had been conveniently laid there.

"How long do you think it will take them to shoot all those cans?" she asked, trying to ignore his closeness.

"I figure we've got about twenty, thirty minutes. Tom's got to wander around the place bragging that he won. Shorty's probably escaping from Delores by putting himself in charge of frying fish, and Mildred is trying to decide if this town can afford Don Ho to sing 'Tiny Bubbles' at the Cornyval."

Beth laughed at the pictures Grant drew with his words. The amazing thing was, he was right. She didn't have to turn around to know that was exactly what was happening.

He couldn't resist the temptation to run the pads of his fingers along the elegant arch of Beth's neck as she tilted her head back to laugh. Her laugh ended on a shaky note.

"Then we really don't have to stay here?" Her voice shook, too.

"Oh, yes, we do. A deal's a deal. I've already been out-shot. I won't be called a welcher or a poor loser. We're stuck back here for at least an hour."

"What happens then?"

"We bribe some hormone-crazy teenagers to take the spot."

"Grant Stephens!"

"What's the matter? Don't you remember what these spring evenings used to be like? All the sap rising, no place to release the energy. I remember we used to find some pretty cozy spots and while away the time, necking. Everybody thought we were getting it on. No one ever knew you wouldn't let me get to first base." He smiled. "Well, maybe second base, but I never hit a home run until after we got married."

"I remember. But I'm not going looking for the teenagers."

"Oh, they'll find us."

They settled more comfortably on the blanket. Grant lay down and stretched out on his side facing Beth. She sat with her knees drawn up and her chin tucked on top of them. In silence they watched the water drifting slowly, reflections of the lanterns and trees mysteriously transformed by the current.

After several seconds of reflective silence, he turned to her. "Beth, I'm really trying to work the demons out of my system about our marriage. You've apologized for going to your father for money, but why did you feel you needed more money in the first place?"

Her breath came in short, jerky gasps. She knew, by the intensity of his stare and the tone of his voice, that this was her chance to make him understand her motives. She wanted, needed, him to know. But she honestly didn't understand herself. How did you say, "I was selfish. I was too caught up in stuff that didn't matter. I worried about people's inconsequential opinions"?

"Beth?"

"I've wondered about that for such a long time." She faced him. "I wish I could tell you this and sound less silly, less superficial. But the hard, cold fact is that I wanted the clothes and the car to impress other people. That was important to me then." She watched his eyes. They were clear, piercing. "But I never meant to hurt you. The truth is, I didn't think about you at all when I did it. I only thought of me."

Grant went still, amazed at her answer. "Thank you."

She smiled. "For what?"

"For erasing a permanent ache."

"Oh, Grant."

The past days had shown him that they had both grown up and expanded their worlds. Could he tell her that now he had a different ache—one he didn't think he would ever be able to rid himself of—the torturous throbbing of his need for her?

All these years the painful memories had buried the clear, clean ones of her. And now he had discovered new and hidden facets of her personality. How ironic. Now he knew the real Beth, but he could never tell her how much he needed her, because he also knew deep in his being that he wasn't right for her. Her father knew what he was talking about. She needed someone gentler, more sophisticated, than he was. But before he could let her find that someone else, he had to have her—had to build his memories for the future.

With infinite care, he curled a hand around the nape of her neck and pulled her down to possess her with his lips. At the first touch she seemed to melt and pour herself into the kiss. Her lips parted, and his tongue took advantage of the delicious invitation. She seemed more than ready for the invasion and met him stroke for stroke. She tasted of peppermint and woman, exciting him more than any woman he had ever known.

He released her soft, smooth neck, and she looked with luminous eyes into his. Never breaking eye contact, she shifted her body so that she was reclining on the blanket beside him. Gently she pressed Grant onto his back and, resting her breasts across his chest, crushed her mouth to his in reckless wantonness.

He felt heat rise so quickly through his body that he thought he would suffocate on the spot. The lush heaviness of her breasts hugging his chest made desire blaze through his veins and pool with a solid rigidity between his legs. Her velvety lips, dancing so winsomely with his own, drove sane thoughts and courtly behavior fleeing from the red flame of passion. He wanted her, and he wanted her now.

"I can't wait any longer for this," he whispered against her ear.

With ease he rolled her under him and continued the kiss from his new vantage. He left a trail of tender kisses across her cheek before he grabbed the delicate lobe of her ear between his teeth and gave it a gentle tug. Then his tongue laved loving attention on the pink shell. He was gratified to hear a harsh hissing come from deep in Beth's chest, and she writhed in response to his sensuous attention.

His mouth claimed hers as his hands found the soft mounds of her breasts. Through the material of her camp shirt, he kneaded them tenderly.

His mouth continued its fiery exploration of the sensitive points of her body. He rained kisses down the smooth column of her throat to the pulse point at the base.

"Oh, Beth, I need to feel you," he declared in a raspy voice as he began unfastening the small buttons of her blouse.

Unhampered now by any barricades, he extended his ardent attention to her body by pushing the shirt open and continuing to place kisses and love bites on the creamy skin of her shoulders and chest. He quickly unhooked the front closure of her bra and drew back to marvel at her exposed beauty. The shadowy twilight and the glow from the lanterns cast a haunting splendor over the perfect womanliness of her. She looked like a goddess, otherworldly and untouchable. But her flushed warmth, quickened breathing and soft moans told him otherwise.

"You were and still are the most beautiful woman I've ever seen, Beth Stephens."

She breathed his name on a gentle wind, and he lowered his head to run his tongue in a tantalizing pattern around and around one breast. The nipple beaded and grew more rigid. Finally he took it in his mouth and suckled, first tenderly and then with a growing urgency.

When Beth began to chant his name as though it were magical mantra, he switched his attention to the other breast and gave it the same pleasure.

"Grant, please, please..." Her eyes were closed, and she was tossing her head back and forth.

"Please, what? What do you want, Beth?"

She didn't answer, just opened her eyes and stared at him with desire rich in them. Then she framed his face with her hands and drew him back so she could drink from the delicious essence of him.

He stroked the firm fullness of her body again before moving his hand down to unbutton the fastening at her waistband. That accomplished, he began to slide the metal zipper slowly down. Suddenly bells began to clang with undeniable impatience.

"What the hell?"

Grant sat up, and Beth rolled to one side and quickly rearranged her clothing.

"Yeah, yeah, we'll be right there!" Grant called out to no one in particular.

She stared at him with wide, serious eyes.

He stood up and ran a hand through his hair, then looked down at Beth. From where she sat she couldn't deny the proof of his fervent desire for her and quickly glanced away when he turned his attention to her.

Leaning over, he cupped her face between his strong fingers, forcing her to look at his boldness. "Don't shy away, Beth. *This is for you.* This is your power over me."

He gave her a long, smoldering once-over. "You were saved by the bell this time, but this isn't finished."

Chapter 8

He hadn't touched her intimately since his declaration. Four days ago. The morning after, they had been stilted and polite to each other, but then their lives had settled into a routine. Grant helped around New Start in the mornings. In the afternoons he worked in the study. He took charge of dinner every other night and was even helping her get ready for the Cornyval. But since that night, he hadn't shown an interest in finishing what had begun on the banks of the White Creek.

As Beth supervised the arrival of a bright yellow school bus, her mind strayed to Grant and what had happened between them at the sighting-in. She could still feel his hands running over her body, his lips devouring her own.

Screams of delight brought her back to the present.

"Okay, kids, be careful getting off the bus," she admonished the twenty first and second graders as they climbed from the bus that had brought them to New Start for a field trip.

Mrs. Jackson, their teacher, peered around the bus door. "Beth, I'm sorry about my knee. You know I love to see all the animals, but I can't hobble around today." She laughed ruefully. "I'm going to give up tennis if I can't play without getting hurt."

Beth smiled with warm reassurance. "It's okay. Since you called ahead to warn me, I've got help. Rest easy. We'll be back in about an hour." She turned to the children. "Hi, boys and girls. My name's Beth. That's an easy name to remember so if you need anything, just call for Beth. Everyone grab a partner's hand and walk over to the shade by the barn." She pointed toward the building. "That's our first stop. We're going to use the buddy system today. Every time we walk somewhere different, be sure you're holding your buddy's hand. That way no one will get lost."

As she talked, she looked around for Grant. He had promised to help with the field trip. There was usually a volunteer or two to help chaperon, but everyone had cancelled today. Delores had gone into town earlier to pick up some hay from the feed store; Grant had offered the use of his rented truck since Red's convertible wasn't built for hauling hay.

Mentally shaking herself, she asked the children, "How many of you have seen a horse up close?"

Several hands shot up, with one boy jumping up and down for her attention. "What's your name?" she asked.

"Chris."

"Chris, do you have something you want to tell me?" She bent close to be on eye level with him.

"I saw horses in a parade once." He looked around as if pleased that he had everyone's attention, including the pretty lady in charge. "They pooped on the street and people had to clean it up."

Several of the little girls exclaimed, "Oh, gross," and "Chris, I'm going to tell Mrs. Jackson." Beth bit the inside of her lip to keep from laughing. She didn't want to give Chris the impression she enjoyed his story. He might feel the need to keep her entertained all morning.

"Well, today there won't be a parade, but you will see some horses and get to touch them." Beth paced into the barn, again scanning for Grant. "Take your partner's hand and come in here," she called to the children.

They trooped into the barn and stopped midway.

"There are two special horses in here I want you to meet." She opened the stall to her right and led Granny out by her halter.

The kids looked on wide-eyed as Granny whinnied and shook her head. "This is Granny. She's the oldest horse we have here."

"How old is she?" asked a boy dressed in Ninja Turtle T-shirt and jeans.

Beth stroked Granny's long nose. "In people years, she would be about eighty."

"Wow, that's old!" proclaimed a redheaded girl with green ribbons in her hair.

"Can we pet her? Can we pet her?" the children all chorused at once.

"Yes, but come up two at a time and pet her gently on her side and her neck."

As she supervised the children touching Granny, Beth marveled at their sense of wonder. To her amusement, one little boy went to Granny's head and began a conversation, asking the horse all about her life and did she sleep standing up.

"No, champ, horses lie down just like we do to sleep," Grant said as he walked up and patted Granny on her nose.

"Well, they eat standing up," Chris announced with authority, "and they poo—"

"Let's meet our other special horse," Beth broke in before Chris could explain more about what seemed to be his favorite topic.

She led Granny back into her stall.

"Sorry I'm late," Grant whispered to her as she turned to open Studmuffin's stall. "Here, let me get this rascal out for you."

"Kids, stand back. This horse is a little friskier than Granny," Beth warned, shielding the children from Studmuffin until Grant walked him into the yard.

"He really is big," said one of the children. "Will he step on us?"

Grant reined in Studmuffin and spoke soothingly to him until the big horse was still. "No, he won't step on you. In fact, if you want, I'll put each of you on his back. Who wants to be first?"

Every child's hand flew up, and they started elbowing each other to get up close.

"Grant, are you sure?" Beth asked, a small worried frown on her brow.

"Sure. I can handle it." He patted the horse's neck, and smiled at Beth. "He's a real gentleman when he wants to be. Now if you can get them into some sort of line, we can get started."

Beth began maneuvering the children into an orderly group. "We're going to go from the shortest to the tallest, to see if you can find the right spot."

"I'm the tallest, so I'm last. I hate that," Chris whined as he moved to the back. "What's the horse's name?"

Beth glanced at Grant. He smiled broadly at her.

"His name's Muffin," Beth said as she looked at Grant triumphantly.

"Ah, that's a girl's name." Chris kicked dirt in a little cloud around his foot.

If he only knew, she thought.

"The thing about Muffin," Grant confided in the children, "is he doesn't like loud noises. So everyone has to keep their voice low and soft."

The children immediately began speaking in hushed tones.

"Great idea," Beth whispered to Grant as she helped each child find his spot in the line.

The redheaded girl was first. "Look, I can almost touch the ceiling," she shrieked. She quickly clamped a hand over her mouth, realizing she'd done something against the rules. The other children admonished her in angry whispers.

Beth stood back and watched Grant as he gently worked with children and horse alike. She noticed how relaxed his face was when he talked with the children, and how he managed to coax a smile out of even the shyest child. He's so good, so gentle with children, she mused. What other secrets has he hidden?

"Chris, you're the last one." Grant hoisted the youngster on top of Studmuffin's broad back. "What do you think? Would you like to have been a cowboy?"

The boy shifted on the horse's back and grabbed his mane. "Yeah, I'd have to get spurs and a rope. I'd be a mean cowboy, shooting bad guys."

Grant smiled. "And how could you tell the bad guys?"

Chris looked down and smirked. "All the bad guys wear black—that's what my mom says."

"I wish it was that easy," Grant muttered as he swung Chris down from his perch atop the horse.

"Where to next?" he asked Beth.

"I thought we'd show them the monkeys and the ducks."

"Monkeys!" the children chorused together.

"Oh, boy, do they eat bananas?"

"Do they swing in trees?"

"Do they stink?"

"Hey, slow down. We only have seven of them." Beth laughed at their enthusiasm. "Grab your buddy's hand and follow me. You can see them for yourselves."

"Are we going to the jungle?" The little red-haired girl's eyes were as big as moons.

"No, silly. We'd have to take a boat for that," Chris said and then turned to Grant. "We're not, are we?"

"No, sport. We're just going over here to this makeshift cage."

Beth, Grant and the children walked over to a large cage that was really several trees surrounded by mesh wire. It was a temporary home to seven primates. The monkeys were making themselves at home. Three were sprawled asleep in the trees, two young ones were playing chase and the remaining two were grooming each other's fur.

"You're lucky, because in about two weeks these monkeys won't be here," Grant explained to the children.

"Where will they be?"

"They've been accepted by a zoo in Pittsburgh," Beth said. "We try to find homes that can take better care of the monkeys than we can. They'll love their new home." She motioned to the group. "Come on. Let's go down to our little pond, and you can feed the ducks."

"Where's the food?" Chris wanted to know.

Beth took a key out of the pocket of her shorts and unlocked a large wooden box secured on an outdoor light pole. Inside was a sack of duck pellets and a bucket. Grant hefted the big sack out and poured food in the pail.

It was such a pleasure to have Grant by her side, helping, advising, she mused. He was so solid. She could depend on him to help her with everything from the physical lifting of objects that were too heavy for her to the emotional experience of delighting these children with a peek at wildlife. She had quickly gotten used to having him around New Start and her. What would it be like when he left?

"Okay, group," he addressed the children as they pressed in close to get a handful of the food, "let's wait until we get to the ducks, and then I'll hand out the pellets. That way everyone will get to feed the ducks."

When they got to the pond, Beth helped pass out a portion of food to all the children. They were careful to keep the children away from the water's edge.

The ducks, used to being fed, rushed the children and quacked, demanding food. Some of the more aggressive ones even pecked at the children's shoes.

"Ouch. That duck bit me," the girl with the red hair complained.

"No, he didn't," Beth told her. "He just wants more food."

"Well, I don't like him." She walked over to Grant and held up her arms. He picked her up.

"Can I feed them from up here?" she asked Grant.

"Sure. But you know, ducks can fly."

"They can?" She looked solemnly at Grant and put her arms around his neck. "You just make sure they don't bite me."

"Yes, ma'am," Grant said.

He looked over at Beth and grinned. "I wish all ladies were this easy to please."

"Remember, she's only six."

"I'll remember that," he said, still smiling broadly. "The older a woman gets, the harder she is to please."

Beth snorted and then turned her full attention to the children. "Let's come over and sit for a minute under the shade of this big oak tree."

When the group was settled, she sat down among them. Grant took a place beside her, with the little girl snuggled in his lap.

After making sure everyone was settled, Beth asked, "What holiday will be coming soon?"

Several hands went up.

She called on one child. "Easter."

"That's right. And what do we sometimes ask the Easter bunny to bring us?"

She got a variety of answers until finally one of the children came up with the answer she wanted. "Chicks."

"Yes, and some kids get baby ducks and some baby rabbits. Everyone loves baby animals, but what do you think happens sometimes because we love little animals too much?"

The children all shook their heads.

"Sometimes baby animals are squeezed to death or badly injured when we're just trying to love them."

Gasps filled the air.

The little Ninja Turtle piped in, "My granddaddy says if I touch a baby animal, its mommy won't take it and love it anymore."

"People used to think that was true. Some still do, but it's not true that a mother bird will reject a baby that's been touched by a human," Grant said solemnly to the little boy.

"If you watch an animal for a long time, and are sure that it needs help, call us. We'll give you a paper before you leave today that has our phone number on it. We have special food we can feed the babies, and we know how to take care of them so they don't die."

One of the kids said, "This is a neat place."

"Yes, it is," Grant agreed and his eyes glowed at Beth.

She hoped the children didn't notice her cheeks pinken. She rushed on to explain one more problem to them. "Since many of you live on farms or ranches, if you find a fawn or some other baby animal that appears to have lost its mommy or daddy, don't bother it. The mother is probably hidden very close by, watching. You can go back later and check on it, though, and if you think its mother really isn't coming for it, call us. We'll come to your house and make a decision about what to do.''

She smiled around at the sea of faces. ''Can you remember all we've told you and tell your parents, too?''

''Yes.''

''You've got it, dude.''

''Okeydokey.''

The honking of the bus's horn told them it was time to herd the kids back.

''Okay, give the ducks the rest of the food and grab your partner's hand. Follow me.'' Beth led the group back to the bus. Grant, still holding the red-haired girl, with her partner walking beside him, brought up the rear.

After passing out the brochures with information about New Start, and shouting twenty goodbyes, the group was finally off.

''Whew,'' Grant exclaimed. ''How often do you do that? Those kids take more patience than most overnight stakeouts I've been on.'' He continued to wave at the departing bus.

''Oh, several times during the school year. School districts from fifty to sixty miles away come to visit.'' She smiled wearily at him. ''Usually the volunteers handle it, though.''

They turned to head back to the barn, but were stopped at the sound of another horn beeping. A truck came roaring into the yard, spraying gravel as it ground to a halt.

''Who in the world is that driving like a madman?''

Beth walked toward the vehicle. Before she could get close, a man dressed in jeans and a dirty blue denim work shirt climbed out of the cab and headed straight for her.

He didn't stop until he was right in her face. She tried not to gag at the foul smell of his breath or the yellowed rot of his teeth. His stance and demeanor shouted he was angry and meant to have his say.

"You the person who come and got my horses?" He poked a bony finger at her throat.

Out of the corner of her eye Beth saw Grant react and move closer. She stiffened, and he stopped.

"I don't know. Who are you?" she asked coolly.

"I'm Dewey Smith, and I own those horses you stole off my property."

"Which horses are you talking about? I rescue lots of them."

"You know good and well. I gots me a ranch out east of town. 'Bout three weeks ago that pantywaist deputy, Joe Clay Phillips, comes out and says they've had a complaint that I ain't takin' care of my horses. Says I got to go into town and answer questions. While I was gone, you stole my animals." His eyes narrowed.

"It took me a long time to figure out where they was. Wouldn't Phillips or anybody else tell me, but I seed a poster asking fer money fer this place in the grocery store. I asked around and sure enough, I figured it out. You stole my horses."

"I do have your horses, Mr. Smith," Beth said calmly. "But as I said before, I didn't steal them. I rescued them."

"Like hell." Smith advanced even closer. "What you done was cause me to lose all kinds of money."

Beth tossed her hair over one shoulder. "I was called by law-enforcement officials to seize those horses. I had the right warrants and permits."

"I don't give a damn about no permits. Those horses are my livelihood and I want 'em back. I need them colts the horses throw. They bring big money."

He was nose-to-nose with Beth. She wondered briefly how one man could smell so bad.

"You want them back so you can starve them, leave them in excrement up to their fetlocks and breed them to death." Her voice rose with every word she uttered. "You won't get those horses back, Mr. Smith, and if I have my way, you won't get any more horses, period."

"Who do you think you are? I made my living off them horses. Now I may starve today 'cause I don't have no money. Them animals were in fine shape. You and that Joe Clay fed that judge a pack of lies."

"We told him the truth and you know it. That filthy dump you call a ranch wasn't fit for even you."

His anger-reddened face turned even redder.

"Lady, they're just animals—not people." He looked around at the well-kept yard, took note of a barn cat lazing in the sun, and the flower basket hanging from the trees and he said with derision, "I wasn't running no camp for kids." He pushed her and she had to step back. "Now, I'm going to get my horses back one way or the other."

"I have court orders forbidding you to come near those horses." Beth wouldn't allow this dirty bully of a man to intimidate her.

"No court's going to stop me." He barged past Beth, heading for one of the barns, and swiped her with a beefy arm. She stumbled.

The furious note in her voice stopped him. "I'm going to call the police."

He turned around and skewered her with a hateful stare. He slowly stalked her. "The police can't keep you safe from me."

"No, but I can." Grant came out of the shadows of the barn, where he had been listening and watching the entire scene. At first, he'd wanted to launch himself at this creep the minute he'd threatened Beth. But he'd held back. Beth had made it clear with her body language that she didn't want him running interference for her. Plus, he wouldn't be here in a few weeks, and he needed to know she could handle herself without him. She'd done just that. But now, with the Neanderthal advancing on her, it was time he got into the action.

His voice was low and deadly as he told Smith, "Get back into your truck and get out of here. And for the sake of your good health, don't come back."

Smith studied Grant for several seconds, as if trying to decide whether he should take him on. His fists knotted. He figured he'd try one last shot. "I need those horses. I don't have no other job. You folks are taking away a man's way of earning a living."

"Try cleaning up and getting a job where you have to do the work instead of using those mares as a foal factory. Come to think of it, Smith—" Grant's eyes glittered dangerously "—that pit you have on your place would be a good place for you to spend a few days thinking about how to treat animals."

"Pit? What you talking about?"

"You know, the pit where you burn the carcasses of the mares after you breed them to death."

Grant walked slowly toward Smith, calmly backing him to his truck. His relaxed stance fooled no one. He was ready to spring.

Beth followed at a safe distance. For a moment she thought Smith was considering charging the other man. He showed a remarkable amount of intelligence when he decided not to.

Grant glared as Smith fumbled with the door to the cab and then got in. From the safety of his truck he threatened, "This ain't over."

Beth's voice rang with anger. "You're right. I'll see you in court."

Dewey Smith jammed the truck into gear and spun out of the yard and onto the road, leaving a cloud of dust in his wake.

"Thanks for coming to the rescue," Beth told Grant, hoping she sounded more confident than she felt. "But you didn't have to. I would have—"

"I know, I know." He pulled her into his arms. "You can handle everything. You've told me. I just wanted that creep to know you aren't alone on this one."

"Do you think he'll be back?"

"He had liquor on his breath. I think it made him brave. I've seen his kind before. His courage is in direct proportion to his booze intake." He looked over her head at the disappearing truck. "I don't think he'll bother you anymore." Silently he vowed to pay Dewey Smith a private visit. Beth might not want his interference, but he couldn't leave Douglas without being sure this particular situation was taken care of.

"I'll notify Shorty about this, just in case," Beth said.

"I think you can do that sooner than you think. That's his car coming up the road now," Grant said, nodding toward the dirt lane.

"This has been some morning," Beth muttered as she waited for Shorty.

When he pulled up, she saw Delores was in the car with him. Shorty jumped out of the car and ran around to the passenger's side, then motioned to Beth and Grant. "Delores needs your help."

"What on earth . . . ?"

"She hit a tree."

"Oh my God," Beth breathed.

She and Grant sprinted to Shorty's car. The lawyer helped Delores get out. Her hair was a mess, and she had a glazed look in her eyes.

"We need to get her to a hospital," Grant directed. "She looks like she's in shock."

"I'm not going to any hospital. I'm fine. Just a little shook up. I wore my seat belt," she told them triumphantly. "Thank the lucky stars that truck of yours had them, Grant. I guess I would've been better off getting hay in the back seat of my convertible." She leaned into Shorty, crushing her large breasts against his arm. "Just help me to that bench over there."

Shorty picked her up and carried her to the bench. Delores, though pale, seemed on cloud nine. She wrapped her arms tightly around Shorty's neck and clung to him.

As he tenderly deposited her on the seat, he said, "I wanted to take her to the house, but she insisted on coming here first." He looked at her with agitation shining in his eyes. "She can be so stubborn."

"We'll talk about all my faults later, sugar." Her skin was pale and her lips trembled slightly. "Right now I want to know why you didn't tell me your brakes were going bad, Grant Stephens."

"What?"

"Your brakes—they disappeared on me. I was going fine until I tried to brake for Mrs. Finney's peke-a-poo. How her little darling got out into the road, I'll never know. But when I stomped on the brakes, nothing happened. Thank goodness I missed the dog. I just let the truck run into the nearest tree."

Grant stared at Delores, a mysterious look streaking across his face. His voice was tight as he asked, "Are you sure about the brakes?"

Delores blinked and said, "I'm sorry, Grant. I'll help you pay for it. Honest."

Grant made sure his face was a careful blank. "It's okay, Delores. I'm not mad at you. I'm glad you're okay. I have only one question, though. Could the shock of the peke-a-poo running into the road have caused you to miss the brake pedal?"

"I know you think I thrive on excitement, and I'll admit I do," she answered with a shaky smile, "but my kind of excitement doesn't include running into trees for fun. Yes, I'm sure about the brakes."

Grant turned to Shorty and said, "Get her up to the house. Beth, you and I will take your truck."

Shorty nodded and turned to Delores. "I'll carry you back to the car."

Delores, recovering rapidly from her trauma, whispered, "My hero," and lifted her arms around his neck. "Oh, Beth," Delores called over Shorty's shoulder, "someone needs to go unload the hay from the back of Grant's wrecked truck."

Beth, amazed that Delores could think of hay at a time like this, nodded.

Grant sat tensely, deep in thought, as Beth drove them back to the ranch house. Just yesterday, he had given his pickup the once-over. The brake line and brake shoes had been fine. He had the sinking feeling someone had tampered with the brakes. Dewey Smith came to his mind, but was promptly dismissed since he hadn't known who Grant was or, for that matter, who drove which vehicle at New

Start. Besides, he didn't have the smarts to alter the brake system. Grant closed his eyes and rubbed his fingers across the lids. The cold fact stared him in the face. He had been found. Someone knew he was in Douglas.

Chapter 9

Grant watched as Beth put the finishing touches on her float for the parade. He had to admit, it was something—all decked out as an Hawaiian island, complete with smoke-spewing volcano. The two veterinary hopefuls who worked at New Start had helped him put it together, and it didn't look half-bad, if he said so himself. Bright flower baskets and real palm trees, on loan from the local plant nursery, helped create the illusion. But the most incredible addition was the Hawaiian princess—Beth. She was already in costume, and as he'd predicted, she looked jumpable in the grass skirt. Her grace of movement was emphasized by the swaying and swishing of the skirt. The teasing glimpses of long limb and firm hips added to the seductive picture. A skimpy, bright yellow halter topped off the outfit.

He intended to keep her in his sight the entire day. Even though nothing else had happened, his cop senses had been alerted by the brakes incident. He'd checked it out and his suspicions had been right, the brake line *had* been cut.

He'd already called for backup, but he wasn't taking any chances. He knew he was the main target, but with these guys you could never let your guard down. His gut instinct told him they'd try to get to him through Beth. And he never questioned his instincts, he acted on them.

Besides, he'd trained himself to think like his opponents. If he were the hit man, he would have already figured out that Beth was the key. He knew his opponents were smart, devious and deadly. Now he had to stay to protect her—to undo what his being there had done. Again, he had been trouble for her.

He wandered over to the float. "I knew you'd look great in that skirt."

"Grant Stephens, don't you make one crack about this." She put her hands on her hips and the grass skirt rustled. His senses went into overdrive with that simple sound.

He held up his hands in surrender. "I'm not the one who said I wouldn't be caught dead in a grass skirt. I'm not the one who said it would be over my dead—"

"All right, all right. I admit I said all that stuff." Beth fluffed the skirt again. "But that was before Mildred said she'd give a donation to New Start if I did this."

"And you'd do almost anything for New Start, right?"

Beth turned at the tone in Grant's voice. Did she imagine the wistfulness? She couldn't read anything in his face. "Almost anything," she whispered.

"Yeah, I remember."

They both flashed to the same memory. A desperate, passionate Beth offering herself to Grant. She lowered her eyes before he could see the confusion in them.

"Hey, you two, we're ready to line up." Mildred, clipboard in hand, grass skirt on body, was sashaying through the crowd, taking charge. "Grant, Beth's float goes right behind the high school band. And, Beth, when the band plays that Hawaiian song, try to do a little hula."

"A what?" Beth shouted after a departing Mildred.

"A little hula, I think she said." Grant covered his laugh with a cough.

"She didn't tell me about *that*." Beth put her hands against her cheeks, trying to cool the heat that collected there.

"Just remember," Grant reminded her, "it's for a good cause."

"Yeah, I guess." She shrugged her shoulders, thinking it would all be over in two hours. Then she'd have the money to buy next month's feed. She wondered if she should bone up on belly dancing for next year. Mildred's thought processes seemed to have run amuck.

She turned to find Grant's eyes on her, desire flaming in their depths. She patted her hair nervously and told him, "You'd better get into the truck. Mildred will have a fit if we miss our place in line."

"You're right." He walked over, gave her a kiss on the lips and then one on each cheek. He explained innocently, "That's an old Hawaiian custom." He released her and jumped off the float. "And remember, my rearview mirror will be trained on your hips, so hula away."

Beth, too startled by his kiss to react, just nodded. That was the first intimate contact they'd had since the sighting-in. It felt so natural. Sighing, she leaned against the standing rail and reached for the leis draped over the fake pineapple plant.

The high school band marched into place. Then, warned by Grant's honk, she grabbed the rail as they lurched into place.

The Cornyval parade started, with Beth Channing Stephens waving to the crowds and doing a hula whenever the band played a twangy Hawaiian number. Grant, looking through his rearview mirror, had the best view.

At one point, his good feelings were smothered when he saw Dewey Smith yell an obscenity at Beth. He had a bottle in a brown paper bag and was reeling against the side of a building. Grant glanced quickly in the mirror but Beth was waving at some children and didn't see Smith.

When Joe Clay had heard about the threats, he'd wanted Beth to press charges, but she had declined. Knowing he wouldn't rest otherwise, Grant had finally paid Smith a private visit. As a cop Grant felt he knew something of people's patterns—the way certain folks acted in a given situation. He didn't think Smith would bother Beth again.

As the parade progressed, he could tell when Beth stopped being self-conscious and got caught up in the spirit of the parade. Her smile became brighter, she called out to people by name and her hips undulated with more sensuousness. He loved the last part. How quickly his body responded to her! The bulge in his jeans was damned uncomfortable, and it had been there since the first moment he'd seen her in the Longneck Palace. He smiled. Beth wanted him, too. She often looked at him with a hunger that made him want to throw her to the ground and bury himself in her softness. But he didn't. He couldn't. He wanted her to make the first move. To say she wanted him. To say she wanted to make love. The only problem was his physical condition was getting embarrassing. He felt like a young stud on the make.

He was sorry when they pulled up into the fairgrounds; it signaled the end of the parade. He wanted to watch Beth dance in slow, exotic movements for a lifetime. His heart jolted. A lifetime with her wasn't in his future, just a few weeks and then back to being a good guy chasing bad ones.

He jumped out of the truck cab and went to help Beth down from the float. Her cheeks glowed from the excitement and the early heat of the day. He wanted to spin her around and give her a great big kiss, but he settled for lifting her down and allowing his hands to linger at the naked skin at her waist. Her skin felt as soft as the finest silk, and its warmth scorched his fingertips. Her delicate fragrance intoxicated him, making him light-headed. "A lot of impressive hip work up there. Are you sure you didn't secretly practice?"

I pretended I was dancing just for you, in front of the fire, wearing only the grass skirt, she thought. Aloud, she said, "Don't be ridiculous."

Their eyes held for several seconds, each reading signs and promises in the depths of the other's.

"Beth, you were wonderful," announced Mildred, flushed from the excitement of being in the lead car. "Everyone just loved the float and you on it. Now where is Tom? He's supposed to be here at the carnival to make sure all the booths are set up." She scoured the fairgrounds with her eyes.

"I'm sure he's inside the gates somewhere. Try the shooting gallery," Grant suggested.

"Okay, right after I tell Delores and Shorty how wonderful they were in that old car of hers. Oh," Mildred said absentmindedly, already waving to her next honoree, "Beth, you'd better get into that gypsy outfit. Remember, you promised to be the fortune-teller this year."

Grant turned to Beth, grinning. "You are a wonder today, Elizabeth. First, a Hawaiian princess and now a gypsy."

"Be careful or I'll put a curse on you," Beth teased. "Now I've got to find Delores. My next costume is in her trunk. She's probably still entertaining somewhere, with Shorty trying hard to hide." She swished away.

Trying to keep Beth under surveillance during the carnival was a joke. Grant tried to keep track of who went in and out of her booth, but the successful advertising campaign had lured thousands of people here. Most of them were from neighboring towns and cities, but trying to spot a stranger was impossible. Nevertheless, Grant still leaned against a tree, and closely watched the brightly colored fortune-teller's tent.

Inside the tent, Beth blew a stray hair out of her eyes. "I see a promising future for you."

"Does that mean I'll get married this year?" asked the pretty eighteen-year-old.

Was that the only prediction these girls were interested in? Every single female, young or old, wanted to know about a tall, dark stranger coming into her life. There weren't that many Grant Stephenses to go around. She smiled at her own thoughts.

"Does it?" The girl pulled her hand away from Beth and leaned forward, waiting for the answer.

"It might mean that, if you want it badly enough."

"Oh, I want it more than anything." The girl sighed. "What else? Does it say how many bridesmaids I'll have?"

Beth hid a smile as she struggled to get herself back into character. This was all for fun, she reminded herself. "Yes, I see the number four here and, wait—" she stroked the girl's hand and paused dramatically "—I see the colors peach and lavender."

"Those are my favorite colors, and I have four best friends," the girl shrieked. "I can't believe it. This is real." She bounced up, ready to leave. "Is there anything else?"

Beth shook her head. "No, that's all the crystal ball tells me right now."

"Thanks, I can hardly wait to tell my friends."

Beth took a sip of the iced tea sitting on the table behind her while she waited for her next customer. She glanced around the tent, impressed with what she saw. She had rummaged through Red's barn and come up with a fringed tablecloth, a crystal ball and a rug with stars all over it which she had hung behind her. She'd thrown a red scarf over a lamp, and voilà, a fortune-teller's room, complete with poor lighting and eerie shadows on the wall.

She stood up to stretch, wondering why it was taking so long for the next person to come in. She'd been busy the entire afternoon. Turning away from the tent's entrance, she reached toward the ceiling, stretching from the tips of her fingers to her toes.

Grant stood transfixed, watching the unconsciously sensual display. He'd come in, trying to convince himself all the while that he'd done so because he was afraid someone had slipped in through the back of the tent. But in reality, he just missed being around her. When a throaty moan escaped her lips, he forgot to swallow. God, she was beautiful. Hair swinging around her shoulders, arms outstretched as if imploring a lover to come and satisfy her. He took a deep breath, not wanting to break the spell, but she must have heard because she whirled to find him standing there.

"Grant." She was breathless. "You scared me. I didn't hear you come in."

"Tired?"

"What?"

"You were stretching." He couldn't keep the low, husky pitch out of his voice. "Are you tired?"

"Oh, no, just getting out the kinks."

There were better ways, like a total body massage, he thought. Aloud, he asked, "Ready to tell my fortune?"

"Yours?"

"Yeah, I figure you need some practice with a man." Grant sat down across from her. "I haven't seen anyone but women coming in here all day." His eyes became cloudy, frosty. "You haven't had another man come in here, have you?"

"No, you'll be my first."

"Again."

Beth gasped. "Grant, I don't think this is such a good idea. The only thing I've been predicting all day is marriage in June with four bridesmaids...." Her voice trailed off as she realized what she'd said.

Grant laughed. "Well, then, you need a break. I don't want four bridesmaids, and I hate the color peach."

"How did you know?"

"I heard your last satisfied client tell all her friends that you were the real thing. You'd even guessed her favorite color."

"It's everyone's favorite this year." Beth smiled up at him.

"Not mine." He held out his hand, palm up, on the table. "Tell me what you see."

Beth lowered her head and picked up his hand, staring sightlessly into it. *What do I see? I see a man who seems to change every day. Just when I think I've figured this Grant Stephens out, he does something like this. The old macho, "I'm the head of the household" Grant was predictable, but the new Grant was a lot more fun.* She stroked his palm, running her tongue along her bottom lip in concentration.

"Beth?"

She jerked back to reality. She ran her thumb over the hard calluses on the inside of his hand, knowing that working at New Start had caused them. They were beautiful, she thought. His body heat flowed out of his hands with such intensity that she thought her own would be consumed by the flames.

"What do you see?" he asked in a husky tone.

"I see a long life line with many adventures notched into it."

"Really?" He leaned over to see what she saw. His face was so close, his every breath caressed her with a whispering softness. "Where?"

He wasn't looking at his hand, though, he was looking into her eyes. The emotions she read in his gaze were confusing, elating, intriguing and sexy all at once.

Grant broke the spell. "Now it's my turn. Let me tell your fortune."

Beth was unable to push words past her constricted throat. Did Grant feel the trembling in her fingers? His nearness played havoc with her control.

"I see a tall, dark, extremely handsome man—in fact, the most handsome man you'll ever meet—in your future," he began as he pretended to study her palm.

Beth raised her eyebrows and teased, "Tom Selleck's riding up on a white charger soon?"

Grant produced a mock frown and continued, "This man will sweep you away on the dance floor tonight. Be ready, my child, he cometh."

She smiled as Grant stood. Slowly—oh, so slowly, he leaned over until his lips were a mere inch from hers. She waited in exquisite anticipation for him to kiss her. Breathing in the smell of his cologne and the special scent that was Grant, she realized that the palms of her hands were clammy. Finally, when she thought she'd faint from wanting his touch, he placed his warm lips over hers.

The kiss was fiery in its intensity. His lips sent out a message and a promise as they moved with masterful purpose across the surface of hers. But before she could respond with all the pent-up emotions she had, Grant pulled away.

Her breasts throbbed and a delicious warmth skyrocketed through her body. The temperature inside the tent suddenly seemed stifling, and she found her chest heaving as she gasped for air. Grant grinned at her before he sauntered out of the makeshift fortune-teller's tent, leaving Beth to still her reeling world and calm the wanton desire for him that threatened to rob her of her independence.

Grant watched through half-closed eyes as Beth twirled and two-stepped her way around the community hall like a pro. She'd always loved to dance. They'd never missed a dance in high school. She had even made him learn to fast dance. Or, more accurately, he had forced himself to learn so he wouldn't have to watch her dancing with other guys, like tonight.

He didn't like her in other men's arms any better now than he had ten years ago. She still wore the gypsy costume and the bright red-tiered skirt swung up and around her, revealing her long legs. Legs that could hug a man with enough strength to make him want to stay between them forever.

Grant ran a hand through his hair and forced himself to look around the room. Everything seemed normal. The Cornyval's success was guaranteed. The community hall was packed, the country-western band played, and everyone from grandmas to grandchildren were dancing and laughing. Even Tom, still in his Hawaiian print shirt, was slapping people on the back, proclaiming what a great idea this theme had been.

I'm just tired, he thought. He hadn't had a decent night's sleep since the sighting-in. He had told himself it was because he was restless and ready to leave, but, no, the real truth was he couldn't get the feel and the taste of Beth out of his mind. Just as he was remembering how she tasted like honey and how she felt like warm silk in his arms, she swept by and waved at him from the arms of another man, Mark, one of the vet helpers at New Start.

The music ended, and he watched Beth excuse herself from the young man. Turning around, skirt swaying, she headed straight for him.

"I had a fortune-teller predict today that I was going to dance with the most handsome man I'd ever seen." She craned her neck. "I haven't seen anyone who fits that description yet, have you?"

"You're mighty sassy these days, Beth Stephens." Grant reached up and sifted his fingers through her hair, marveling at the golden shower of silk as it fell back into place. "I haven't seen that guy, but how about a dance with a broken-down jock?"

"What a sweet proposal," she said and batted her eyelashes at him exaggeratedly.

There was nothing sweet about the fierce and determined way he swept her into his arms. The band struck up a slow ballad, and the dance floor filled quickly with lovers holding each other tightly.

Beth's heartbeats kept time with the steady cadence of the music. Both hands wound around Grant's shoulders, where she could feel corded muscle purl under her fingertips. She tilted her head up and tucked her lips against his ear, wanting to nibble and taste but not daring to. Her nostrils were filled with the scent of Grant—the woodsy, outdoorsy scent that held bittersweet memories for her. During their marriage, when Grant would leave their bed early for work or practice, she would bury her face in his pillow, taking in his scent and imagining that he was still with her. After their divorce, whenever she'd caught the aroma of his cologne, a pain had knifed through her gut, and she'd thought she would die from wanting him so.

Now his hands brushed up and down her waist lightly, and the easy pressure made her ache with a hunger that only Grant could satisfy. She shifted in his arms, pulling back to study him. His eyes were the darkest blue she had ever seen them, and they reflected her longing. Gazing lower, she studied the springy black hair that peeped above the buttons of his shirt. Lord, how she wanted to press her lips against that ebony carpet and taste him. She wanted to glide her tongue over every last inch of his body, devour him, consume him.

Grant watched Beth stare at the tuft of hair sticking out of his shirt. During their marriage she had been an innocent yet passionate lover, but the messages she was sending out tonight were more like those of a tigress ready to mate.

His fingertips burned where he stroked the sides of her body. Her delicate fragrance wafted to his brain, filling his mind with erotic, tantalizing thoughts. He wanted Beth in his bed, naked, writhing in shared ecstasy. He wanted to trail hot, hard kisses from her lips, down the column of her throat, across her shoulders, to the high peaks of her breasts. When she screamed her pleasure and begged him to sheathe himself in her, he would drift lower, teasing her with kisses down her tummy, in her navel, and advance down the silken length of her thighs. She would flower for him, opening her limbs to invite her lover's favor, finding fulfillment with just the flick of his tongue.

"Grant, the music's stopped." Her voice was a throaty siren's song.

His feet stopped, but he didn't let her go. She fit the contours of his body too perfectly.

She stirred, glancing around at the other dancers. "It's a warm night for March. Would you like to get some punch?"

He let his hand ride at the small of her back as they wove their way through the crowd, chatting with friends as they went. The gesture was not lost on many of the men who'd had their eye on Beth. Grant was staking out proprietary rights.

The punch was refreshing but sour. Beth made a face after taking a sip, but Grant downed his in one swallow and ladled out another serving.

"I saw a lot of old friends from high school and college at the festival this afternoon," he told her.

"Really?"

"Yeah, I was trying to keep an eye on your booth but several times I got caught up in conversation. Remember Jimbo O'Neale?"

Beth nodded. He'd been a quiet, brainy type who was like a computer when it came to dishing out sports statistics.

"He's living over in Slater. He spirited me away for a while to meet his wife. They have a new baby, and nothing would do but that I had to see it."

She glanced at the door by the refreshment table that led into the kitchen. "I'm supposed to check in with the refreshment crew every now and then and see if I can help. I..." Beth's words drifted away as she looked toward the doorway.

Grant's eyes followed her gaze and saw Martin Channing greeting people near the entrance. "Damn," he muttered under his breath. Why the hell did he have to show up tonight?

Grant had only seen him the one time at the ranch house, but that once was enough. He knew that Beth talked to him every week on the telephone, but he never asked nor wanted to know what was said between them.

Channing's eyes covered the crowd, pausing for the briefest second on Grant. In that instant, anger and repugnance flashed across Martin's features. His eyes moved on to rest with love and pride on Beth.

He excused himself from the couple he was talking to and strode across the room to give Beth a kiss on the cheek.

"Hello, my dear. You look lovely tonight." He inclined his head marginally. "Stephens."

"Hello, Daddy. It was nice of you to join the festivities."

"You know I support all of the town's functions. I made a major donation to the Cornyval fund because a portion of the proceeds are going to the library."

Grant watched the exchange, eyes narrowed. He kept his silence, not wanting to give Martin fodder for an argument or Beth a reason to be unhappy.

The band began a stilted version of a waltz and Mr. Channing took Beth's arm. "How about a turn around the floor with your old man?"

"I'd love it," she said and laid her empty punch glass on the table.

Grant melted into the background to scrutinize the scene. Martin Channing was an excellent dancer, and father and daughter moved with an easy grace. Beth laughed at something her father said, and Grant felt his stomach contract. Why was he so jealous of Beth's relationship with her father? The answer was as complex as it was simple. Martin always made him feel inferior, inadequate in the role of taking care of Beth. Years ago, just when Grant had thought he'd proved Channing wrong, Beth had betrayed him. He was finally through blaming Beth, but the older man still had the ability to make his blood boil.

When the dance was over, Martin took Beth's arm and ushered her to the side of the dance floor to converse with a young man Grant didn't recognize. The man was dressed in a starched, button-down collar, and Grant would have been willing to bet a month's wages that he was probably a banker or lawyer. Certainly someone Martin Channing deemed suitable for Beth.

His gut tightened more, and he shoved away from the wall, missing the glance Beth tossed him over her shoulder. He cursed under his breath. He needed some fresh air. The atmosphere in the hall was stifling and muggy. Heading for the door, he didn't stop until he was well away from the hall, breathing in clean air. Locating the keys to Beth's truck in his pocket, he opened the door and sat down, leaving his legs hanging out the open door. He turned the key, switched on the radio and lay across the seat. The bluesy tones of Bonnie Raitt filled the night.

Hoping to rid his mind of Martin Channing, he concentrated on the counterfeiting case and decided to call the Houston office to see what was up. Picking up Beth's car phone, he dialed the special number he was given by his office in St. Louis.

"Culpepper? Stephens." He listened intently and his eyes narrowed. He sat up straight.

"Got it. Will do." He pressed the disconnect key and dialed 9-1-1. "Yes, get me the sheriff's office." He waited. "Come on, answer." Finally he heard the click.

"Sheriff's office. Joe Clay Phillips here."

"Joe Clay, this is Grant Stephens. I need your help."

Grant burst his way through the door of the community hall and headed straight for Beth, who was by the bandstand with Delores. They were both laughing. He grabbed her arm and swung her roughly around to face him.

"Get your things, Beth. We're going," he told her. "We have some serious talking to do."

Her eyes widened. Without another word, she gathered the suitcase with her Hawaiian outfit in it and followed him out into the warm night.

When they were out of earshot, he turned to her. "I got a call a few minutes ago on the car phone." His voice was level and gave no hint of his emotions. "There's trouble here in Douglas."

Beth frowned. "Trouble?"

"I may be in danger and, for that matter, so could you."

"Grant—"

"Listen to me, Beth. This isn't a game. There's a backup, another agent, positioned at your house right now. We want to pull the guy out who's after me into the open, so I'm going to be the bait to hook and reel him in."

"No." Her voice was a thin whisper on the gentle breeze.

"Yes. I've called Joe Clay Phillips and the local sheriff's department will take you somewhere safe." Grant's features were hard in the dim light.

Beth's mind whirled at his revelation. She thought of what he wanted her to do, but her resolve stiffened against the idea.

They both looked up as a police car wheeled into the parking lot.

Beth grabbed Grant's arm. "I'm going with you to New Start."

"Absolutely not." Grant's eyes flashed in the moonlight.

"Absolutely *yes,*" she said, and steely determination laced her voice. "I live at New Start, and I'm not leaving it."

"I'm not asking you to leave it, Beth," he said with gentle persuasion, "only to spend a night or two away."

She pulled him closer and spoke with her heart in her eyes, "If you're going to face this danger, I want to be there with you. We're in this together."

Grant read the concern and a deeper emotion in Beth's eyes, but there was no way he would let her risk her life.

"Sorry, Beth."

"Grant, I'm going. If you don't take me, I'll drive there myself."

Joe Clay stopped the police car in front of them. Grant grabbed Beth's arm firmly, yanked open the door and shoved her inside. He slammed it shut and leaned down to inform Joe Clay, "I'll call in a report, but for now just keep her safe."

"Grant—" she began.

"I've got to do this alone."

Chapter 10

Grant had just finished giving the house a thorough once-over, checking the windows and doors, switching lights on and off, opening closets and closing them. The doorbell's musical chimes made him stiffen and grab the butt of his gun, which he'd strapped on as soon as he'd arrived at the house.

He approached the door cautiously and lifted the curtain a notch to peer out.

"Marshal Stephens, this lady just drove up and says she needs to talk to you." Grant recognized the voice of the deputy who'd been sent to help him.

Grant closed his eyes as his breath hissed through his teeth. The little fool! He would wring her gorgeous neck.

"Grant, open this door right now." Since when had she developed this bossy streak? he wondered.

He unlocked the door and stood face-to-face with a furious Beth.

He glowered. "I see you've already met Deputy Mullins."

Beth glared at the flustered deputy. "This...this man accosted me when I drove up and wouldn't let me use my own key to get in my own house."

"Marshal—"

"It's all right, Mullins. This is Beth Stephens and she lives here." He grabbed Beth's arm and jerked her inside. "I'll handle her from here."

"Okay. Good night." Deputy Mullins looked unsure as to what he should do, but Grant slammed the door and left him gaping on the porch.

"How'd you give Joe Clay the slip?" His eyes bored into her.

"It was pretty simple." She tried to smile in the face of Grant's anger but it wavered. Anger still sparked in her eyes, however. "He took me to his sister's house. I said I was going straight to bed, but instead I climbed out a window and took his sister Sharon's car."

"Nice work," he said sarcastically. "I'll call him and tell him you're here and that the car is in one piece."

Beth followed him to the kitchen, where she reached for a glass in the cupboard. "Grant Stephens, you need to explain this to me right now. The call to Joe Clay can wait. You've scared me half to death. I'm afraid for you, and I don't know what to be frightened of." She motioned to him with the glass. "The *not* knowing is scarier than anything else."

Grant refused her offer of a drink. He let out a long breath and even managed a half smile at her before saying, "Yeah, it's time you heard the whole ugly story. Come on." He took her hand.

He led her into the living room and gently pushed her into the cushions of the sofa. She popped back up, refusing to bow to his high-handed treatment. Rubbing her hand where he'd gripped it so tightly, she stared at him warily.

Grant settled into one of the chairs and grimly faced her. "Remember the case I told you about?"

"The one with the counterfeiter?"

He nodded and picked up a horse statue from the side table, studying it for several seconds.

"You told me everything was under control."

He put down the knickknack and looked directly into Beth's eyes. "I also told you I'm the eyewitness who saw the counterfeiter using the copier and plates."

Something prickled at the back of Beth's neck at Grant's taut stance and reluctant tone. Her body grew suddenly cold despite the pleasantly warm night. "That makes the case airtight, you said, but he has friends in high places who want him out to make more phony money, right?"

"Right," Grant agreed. "The counterfeiter's bosses know we can put him away for a long time. If he cops a plea, their little operation is in big trouble." He took a deep breath. "We received information that the crime bosses are looking for me. That way, our case would only be based on circumstantial evidence, and the counterfeiter would, in all probability, walk free."

Beth sat as motionless as a statue. Her voice was a reedy whisper. "Why are you telling me this in more detail now?"

"Because they've found me."

"You're sure?"

"Nothing's ever certain, but events are starting to add up." He stood, but then flopped back down in his chair. "My office instructed me to lie low here. I wasn't taking a vacation—well, I was, but I was ordered to. My boss felt Douglas was as safe a place as any to hide." He smiled tensely at her. "After all, nothing exciting ever happens in Douglas."

She tried to smile back at him but the attempt was a miserable failure. Her prophetic words that nothing exciting ever happened in Douglas had come back to mock her in a sadistic way. Solemnly, she forced herself to ask, "What did you mean, 'events are starting to add up'?"

He sprang up and paced around the room, restless. "I suspected something when the brakes on my truck failed the day Delores borrowed it." He paused to look at Beth. "I'd just had everything under the hood checked a few days before. After the wreck, I discovered the hose to the brake fluid had been cut."

Beth gasped.

"Dewey Smith was the only culprit I could think of in Douglas, but we had our argument only moments *before* the accident." He cocked a thumb at his own chest. "*I* should've been driving that truck, not Delores. The brake failure was meant for *me.*" He slammed his balled fist into the palm of his other hand.

Beth sat still as a stone, watching Grant pace like a caged animal. Her mind flashed back to the sighting-in, when the gun he'd held had become a part of him. As she watched him now, she knew she was seeing the real Grant, powerful, dangerous and lethal. But instead of being frightened by this barely controlled strength, she was comforted, knowing that he would use his strength wisely in dealing with these criminals.

She eased out of the chair and stood in front of him. Quietly she asked, "What do we do now?"

"*We* don't do anything." He walked to the stereo and found a country-and-western station. He motioned her to his side. "Since you're here, you might as well stay. At least this way I know where you are. While I'm wrapping this up, you're never going to be out of my sight or Deputy Mullins'."

"But what about New Start? How am I going to get anything accomplished with you dogging my heels?"

He pulled her to him, crushing her breasts against his chest. "You're not getting the picture, Beth. These guys play for keeps, and they don't make mistakes." He reached up and rubbed a finger across her lower lip, staring for several seconds at her lush mouth.

"Grant, you're scaring me."

"Good. I want you to be scared. I want you to understand that your life may be in danger. And I want you to do exactly what I say."

She stiffened, searching for some measure of gentleness within his rugged features. Her gaze settled on his lips and as she watched, they slowly lowered to hers.

"Damn," he whispered into her mouth as his lips claimed hers. His aggressive act was smooth but masterful and in spite of herself, she felt a lethargy begin to steal over her, and she began kissing him back. He slanted his lips across hers, at the same time drawing his tongue across her lower lip. She sighed deep in her throat and opened her mouth to give his questing tongue more access.

Beth felt the tender assault throughout her entire body. Tiny erotic messengers fluttered along her nerves, alerting her body to a marvelous sensory experience. They tickled and teased as they visited every erogenous zone she had, from the hollow of her mouth, to the tips of her breasts, to the inside of her legs, to her toes. But they finally gathered in the apex of her thighs to rejoice and enjoy this electrifying sensation.

Grant. He was here kissing her, protecting her, igniting flames. His scent—woodsy after-shave, soap and male—surrounded her in a dizzying fog, and she surrendered herself to the thrill of it.

Their lips couldn't seem to get enough of each other's taste until she thought she would go insane from the pure pleasure of their mouths blending. Then Grant ran his hands up and down, up and down her back in a slow cadence, at the same time taking love bites from the silken column of her neck.

His hand stole around her side and claimed the womanly lushness of one breast. She sighed into his mouth.

"Baby, you're so soft, so sweet." He kneaded her breasts gently, coaxing the tips into tight buds while Beth whispered his name against his throat, pressing herself against him.

Common sense and good judgment fled as Grant immersed himself in the feel and smell and taste of Beth. He wanted to brand her touch into his brain, her kiss into his body, her soul into his soul.

Slowly he brushed the gypsy blouse off her shoulders to expose her trembling breasts. Gently, lured by the soft sounds she whispered into his ear, he lifted them free from their dainty prison of silk and lace and explored their fullness. He teased and manipulated, watching her face and the myriad emotions that flashed across it—pleasure, joy, bliss. Finally he leaned down and entrapped one with his mouth while the other's crest was finessed into a throbbing pearl by his fingertips.

"Grant, Grant." Beth whispered his name as her hands clutched at his thick hair, drawing him closer to her. "Please." She pulled on his shirt, tearing it out of his jeans.

Her urgent whispers and hands brought some sanity to his love-starved brain, and he remembered. This was the way he wanted Beth, clinging to him, coaxing him to love her. But not *now*. He knew, from all his work in the field, that she was reacting to the *situation*, not to him. He'd seen people, scared half out of their wits, do emotional, irrational acts that they regretted later. When he made love to Beth, it would be because she wanted him. It wouldn't be in a moment of fear, because of the thrill of danger, or as a fulfillment of the allure of lust.

Once they made love, he'd never let her go. He swore under his breath as Beth's hand clenched around him. Why hadn't he thought about this? He should have left town right after the will reading. Now they'd found him, and they probably knew Beth was important to him. He'd suspected when the brakes had been tampered with, but now he knew and damn it, it was too late. Beth was involved. His work was lethal, and he could not expose her to that.

He pulled away slowly and smoothed her top over her breasts. Taking a deep breath, he rested his head against her forehead. His voice was low and teeming with emotion. "We can't do this. *I* can't do this. Not now. Not like this." He ran a hand through her hair. "I'm sorry I got carried away."

He heard a strangled cry and quickly pulled back to look into her eyes. "Did I hurt you?"

"Grant, I don't understand. I can't keep going through this teasing dance."

"Do you think I want to?" He searched her face for the answer. "Beth, you're reacting to the situation, not to me."

"Don't tell me what I'm reacting to. I'm reacting to you, not this crazy mess we're caught up in."

He pulled her head onto his shoulder, effectively silencing her. "Shh. I'm sorry, but you have to trust me on this one." He kissed her hair. "I'm going to check upstairs one more time. You stay here until I call you."

Beth watched in confused silence as he walked out of the room and took the stairs two at a time. She waited, not moving from the spot.

At his all-clear signal, she turned off the music and slowly climbed the stairs. Searching for Grant, she saw the door to his bedroom closing as she rounded the corner. Her body was still rioting with the feelings he had awakened.

She paused for a second at his door, hand poised to knock. She heard his voice, low and calm. Who was he talking to at this time of night? Was it Joe Clay, discussing this deadly game with him? Was it one of the men he worked for? She shuddered and continued on down the hall.

Slipping into her room, Beth stared at herself in the mirror. How many more times would they do this? Come to the boiling point, then shut off? Never, if she had anything to do with it. What did he want? Her walking naked into his room and falling all over him before he believed she wanted him, needed him?

She stilled. That was exactly what he wanted. He wanted their joining to be her choice, her decision, her giving. And that was exactly what he was going to get.

Swiftly she ran into her bathroom and turned on the spigots to draw water. Hastily stripping, she paused to pour cologne into the bath before stepping in and rinsing away the residue of the long and hectic day.

Five minutes later she rummaged through the back of her closet, rediscovering a silky, midnight-blue robe. After a quick, silent debate with herself, she belted the robe loosely around her body. She wore nothing else. After dragging a brush through her hair, she surveyed her image. Her reflection revealed a tall woman with blond hair and blue eyes that smoked with desire.

"Well, this is it, baby," she said out loud. She giggled nervously and realized that she was almost as jittery as she had been on her wedding night.

Taking a deep breath, she turned and hurried to the door before all her courage fled....

The cold shower had done nothing to make Grant relax. He sprawled naked across the bed, staring at the ceiling, arms behind his head. The door opened and slowly he turned his head. His breath caught, and he jackknifed to a sitting position.

"Beth?" He hastily yanked the covers over his lower body.

"Grant, I think it's time we stopped torturing each other like adolescents." Her voice was a throaty rasp that twisted in a silken knot around his brain and caused that ache in his groin to blossom.

She walked over to the bed and slowly slid the covers off him. "And I think it's well past time that you delivered what your kisses promise."

He held her gently away by her shoulders. "I can't promise you anything permanent, Beth."

"I know." She kneeled on the bed and leaned toward him. "I don't want a promise for tomorrow, I just want tonight."

She pushed him down on the bed and began kissing his exposed chest.

"Beth." His words came out a strangled cry. She silenced him by nibbling on his lips, hushed him as she nipped his jaw.

"Beth, in a few more seconds, I won't be able to stop myself from taking what I've wanted since the reading of the will. Are you sure this is what you want?" He grabbed her head between his large hands, forcing her to look into his eyes.

She smiled. "I don't ever want this to stop."

Grant groaned then swore, muttering something dark and sexual, before he crushed his lips to hers. Her lips felt like velvet, burning velvet.

Beth squirmed, causing her robe to open completely. Her breasts pressed against him, rubbing against the hair that dusted his chest, those soft pillows of warm flesh squeezed tightly to him. Self-imposed restraints gone, Grant created a symphony of sensation. He stroked up her back and then down her side, stopping to tease the side of her breast. Her back arched, allowing her full access.

He sucked strongly at one stiff peak while he molded her other breast with his hand. Rivulets of pleasure so strong she thought she would die coursed through her body. The secret place between her legs was bursting with delicious sensations.

The movement of his hands and mouth encouraged her to bring her softness in line with his hard length, and Beth's groan soon mingled with his own throaty growl. With a will of its own, her body ground again and again against him, seeking release from the building tension.

"It's been so long. I'm ready for you now. I've been ready for you forever." Grant's voice grated with emotion.

A sense of urgency fed their passion. He peeled her robe off and sent it in a whispering blue cloud to the floor. Their fingers and lips glided with frenzied pleasure over sensitive flesh. Each was a slave to the other's body, but neither wanted the bonds to be broken.

She entangled her hands in his hair and pulled him to her breasts again. His mouth worshiped them. He laved them into wetness and then blew them dry. He watched the tips pout tighter, and reveled in her throaty cry.

Slowly sliding his hand in between her thighs, he found her silken wetness. "I want to be inside you. Now. I can't wait."

He palmed her mound as she writhed beneath his touch. She dug her fingernails into the muscled surface of his back.

At that moment she cried out and showered her sweetness against his questing fingers.

He felt stunned. "God, you react so beautifully. You're all I've ever wanted, Beth."

Beth opened her eyes and turned her head away.

"What is it?" Grant touched her chin, bringing her head around to face him.

"I'm so embarrassed, Grant. I don't know how I let that happen."

He lovingly turned her over on her back and smiled tenderly down into her eyes. She had given herself to him and his heart pounded with excitement at her abandonment. "It was beautiful. It was the most precious gift you could have given me." He gathered her into a crushing embrace and kissed her.

Then he slowly let her go and watched in the moonlight as his fingers sifted through the hair between her thighs. She shifted restlessly, opening for him.

"You're so warm, so soft." Grant kissed her stomach, feeling the quivers that shot through her. He rose up and settled between her thighs. Kissing her ear, he whispered, "Take all of me, Beth. I can't wait any longer." He buried himself in her silkiness with one deep plunge. "That's right," he murmured. "Hold me tight inside." Her shallow breaths mirrored his own.

Slowly, then with more speed, he began moving, each time almost pulling out, before reentering the mysterious haven. The tempo increased until he hung on the edge, striving for the final crescendo. Just as he reached it, he felt Beth's release, and he sank into an exhausted, harmonious peace.

Darkness cushioned Beth as she woke from what seemed like a long, deep sleep. She couldn't remember having felt this rested in ages, not since before... she couldn't pinpoint when. The blackness was soothing, dreamlike, far removed from reality. It sheltered her, allowing all of her senses to be attuned to her body.

Even now, she could feel the afterglow: behind her knees, between her legs, around her mouth. Her stomach fluttered as she remembered Grant's love nips. But of all the places sensitive from his touch, her breasts ached the most from his attention. They felt large, full, as she imagined they would during pregnancy.

As her mind lounged within the erotic darkness, she tried to stretch her body. Grant's hard, warm length curled next to her. She opened her eyes and when they adjusted to the dim light, she saw that he was sprawled out with one of his hands tucked under his cheek, the other flung over her breasts, softly caressing them. She smiled and gently stroked his arm.

No wonder I woke up needing him again, she thought. Sudden shyness made her try to push his hands away carefully, but his hold only tightened possessively. She groaned. This was the way she had felt every morning during their marriage. Beautiful and whole. The empty ache that had throbbed in her heart since the divorce was gone.

She raised her eyes to the ribbon of light that intruded between the heavy drapes. Sometime during the night, Grant must have closed them. He had shut out reality. What would happen when light penetrated this dreamworld? She squeezed her eyes shut, trying to hold on to the security of darkness.

Beth focused her mind on their lovemaking of the night before. Only one thing was wrong. Although Grant had whispered erotic words, even loving words, he had never said "I love you."

He'd warned her that he wanted only her body and had made no promises. And she had wanted his body. Their cravings for each other had been mutually satisfied and that was all. At least for him. He didn't love her, but she loved him, body and soul. And if it took the rest of her life, she would heal his wounded pride and make him whole again. And when he was whole again, he would love her. She'd make him see that their love could overcome the deceit and heartache of the past.

"Grant?" She softly blew the mahogany hair that fell across his forehead.

He sighed deeply and a reflexive movement of his hand completely covered her breast. Trying again to wake him, Beth shifted her entire body. He possessively pulled her closer.

"Be still, woman. It's not morning yet." He didn't open his eyes.

"How long have you been awake, you sneak?" Beth pushed against his arm.

One eye popped open and pinned her with its electric blue intensity. "Long enough to grow hard again just thinking about you."

Beth blushed in the dim light and closed her eyes. "Grant!"

"It's too late for shyness, Beth."

He pushed the covers down and stared at her breasts. He frowned and ran a finger gently around the crest of one. "I left my mark on you last night."

Beth's eyebrows hiked and she looked: light abrasions visibly showed on her translucent skin.

"Did I hurt you?" His expression was concerned and filled with self-disgust.

"Of course not. It was wonderful."

"I acted like a young stud, thinking only of my own pleasure. You broke down all my common sense when you came in here half-naked, smelling so sweet." He planted several kisses in the valley between her breasts. "I want to return your gift this morning. I want to do such exquisite things to your body that I'm the only man you'll ever remember."

"You *are* the only man, Grant."

He cursed and crushed her to him, raining kisses across her lips.

Dear God, he *was* giving to her. She wanted to laugh and cry and scream and moan all at the same time as he touched her all over. She'd remembered him as a tender lover, but he was now concentrating solely on her pleasure. Her heart swelled with feeling.

Kisses as soft as snowflakes landed around her ear causing her to gasp with pleasure as desire poured like molten lava through her veins. When his tongue dipped into the delicate center, a moan that was almost a purr rose to her lips.

His lips traveled down to her breasts and he placed careful kisses on the reddened areas his passion had left the night before. His hands gently shaped and reshaped the firm flesh, and finally he suckled the tips, causing them to bead in arousal.

Beth was almost delirious from the stunning sensations radiating through her body. She reached for Grant. "Let me love you, Grant. Let me."

He raised his head and smiled. "You are."

He continued his tender assault by moving lower. First, her navel was given exquisite attention, then her stomach. Kneeling between her thighs, he brushed his knuckles along the smooth expanse of one leg.

"Your legs go on for miles, Beth. They drive a man crazy because he knows when he gets to the end of them, heaven will be waiting."

Picking up a foot, he massaged and kissed each toe. Ecstasy, almost painful in its intensity, shot through Beth. Whispers and moans floated through the air like a lover's concert. His tongue traveled up and around her calf, pausing to nip and nibble the back of her knee.

"Grant, Grant." She chanted his name.

She reached for him, to force her lover to complete his sensuous pursuit. But he evaded her and turned the same attention to her other leg.

Finally he looked at the wanton picture Beth made lying on the big bed. Her hair was a golden fan across the pillow. Her eyes partially closed in desire. Her breasts quivering in anticipation. The delicate blond curls between her legs beckoning his touch. Her long legs smooth as a baby's cheek. God, he loved her. He wanted to make her happy. He wanted to take her to paradise.

He lay beside her and kissed her fully and completely. His hand slipped between her thighs and found the tiny nub that sparked the fire in her.

"Yes . . . !" Her breathless cry begged for release.

"That's right," he said deeply, sensually. He touched her inner core with his fingers and she arched against his hand. "Show me how I make you feel. Do you like that? Do you want more?"

As he talked, his fingers performed their magic. She felt adrift in a sea of sensations, whirling out of control; Grant her only anchor.

He smiled, kissing her tenderly.

"Grant, I . . . I . . ." She looked at him, her eyes shining with desire. She turned to him, kissing his chin, his eyes, the inside of his ear. She was frantic to return his gift of loving.

"Easy," he warned her.

She reached for him, and it was his turn to arch into her palm. "Beth, honey, yes." Then the only sound in the room was that of their labored breathing.

He had known several women in his years away from Beth, but none of them could incite the same fire in him, arouse the same tenderness. She had been beautiful last night, offering herself to him, but today he'd sought to give her that same pleasure. Amazingly, he found that he was still the recipient of the greatest gift, because of the joy her fevered responses gave him. She was no longer the innocent girl he'd left years ago. She was now a woman who knew what she wanted, a woman capable of making her own decisions. She was a vibrant, challenging woman, and he found the new Beth gorgeous and extremely sexy.

Damn, what had he gotten himself into? He was falling heavily under her spell again, but he was determined he wouldn't let himself become vulnerable to her charms. The pit at the end of the pleasurable path she was leading him down was dark and painful, he knew. He'd been down it once already, and he had to keep himself from plunging into it now.

On a hissing breath he covered her hand with his and stopped its motion. "I've waited forever to feel you holding me like this. You used to be embarrassed to touch me."

"I used to be a girl," she told him. "But no longer." She rubbed the tip of her nose back and forth across his chest.

Grant couldn't stop himself from brushing feathery kisses on the top of her shoulder before he touched her again at the heart of her womanhood.

"Ohh, Beth, you're so wet and ready for me."

Silently cursing himself for his lack of control, he knew he couldn't wait any longer. He rolled her on top of him and gently positioned her, with one thrust reaching the limits of her womb. He smoothed his hands on her buttocks, guiding her, moving her. Then he cupped her breasts and fingered the tight buds of her nipples. Her half-closed eyes were a blaze of emotions.

As they moved together, their bodies spiraling to breathless fulfillment, Grant shut his eyes to block out the sight of Beth's glowing body and sensitive face moving above him. And as his senses exploded into a thousand fragments, shattering his soul with the strength of his release, he swore at Beth, the gods, life in general and most of all, himself for becoming caught up in her life again.

Deep in his heart, he ached.

Chapter 11

Grant stood in the doorway of the bedroom, studying Beth's face as she slept. Her childlike innocence was never more apparent as when she was asleep. He remembered the joy he'd taken, during their brief marriage, in waking before her and soaking up her beguiling charm while her body was still flushed with sleep's warmth.

Damn. He shut his eyes to block out how beautiful she was as the sunlight showered her with golden light, setting her hair on fire and making her skin glow. He'd worked harder to forget her in the ten years he'd been away than he'd ever worked on anything in his life. Next to obliterating her from his mind, dodging a two-hundred-pound tackle or disarming a drugged-out psychopath was a breeze.

Just when he'd thought he'd accomplished what he'd set out to do ten years before, fate had thrust them together again. And instead of finding himself immune to her, he'd found just the opposite. Her womanly body, intelligence and independent spirit worked like a drug on him to make him ignore his vow to forget her and get on with life.

In just one night he'd let her tear down the wall he'd carefully mortared and bricked around his heart for ten years. He didn't like it, and he wasn't going to let his guard slip again.

That was going to be hard, considering he had to put her in his protective custody. Grimly he determined to do his job, salvage what he could of the pieces of the wall around his heart and leave town as soon as he could fulfill his obligation regarding New Start.

Suddenly Beth jerked awake and peeked at the bedside clock. It was nine-thirty.

"Good morning." He pushed the door wider and stepped into the room. "I've brought you a cup of coffee. It's time to get up."

After he set the cup on the bedside table, he sat down on the edge of the bed. A bright smile lit Beth's face.

A rosy color suffused her cheeks and he found her more irresistible than ever. It was self-inflicted torture to be so close to her. His hands ached to touch her, but he slammed shut the door to his desires, brutally reminding himself of his vow.

"Good morning." Beth's husky voice carried satisfaction from the night before and promises of more.

She sat up and the sheet fell to her waist, exposing her creamy breasts to the morning light. Grant jumped off the bed, grabbed her robe from a nearby chair and tossed it to her.

"When you get dressed, meet me downstairs. We need to talk." On that note he ducked out the door and headed down the hall.

She stared after him. What was going on? He acted as if nothing had happened, as if their lovemaking had been a figment of her imagination. But then she moved her body and felt the soreness, and she knew she hadn't dreamed his caresses, his kisses, his whispered phrases.

Determined to get to the bottom of whatever was going on, she threw off the covers and shrugged into her robe. Marching into the kitchen, ready to pounce on Grant, she was stopped short by the sight of him hunched over the table, looking at a map and marking it with a red pen. He looked up for a moment.

"I poured you some orange juice. There's some toast, too." He gestured toward the counter. "Grab it and sit down."

Puzzled at his high-handed manner, she didn't move. She couldn't. She wasn't sure what she'd expected but it hadn't been this man. This monosyllabic, steely-eyed man who had trouble meeting her gaze was not the Grant she'd slept with last night. She tried breaking through the shell. "Grant?"

He looked back up from the map he was studying. He saw confusion playing on her face. "Beth, I'm sorry. I know this isn't the morning after you wanted."

He saw her back straighten. "How do you know what I want?"

"I haven't forgotten what our other morning afters were like. If you'll remember, Beth, sex was always our strong suit." He used the word *sex* purposely dehumanizing the beauty of their lovemaking. "It wasn't the hours we spent in bed that ruined our marriage, it was the hours we spent out of it."

"How foolish of me! I thought last night was special."

"We haven't gained any new territory because of last night. And right now, we have more important things to talk about."

Beth's temper simmered. "What could be more important?"

"Your life."

"What?"

"Get your juice and let me tell you my plans."

She picked up the glass and took a sip. "Am I allowed a say in these plans?"

"Actually, no." Grant shoved the map aside. "Sit down."

He waited for her to comply with his order before continuing. "You're going to stick to me like glue all day. Then tonight, you're going to do the same thing."

Beth stared at him a moment, angry over his domineering attitude and hurt over his insensitivity after the night they'd shared. She didn't even try to keep the sarcasm out of her voice. "As much as I would enjoy all the attention, I have to go down to the barns and take care of the animals today."

"Damn, I forgot about that." Grant wiped his hands over his face. He headed for the phone and picked up the receiver. "Don't worry, I'll take care of it."

Beth set her glass down quickly and spilled some juice on the map. "No, Grant." She wiped up the spill, ignoring his scowl. "It's my turn, and I'm going to do it. We can take care of the animals and then stick to each other like glue."

It was then that he knew he would have more trouble with Beth than he'd anticipated. He should have figured on her possessiveness of New Start and her stubborn determination to do her job. He couldn't let her go to New Start, though. He had to make sure she was safe. Hanging up the phone, he sat down opposite her. "I didn't want to bring this up right away, but I guess now's the time."

"Bring what up?" Beth's voice rose an octave.

He smiled grimly at her. "You're officially under the protection of the U.S. Marshal Service, now. You're not going anywhere without me until we can get you to a safe house."

"What are you talking about?" She sat up straighter, holding on to the edge of the table.

"Last night, I called my boss, Bill Johnson, and told him the story." He gave her a hard, level look.

"I heard you talking on the phone, but I figured you were telling Joe Clay where I was."

"I called him, too, and squared it about your escape from protective custody. They hadn't missed you or his sister's car yet." His eyes narrowed on her. "They'll be out this afternoon to pick it up."

"What did your boss say?"

"He reamed me out for getting you involved, and I deserve it." A muscle ticked in his jaw, and his eyes had gone utterly cold. "I should have left long ago. This never should have gotten so complicated."

"How could you know—"

"It's my job to know," he interrupted. "But, hell, nothing's been normal on this case. Least of all, you. Anyway, you're under the U.S. Marshal Service protection service now." He looked at her through half-closed eyes. "And that means you're my responsibility."

"But why?" Beth frowned. "Surely this person is wiser than to mess around with an ordinary citizen. Do you really think he'll bother me?"

"He knows who you are. He could use you to get to me." Grant's jaw tightened as he looked at Beth, assailable and innocent, sitting across from him. He forced himself to look away from her wide, blue eyes. Getting up, he walked over to the counter. "So, for the time being, you have to go to a safe house."

Beth thought about this for a minute. "What do you mean by a 'safe house'?"

"A safe house is a common, everyday house in a common, everyday neighborhood where anyone out of the ordinary sticks out like a sore thumb. One of the marshals from St. Louis, Culpepper, and one from Houston, Kevin Timmons, are stocking a house like that right now, and we're going to stay there for a while."

"When did you put me under protection?"

"Last night."

"Oh." Beth stood, hugging herself in a self-protective gesture. She couldn't speak for a second. When she could, she said, "Is that what last night was about? Just part of your job?"

Grant studied her for several minutes, waging an inner battle as to how much he should confide in her. Although she stood stiff and unyielding, he pulled her into his arms.

"Being under my protection had nothing to do with what happened last night." He grazed her hair with his lips. "Last night I was not a federal marshal, just a man with a woman."

He kept her anchored close to him so she couldn't see his face. He felt her softening against him and knew that he could have her again right here, right now. He gently pushed her away from him, groaning inwardly when he saw the light in her eyes. Lord, he had to make her see this for what it was. A walk down memory lane but nothing else.

"Get dressed. We've got to move."

She jerked, then shook her head as if clearing it. She blinked at him. "I can't just disappear for several days. I've got New Start to run." She planted her body in front of him.

"This is not the time for one of your obstinate attacks, Elizabeth Channing Stephens. Your life is at risk." Grant, eyes snapping, took her arm and pushed her toward the stairs.

"This man is a hired *killer*, Beth. This is not a movie. It's worse." His lips thinned. "You have no idea what a person like this is capable of."

She stared at him for a long moment, then said, "Life can be so cruel. I've worked for years to establish this place. Red helped by allowing me to make my own decisions. Yet Red, who helped me so much, played the cruelest of all his practical jokes on me." She ran her fingers through her hair. "He brought you back in my life to save New Start, but instead you're destroying my independence and New Start at the same time."

He hauled her against his body. "You'll get it all back, I promise. New Start, your independence, everything. But right now you've got to play this game my way." His eyes shot sparks of liquid fire. "There's somebody out there who's been hired to kill me. He's being paid more than your entire budget for New Start in the last five years. You can't take any chances."

Beth didn't struggle against his rigid embrace. She was hypnotized by the vehemence of his voice, the hard lines of his mouth, his stance. She knew his anger wasn't directed at her, but she also knew whatever caused it stood between them. They could enjoy sleeping together, but that was as far as the togetherness went for them. They had no future.

"You chose me instead of Joe Clay, so you have to play by my rules." His eyes shone with dark lights as he looked into the depths of her clear blue ones. "I don't want to have to worry about where you are. That would make me more vulnerable to attack."

The strength rushed out of Beth's body like a deflated balloon. Risking his life, endangering it anymore by virtue of her stubbornness, her pride, was something he could not do. How had he known that was the only way to gain her compliance?

His fingers relaxed their grip on her arms and roamed up to frame her face. His thumb traced the pout of her bottom lip. "I swear no one will harm you, Beth. You can trust me on that, but you have to cooperate."

He kissed her then. A kiss born of desperation. She felt the pain and pleasure, the longing and possession. And fear. She gripped Grant's shoulders, trying to steady her topsy-turvy world. What had happened to the sane, cozy existence she'd worked so hard to build? She knew the answer, of course. She'd fallen in love with Grant—again.

He ended the kiss and studied the depths of her eyes once more before releasing her.

"All right," she whispered as he moved away from her, knowing that in the past few moments, somehow, she'd made a decision. They had no future together, but she would take and cherish each moment they had. "I'll do what you want me to do, but what about New Start?"

"We'll work all that out," he promised. "Right now, I'm going down to the barns and take care of the animals. They're probably having a fit that breakfast is so late this morning." He gave her a half smile. "You'll be safe enough here with Mullins on guard. I want you to pack and get everything you need. Call Delores and tell her she and Shorty are in charge for a while."

"What reason should I give?" Beth's voice betrayed her mild panic.

"I don't care." Grant tucked his shirttail into his jeans. "Tell them we're going on a lover's holiday." He snapped his fingers. "That's it. Tell them we're going to Houston for a couple of days. We want to check out the ballet, the record stores and get in some heavy-duty reacquainting. They know we're ready for that, so maybe they won't think anything's out of the ordinary. Don't tell them the truth, unless you want to put them in danger."

He went to one of the kitchen drawers and slid it open. Beth's eyes widened as she watched him take out a pistol and coolly check the firing mechanism.

She knew he kept a gun in the bedroom, now this one. How many guns did he need? The seriousness of their situation suddenly registered.

He was totally absorbed in what he was doing, his fingers efficiently examining the firearm. Her breath caught in her throat when he extracted a holster out of the same drawer and strapped it on his shoulder. Sliding the gun into place and snapping it securely, he turned and nodded to her, before heading for the door.

"Grant?"

He turned, and she warred to keep the fear and loneliness she felt from appearing on her features. She must have failed, though, because he crossed to her quickly and took her into his arms.

"Beth, I'm sorry." He stroked her hair. "Remember that I'll be here for you." He looked deeply into her eyes. "Trust me."

"I do, but this is all so new for me, so different."

He held her away from him. "I'll lock the door on my way out. You'll be all right. This creep is too smart to come straight up to your front door. If you need anything, just ask Mullins. I'll be back as soon as I can."

He was almost out the door when he swung around to face her. "And eat your toast."

The door closed with a click. Beth, dazed and disappointed, totally ignored his last statement since her stomach felt like a lead weight sat in it. She shook her head and took a deep breath. She padded up the stairs and down the hall to her room, not stopping until she was in her bathroom. Shedding the silk robe, she stood under the hot jets of water in the shower for a long time, letting the rivulets of liquid soothe and pamper her confused emotions.

She let her mind stray to the lovemaking of the night before. The frantic urgency of the first time had seared Grant's body into her brain. The gentle sharing of the second time had branded his spirit into her soul. Looking down at her breasts now, she traced the faint abrasions with a fingertip and watched in awe as the tip became a tight bud. Just the memory of his wild, heated passion aroused her body with hair-trigger quickness.

She smiled, remembering. Never had she thought her toes to be an erogenous zone, but under Grant's tender onslaught, she'd gone up in flames. Even now, she ached for his magic, surely he'd felt some loving feelings for her?

The perfection of their joining had to have struck a chord with him, too. Last night had eclipsed her wildest dreams. Grant had been a ravenous lover, never giving her time to breathe, to think. "Tonight is for feeling," he'd told her, just before he'd made her feel him from the top of her head to the tips of her toes. She blushed at the memory.

Then, in the pearl gray of predawn, he'd made love to her again. It had been like a fairy tale. He'd showered her with gentleness, cherished her with tender care. And she'd known she still loved him. But he didn't love her. Wanted her, yes, but loved her? No.

Trying to reroute the path her mind had taken, she turned off the faucet, quickly toweled off and dressed in jeans and a T-shirt.

She went to the kitchen to straighten up. She saw the map laying there and stopped to examine it. She noticed the red markings around streets in Houston—the safe houses, she guessed. Sitting down, she studied the map in earnest, determined to regain some control over her life by at least knowing where she'd be spending the next several days, weeks, months. She realized she had no idea how long she'd be in hiding with Grant.

The moment she began to think of spending time with him, her mind latched on, analyzing their relationship. He had definitely changed, and she had to admit it, she liked the new Grant. He was still the charming rascal, but the chip on his shoulder didn't surface nearly so often. She smiled. He was still arrogant, but there was something different about even that. His arrogance was no longer the quick, macho attitude of a teenager, but a pride-filled assertion that he could get a job done. He had also learned to give with grace as well as receive.

She loved him so much, her heart ached. If she'd declared her love, would he have said anything in return? He'd murmured many things in the night, but none of them had been close to the three words she wanted, needed to hear most. His actions this morning confirmed her fears. He didn't love her. She would have to keep the words bottled inside her.

How quickly he changed from tender lover to the federal marshal, talking in clipped sentences, making her feel afraid. When he'd checked his gun and strapped it on, she'd felt the same horror she'd experienced at the sighting-in. He understood guns and violence and fighting. He wasn't really a part of her world anymore.

Grant was glad of the physical labor. He'd given the animals water and feed, and was now mucking out the stalls. The hard work kept him from lingering on the memory of Beth, her softness, her innocence.

Being around her made him forget the deadly business he was in. He was supposed to be one of the best marshals in the service. Why, then, did he allow her to stay with him? It tormented him that she could be a target for this killer, too.

He'd told himself if she was going to be so pigheaded as not to stay where he put her, then he'd just have to watch her himself.

He couldn't excuse himself, hadn't tried to when his boss, Johnson, had screamed at him the night before. But he'd known what it was that had made him make the mistake. It was this town; it was Douglas. And in particular it was Beth.

He'd drifted back into the past, the complacency of a small town, the lull of the slow pace, the beauty of Beth as a self-reliant woman. Then he'd been blindsided. The killer was here in Douglas. If life had taught him anything, it had been never to let your guard down. Hell, Beth had taught him that with her daddy and his money.

Now he had to conduct damage control: get Beth to a safe house and stay there with her. The trial was in two weeks. Surely he could survive with Beth around twenty-four hours a day for two weeks.

Who was he kidding? Being around her was going to kill him as surely as any bullet would. He would spend his time wanting her with every breath he took, knowing that after the trial, it was finished for them.

All his waking dreams about staying on and seeing her make a go of New Start had blown up when the killer had stalked him here. He couldn't, he *wouldn't* subject Beth to this kind of life, always living on the edge. He could never be certain the next case that came along, the next criminal that came along, wouldn't have an even more sick, more evil mind. Might set out to destroy him and those he loved. He was always on the edge, always after the worst bad guy he could find. And he loved Beth enough to want her safe... and that meant out of his life.

Wanting to hurry and finish his job so that he could get back to Beth, he walked over to the end stall and opened the gate. The horse inside just barely lifted his head.

"Damn," Grant muttered under his breath. That bastard Dewey Smith had almost starved this one to death. It was a mare, and she had been in the pit when they'd rescued her. After several weeks at New Start, she still looked bad.

He patted her neck and crooned to her, "Come on, you've got to eat. You still afraid Smith might come back? Don't worry about him. I had a little talk with him, and you'll never see him around here again."

He kept his voice soft and gentle as he spoke to the horse. His memory of Smith made him sick. The filthy mongrel had been drunk and reeling when Grant had located him at a seedy tavern on the west side of town. He'd taken Smith out back and thrown him up against the wall, reminding the creep of his threat to harm Beth. Smith had proved himself to be nothing more than a pathetic bully—he had started to cry. Big, blubbering sobs. Grant had gathered him off the ground and instructed him to seek help from a local clinic or church, but whatever he did, if Grant ever heard of him owning another animal or threatening Beth, he would make the rest of Smith's miserable life intolerable.

He let his breath out slowly and combed his fingers through the mare's mane. "Pretty soon you'll be able to go out into the corral, and I'll introduce you to Studmuffin. The talk around here is he's a real hunk."

He chuckled and was rubbing her nose when he sensed someone behind him. Before he could react, an explosion went off in his head, and the world turned black.

Beth looked out her bedroom window and saw smoke rising from the direction of the New Start barns. Grant! She had to get to him. Rushing out of the house, she dashed to her truck. She floored the gas pedal, but it seemed to her that she had driven a hundred miles before she careened into the driveway in front of the barn. "Oh my God," she breathed as she hurdled out of the truck and took off running toward the barn. She frantically pulled on the door.

It wouldn't budge—*it was locked from the inside.*

Calling out his name frantically, she became even more worried when she got no answer but the faint popping and wheezing of flames.

Wasting no time, she ran to the corral that bounded the back of the barn and scrambled over the fence, but the back door was bolted from the inside, too.

She could hear the horses inside whining and stamping and bile rose in her throat.

"Grant! Grant! Where are you?" She stood still for a minute, listening, but no reply came. She pounded on the door and then, standing back, tried to kick it in. Her pathetic attempts didn't inflict any damage on the door. "Grant, what's happened to you? Dear God, please be all right," she whispered as she hurried around to the west side of the building.

There was a double hay door high above her head. The doors were open and a rope and pulley dangled from the end of an iron rod. The device was normally used to hoist the hay into the loft.

She looked around wildly, searching for a ladder or something to get her up to the open door. She knew she didn't have the strength in her arms to shinny up the rope.

Running back to her truck, she ground the engine to life and backed it to the side of the barn. At the same time, she dialed Delores on her phone, the only number she could think of in her agitated state.

"Delores? This is Beth. Send fire trucks to the barn area." She slammed the phone down and clambered out of the truck. Hopping into the bed of the pickup, she climbed onto the roof of the cab and was able to pull herself over the frame of the hay door and roll into the loft.

Smoke, black and acrid, made her eyes sting, and she coughed. Quickly she found the ladder and scurried down. She could see yellow-and-red flames leaping near the end stall. She crouched, knowing from her first-aid training the lower you were to the ground in a fire, the easier it was to breathe.

Going from stall to stall she opened the doors. Only a few had horses in them, and they were nervous and jittery. One of the horses they'd acquired at Dewey Smith's was already out of her stall and prancing about.

Beth ran to the back door, hefted the bolt from the latch and swung the door wide. The horses bolted past her into the corral.

Grant! Where was he?

Frantic now, because she knew Grant would never have left the animals in the barn unless he was hurt, she went in search of him. The fire was licking at the walls and climbing to the roof. The hay in the stalls was catching, sending sparks and pops all around her as she dashed down the middle of the barn. Her eyes were streaming with tears from the heavy smoke, obscuring her vision. *Where was he?*

Suddenly she was sprawled on the ground. She rose to her knees quickly and felt for what had made her trip. Jean-clad legs stopped her questing fingers. It was Grant.

"Grant," she called softly to him as she bent over his prostrate body.

He groaned and stirred.

She wanted to get up and shout for joy, but knew she had only precious seconds to get him out of the spreading inferno.

"Wake up, Grant. You've got to help me get you out of here." She coughed. "You're too heavy for me to lift."

He moaned again and coughed, before turning over. She struggled to push and pull him to a sitting position. He stumbled as he stood. Staggering and leaning heavily on her, he slowly made his way out of the barn.

Just as they cleared the door, the loft above the stall collapsed and the entire place blazed. Beth was seared by the heat, but she kept moving, half dragging, half pulling Grant as far away from the barn as possible. She looked around in the corral and saw that the horses had bolted for the far side and stood huddled together, their eyes wide with terror. She smiled grimly when she noticed Studmuffin standing proudly in front, as if protecting his herd. Thank God, they appeared to be okay.

When she had Grant close to a water trough, she stopped. Ashes from the fire were flying all around, but her only thought was, *if worse comes to worse, I can throw us both in the water.* Better to drown, than burn. She giggled hysterically and for a second considered that she might not be entirely rational at the moment, but then dismissed the idea. A spasm of coughing convulsed her body for several minutes before she could get it under control.

She sat Grant down so that he leaned against the trough. He was in a semiconscious state. She pulled hard and managed to rip a piece of material out of the bottom of her T-shirt. After dipping it into the water, she sat down and cradled his head in her lap.

As she cleaned away the soot, his head lolled in her arms, and he groaned in pain. Gently she ran her hand through his hair and felt a lump. She investigated still further and came away with a bloody hand.

"Oh my God." She took the wet cloth and tenderly cleansed his head. Someone had hit him and left him to die in the fire. Beth bit her bottom lip until she tasted blood. He had almost been killed.

She was leaning over him, patting his face, crying when she heard the sirens. She looked up to see the volunteer fire trucks followed by a parade of local trucks and cars rolling into the drive. The men leapt off the truck, shouted instructions at each other and went to work spraying foam on the burning building. They were unaware of Beth.

Delores spotted her first and yelled for Shorty, then she came running, going down on her knees by Beth and Grant. "Beth, are you okay?"

Beth looked up and nodded, dazed. "Grant's hurt."

"I'll get a doctor. You stay right there," Delores instructed needlessly.

Delores sprinted around fire trucks, men and equipment to a blue station wagon. "Doc, Grant's been hurt. He's behind the barn with Beth."

"Let me get my bag." He grabbed the black case and followed Delores to where Beth, Grant and now Shorty were.

Shorty was telling Beth, "They rolled your truck away from the fire. It's going to need a new paint job, but other than that, it came through the fire pretty well."

"Dr. Jergins." Beth zeroed in on help for Grant, not caring about her truck.

"Beth, let me examine him." The older man moved Shorty aside.

She held Grant's head in her hands and looked at the doctor blankly.

"Beth, I've got to be able to examine him. Let me move him so I can see him."

"No!"

Shorty and Delores exchanged glances before they both gently pulled Beth away from Grant. Delores held her as the doctor worked on Grant. Grant's breathing was shallow and his coloring gray. The doctor prodded the lump on his head, lifted his eyelids and felt for a pulse.

Shaking his head, he said, "He took a nasty hit on the head. He's probably inhaled a lot of smoke, too. I need to check him further because I think he's got a concussion and maybe lung damage."

Beth sucked in her breath sharply.

"What can you do?" she whispered. "He's going to be all right, isn't he?"

"We need to get him away from here. I'd like to take some X rays to see about the head and run a few tests on his chest. But he's a strong young man. He'll probably be just fine." He looked up to search the caravan that had found its way to the fire. "The EMS is here. They'll take him to the county hospital. I'll meet you there." He folded up his equipment. "Shorty, tell them to bring the stretcher over here.

"And young lady—" the doctor turned back to Beth "—I think I'll check you out at the hospital, too. Never know about smoke damage to lungs."

Beth, still in shock, watched dazedly as they lifted Grant's body onto the stretcher. As they strapped him in, he moaned. She flew to his side and took his hand.

She walked beside him, hoping for another sign that he was conscious, but none came. As she sat in the ambulance, staring at his face, his eyes, watching for a sign, she made a vow. She would protect Grant. He was in this mess because of her and New Start. No one would hurt him again. Even if it meant giving up everything, she would make sure he was never hurt again.

Chapter 12

Beth sat in the plastic hospital chair at the side of Grant's bed. She hungrily watched his easy breathing, looking for any signs of distress.

Minutes dragged by. Her mind wandered to the doctor's words after he'd examined Grant. "He's a lucky man. Only a few minutes more and he wouldn't have made it." He had given Grant oxygen to help clear his lungs, taken X rays and done a CAT scan. All had been negative. "You're a brave lady for pulling him out."

The doctor's prognosis echoed in her ears: *Grant would be all right.* Mullins, the deputy keeping watch, had been knocked out also, but he was okay now. The horses had survived the inferno, as well.

After the doctor had given her a brief physical, she'd insisted on staying with Grant.

She could have kicked herself! Guilt licked at her conscience. If she hadn't convinced him to stay at New Start to fulfill the terms of that damn will, he'd be safe and out of harm's way.

Beth reached for his hand, turned it over and gently kissed the callused palm. She scanned his face, noticing for the tenth time how gray his skin looked. Her eyes misted.

"Delores, I don't think this is a good idea."

"She's been here for eight hours." Delores pushed the door open, shaking off Shorty's arm. "Beth, it's time you got out of this room for a few minutes. I've brought Shorty to sit with Grant. You and me are going to get something to eat."

"I'm not hungry."

"I don't care." Delores tugged on her arm, succeeding in pulling her out of the chair. "I am."

Shorty moved from behind Delores and sat in the chair. He crossed his arms across his chest. "Beth, Delores is right. You need to get out of here for a while. I'll stay and look after Grant."

"I want to be here when he wakes up."

Delores rolled her eyes. "We're not going to be long. If he starts to wake up, Sugar will come and get us." She turned to Shorty. "Right?"

Shorty smiled. "Yes. I promise."

Beth took one last look at Grant and then allowed Delores to pull her out of the room. But before they had gone even ten steps, she had spun around and hurried back into the room. Delores stormed in behind her.

"Girl, this man is not going to wake up for hours." She stood with her hands on her hips. "Tell her, Shorty. Tell her what the doctor said."

Beth looked at Shorty expectantly. He shifted uncomfortably in the chair. "We spoke to the doctor before we came in here. He told us Grant would probably sleep straight through the night." He looked apologetic. "We wanted you to get some rest."

"Did the doctor say anything else?" She watched Shorty and Delores exchange a sideways glance. "Well, did he?"

"No, honey, he didn't," Delores hastened to assure her. "He just said you needed your rest, too. He did say Grant would have to take it easy when he woke up, though."

Beth, standing at the foot of the bed, looked again at Grant. She prayed he'd open his eyes and recognize her. He didn't, of course, and she squeezed her eyes tightly shut. The whole situation was a nightmare. She turned to Delores, wiping the tears out of her eyes.

"It's my fault he's in here, isn't it?"

Delores looked shocked. "No, of course not. You didn't set fire to the barn. We've all been wondering how the fire started, though, and how Grant got that bump on his head. And what was that other marshal doing there?"

Beth looked at Delores, then at Shorty, remembering Grant's warning not to involve anyone else in this. Two people had already been hurt. She couldn't put her friends in danger, but she needed help.

She'd kept her explanation simple. That way, it would be better for all concerned. "This entire mess has to do with a case Grant is working on. There are people who don't want him to testify at a trial in two weeks."

"What about that other policeman who was injured at your house?" Delores watched Beth, her eyes sharp.

"The Marshal Service sent him to help Grant."

Beth's body was so tightly coiled, she thought she'd break if Delores asked her another question. Delores's next words, however, attested to the fact that she had picked up on Beth's body language.

"Well, everybody's gonna live, so put a smile on your face, girl." She looked over at Shorty. "I've got an idea.

When Grant is healthy again, why don't you and him go on a vacation? Man deserves a vacation after bumping his head and almost being burned to death."

Beth stared at Delores, considering what she'd said. This was the perfect alibi for going to the safe house. Let Delores and Shorty think they were on a vacation in Houston.

"That might be a good idea," she said slowly. "As soon as he gets out of the hospital we could go to Houston and see a basketball game, attend a ballet. He'd promised . . ."

Delores turned concerned eyes on Beth. "Are you sure he'll be up to all that?"

"I'll make sure he doesn't overdo it." She shifted under Delores's gaze. "But I think it would be good for us to get away."

Delores nodded. "I always liked looking at those guys in tights." She winked at Shorty. "You'd look great in a pair of hot pink tights."

Shorty stood up abruptly, not liking where the conversation was headed. "I agree with Delores. You need to get away. We'll take care of New Start. You just take Grant and have a good time."

Beth gave them both a tired smile. "Okay." She looked at the man in the bed. "I hope Grant agrees when he wakes up."

"Don't give him a chance to argue. Just get him in the car and take off," Delores advised. "That's how I got Shorty to take me to Las Vegas. I just piled him into the car and the next thing he knew, we were listening to Wayne Newton and feeding one-armed bandits."

Shorty shook his head and took her by the arm. "Let's reminisce another time." He walked to the door, Delores in tow. Over his shoulder, he directed his parting comment to Beth. "If we can't persuade you to go, we'll be back tomorrow morning."

* * *

Grant woke to hard, blinding pain. His head felt as if a jackhammer were pounding on the inside, searching for a way out. Slitting his eyes to let only a glimmer of light through, he tried to determine his location. He saw nothing but white—a light, a ceiling, a wall.

A hospital. He was in a hospital. That, at least, meant he wasn't dead. He'd somehow made it out of the barn. He tried turning his head a fraction of an inch and the jack-hammer tripped into overdrive. He stayed still, trying to remember exactly what had happened.

His brain didn't want to cooperate. It was having trouble maneuvering past the agonizing throbbing. Forcing himself to concentrate on the barn, his memory slowly came back.

He'd gone into the barn and been talking to the mare in the last stall when someone had clobbered him. But what had happened after the blackout? Regardless of how he tried, he couldn't get a clear image.

What he did get was the vivid memory of an acrid smell, pain with every breath and a slow suffocating feeling. It was hazy, but just at the moment his world exploded, he could hear an ugly, sinister laugh.

Digging deeper into his subconscious, he remembered being pulled onto his feet, and then stumbling into fresh air, helped by someone. Who? Then he felt the soft, clean touch of water on his face and the sound of murmuring, crying. *Beth*. It had been Beth who had saved him from sure death.

He took a deep breath and again tried to open his eyes, this time letting in more light and at the same time turning his head. As soon as his eyes opened, he saw her. Sitting on a chair, leaning against the bed, she had cushioned her head on her arms. He tried to reach for her, and with just that small movement, she jerked awake and searched his face.

"Grant?" She looked into his smoky blue eyes as if searching for something. "How do you feel?"

"Like the devil's doing a tap dance in my brain."

"Do you want me to get the nurse?" She made a move to push the call button by his bed. He grabbed her hand, then groaned.

"Oh, Grant, don't move. You're not supposed to move."

"Too late." He closed his eyes again. "Are you the one who pulled me to safety?" He squinted at her.

"You'd been hit on the head and were barely conscious." She brushed his hand with hers and he clasped them. "I just yanked you up and out and then the ambulance came."

"You saved my life." He tried sitting up but couldn't, falling back. "Thank you."

She was gulping back tears. "It's my fault you were there in the first place."

"Beth, you had nothing to do with it." He gave her a weak facsimile of a smile, and then tried again to sit up, but again he failed. "Damn, I'm as weak as a newborn foal."

"Don't do that. Stop moving. You're scaring me." Beth's voice rose an octave. "The doctor wants you to stay still."

"Look, I've got to get out of here. I've got to call my boss and tell him what happened. I don't want to use the hospital phone." Grant gritted his teeth and forced himself to sit up. Sweat broke out on his brow, but he managed to hoist himself into a sitting position.

She grabbed the bed controls and cranked the bed into a sitting position. "If you have to sit up, do it this way."

"What have you told Joe Clay?" He drew deep, long breaths.

"He already knew you were working on a dangerous case since you'd told him some of the details last night. I didn't add much to the story. I said you'd fill him in when you were able.''

"Good girl. Now is not the time for information to leak. I'm not sure who's trustworthy around here.'' He closed his eyes a minute, but opened them quickly and focused on her. "What about Mullins?''

"He'll be okay. He's got a pretty nasty bump on the head, though.'' A shudder ran over her body.

"Thank God he's going to be okay.'' He looked down at his hospital gown. "Where are my clothes?''

"You can't leave.'' Beth looked toward the door. "You still need to rest.''

"Beth.'' Grant swung his legs over the side of the bed. Red-hot pain made him suck in his breath, and he waited until he could speak without gasping. "Clothes or not, I'm getting out of here. The guy who tried to kill me is not going to give up. I'm totally vulnerable in this bed.''

"But, he's not just going to walk in here, in the Douglas County Hospital for Pete's sake, and…and hurt you.'' She swallowed past the lump in her throat.

Grant shook his head. "He can do anything he wants.'' He looked over at the clock on the nightstand. "What day is it?''

"Monday.''

"I've got to check in today or all hell will break loose.''

"Why?''

"You haven't forgotten everything I told you yesterday, have you?''

"No.''

"Good. I'm supposed to check in today and give our location. If I don't do that, my boss is going to assume I'm in trouble and bring out the cavalry. We don't need that right now.''

"Oh.''

"So, you've got to get me out of here."

"You can use the phone in here. I'll go out in the hall and give you some privacy." She tried to stand.

Grant grabbed her hand. "No. I don't trust what goes on in a hospital. There are any number of ways this creep could intercept my call. We've got to get out of here first. Now, where are my clothes?"

Beth looked at him and then at the closet. "Over there, in the closet."

"Get them for me, please. This outfit is definitely not the real me." His attempt at humor was wasted on Beth, but he smiled wanly at the hospital gown.

"I don't know." She looked uncertain.

"Come on, Beth. The guy could be here to finish the job any second."

That did it. Beth scurried over to the closet and brought back his clothes.

Showing not the slightest embarrassment about his nakedness, Grant slid the hospital gown off and began putting on his clothes. Several times he wobbled, becoming light-headed with the exertion of pulling on the garments. The first time it happened, Beth grabbed his arms to steady him. He pushed her hands away with a curse.

"I can handle it. Don't baby me."

"I'm trying to keep you from falling on your face, Grant Stephens. If you weren't so eager to keep your pride intact, you'd have figured that out," she said, fuming.

He pinned her with an icy stare. *"I am okay. Leave me alone."*

Her stoic pose belied the tears that misted her eyes.

After studying her for a few seconds, he reconsidered. "All right. Get my shoes and help me get *them* on."

That job accomplished, Grant eased himself to the floor and let the room stop spinning before he tried to take a step.

Once he'd discovered he could walk while leaning on Beth, he searched in the closet for the rest of his things. He found his wallet, but not what he really needed—his gun.

"Did you see my gun when you helped me from the barn?"

"No." She hadn't had time to think about it then, but now she thought back to when she'd found him sprawled on the barn floor. "I'm pretty sure it wasn't there. *He* must have taken it."

"It'll be a nice souvenir for him to have a federal marshal's .357 Magnum. I'll have to go by the house and get my backup then." Grant sounded disgusted. "Come on. I want to get out of here."

Beth helped him walk down the hall, past the nurses' station. Only two nurses were there and they had their backs to the hall, discussing a patient's chart. She was amazed when no one stopped them. She looked at Grant, and noticed he was trying to keep his gaze focused on the wall at the end of the hall. "Can you make it?"

"I have to make it," he muttered. "Just get me out of here."

"Your truck's here. Delores brought it for you, just in case. The brakes are all fixed."

They made it to the garage and located the pickup.

"Of course he knows this truck." As Grant considered the situation, he wiped away a thin beading of perspiration that dotted his upper lip.

"We've got to have transportation." She looked around. "Do you want to go by Jake's and rent another one."

"Too risky. Too many people involved." Grant leaned against the truck. "We'll take this—for now."

"Get in. I'll drive." Beth tried to help Grant into the passenger's side.

"No, I'll drive." He shifted himself over to the driver's seat. "Get in."

Beth muttered something about pigheaded men, but climbed into the truck.

"Come on," Grant instructed a he stopped the truck behind the ranch house.

"I'll go in first and check out the house. Keep the door locked until I signal you."

Before Beth could protest, he had levered himself out of the truck and was inside the house. In minutes he was back.

"Change your clothes." He nodded toward her torn T-shirt. "Pack a small bag with a change of clothes and whatever else you need. Bring a sweater or a light jacket, too."

She was amazed at Grant's determination as he trudged up the stairs and staggered into his bedroom. She hurried to her room and took a quick shower before dressing in blue jeans and a blouse. She packed a small suitcase and was ready. She went back to Grant's room.

He was sitting on his bed, bag and rifle case by his side. She flinched at the sight of the rifle but didn't say anything.

"What kept you?" he growled.

She leaned down and put her arm around Grant's back, helping him up off the bed.

"I took a shower. Sorry, but I couldn't stand myself. I've been in the same outfit since the accident."

He took a deep breath. "You smell great." He hugged her to him. "And you know it wasn't an accident."

"I know. I just don't know what else to call it."

When they got to the truck, Beth guided Grant to the passenger side.

"What do you think you're doing?" He pulled away from her and stood up straight, wincing but voicing no complaint.

"I'm driving this time." She opened the door and threw their bags and his rifle case in the backseat. "Get in."

They stared at each other, eyes clashing, until finally Grant blinked. Without a word, he settled into the seat, laid his head against the headrest and closed his eyes.

Beth smothered a smile and got in the driver's seat.

"Get on Highway 37." He never opened his eyes as he spoke. "Drive the speed limit, not too slow, not too fast. In thirty minutes, wake me up." His eyes opened then, and he grabbed her wrist. "You'll wake me in thirty minutes, right?"

"Yes, of course," she reassured him. "Where are we going?"

"Houston."

"We are?" Beth's surprised voice made him look over at her.

"Yeah. Kevin Timmons is meeting us at the safe house. Why?"

"Oh, I told Shorty and Delores we were going there to see a ballet. I wanted to keep them from knowing where we really were."

"When did you talk to Delores and Shorty?"

"At the hospital. They're going to take care of New Start."

Grant made no comment and Beth searched his pale visage for a moment. She ran her hand lightly across his forehead, smoothing the jet hair that had tumbled there. He was already asleep.

"Grant. Wake up, Grant."

His eyes opened to glaring sunlight, and he groaned. Where was he?

"Grant, are you all right? Is your headache better?"

Beth's silky voice brought him to reality. They were speeding down a highway on their way to Houston and a safe house. He took inventory of his body. The pain in his head was dull now. He shifted positions. He was sore here and there, but he'd make it.

"I'm just dandy," he informed Beth with sarcasm dripping in his voice. "Where are we?"

"Thirty minutes down Highway 37, just like you instructed me, boss." She smiled at him and was rewarded with a grin. She marveled at how the small amount of sleep had apparently rejuvenated him. The pain lines around his mouth were faint now.

"When we get to the next town, pull off the highway. I need to call in. Also, I've got to call Timmons in Houston and have him get us another vehicle."

Beth shook her head as she exited the expressway. "I can't believe any of this. Do you get a high on this kind of excitement?"

"Hardly." He chuckled mirthlessly. "I suppose when I was younger this kind of thing kept my adrenaline pumped, and I even thought it was glamorous in a way. Pull into this convenience store." He interrupted himself. "But I must be getting old. This is not how I would choose to spend my time anymore."

Beth doubted his words as she watched him get out of the truck and go to the public telephone located on the side of the building. He *did* seem to thrive on this cloak-and-dagger routine. She couldn't imagine him stuck in the everyday rituals of New Start. That thought made her swallow the sadness that engulfed her. He dropped several coins in the slot and dialed a number. The conversation lasted less than five minutes. When he returned, his eyes were icy.

"What's the matter?"

"Well, they're going to take care of getting us another car. We'll soon make a switch so this one can be returned to New Start."

"And . . . ?"

"There're problems with the office red tape. Culpepper wants me to call again at twenty-two hundred hours."

Beth swiveled her head to face him.

He smiled grimly. "Ten o'clock tonight. We'll get our instructions for the safe house then."

"From Culpepper?"

"Him or Timmons."

"What do we do now?" She glanced around at the small-town activities.

"Now we get a bite to eat and check into a local motel."

Again Beth's eyes searched his.

He explained, "We need to stay out of sight for a while, and I could use a little more sleep to lick this headache."

It was a simple procedure to find a hamburger place and satisfy their hunger pangs. It took a little more doing to find the motel Culpepper had suggested. It was an older, twelve-cabin motel that featured a kitchenette in each cabin. Because of its age, it was located on the old highway. It was quiet and clean and cheap.

"Thanks," Grant told the manager as she handed him the key.

"Do you want to pay for more than one night?" she asked.

"We're on our honeymoon, ma'am," he told her and smiled at Beth. "We may just jump in the car tomorrow and take off for somewhere else. We'll let you know."

"That's lovely. Enjoy yourselves." She clucked and closed the door as she let herself out of the cabin.

Grant watched her through a window and when she had gone in the motel's office, he went back out to the truck and brought in his rifle. Then he locked the cabin door, angled a chair under the knob and turned back to Beth.

"I'm going to shower and sleep for a while. Will you be okay?"

Beth, amazed at his resiliency, nodded. "Go right ahead. I packed a book to read."

He went into the bathroom, and she could hear the water running and him splashing. She couldn't concentrate on her book, however. The terrifying events of the past few days held her in an unrelenting grip. Grant came out of the shower with only a towel wrapped around his waist. He sank down on the bed and was asleep in seconds.

Laying down her book, Beth went to the side of the bed and watched him sleep. Love and tenderness flowed through her. What would her world be like if she lost Grant again? The question tormented her.

But did she have the right to tie him down? Could he be happy with the mundane?—for that was what her life was—mundane.

Carefully she eased herself down beside him. Settling her
head on his shoulder and wrapping her arms around him,
she drew warmth and comfort from his body. She slept, too.

The world was a delicious place. It was summery; it was
thrilling; it was arousing. Not knowing if she still slept and
was having a dream or if this was reality, Beth's universe
centered on textures and smells and sounds.

Grant was rasping the zipper of her jeans down and tug-
ging them off her legs. She shifted and lifted her body to
help him as her clothing suddenly seemed a burden. She
wanted to feel her naked skin next to his. Her blouse was
next and then her bra. The bit of lace and satin around her
hips disappeared last and her body was free.

His body covered hers and when she felt the surging heat
of his manhood, she knew she wasn't dreaming. This was
real, Grant was real.

He rose up and drew his chest in tantalizing circles across
hers. The thick, dark hair on his torso teased and tickled her
breasts and made the nipples peak tightly. Her own fingertips found his nipples and when they beaded under her caresses, she heard him whisper her name.

He kissed her then. Lightly, lingeringly. His lips sipped at
the wine her mouth offered.

She melted into him. Her whole being became one with
his through the joining of their lips. His tongue delved into
her sweetness, and she felt the tension only Grant's body
could relieve building between her thighs.

Ending that kiss, he rained kisses everywhere, sending her
whirling into spasms of ecstasy.

He toyed with the fullness of one breast and studied it in
the pearly light. "Your breasts are perfect. After our di-

vorce, I used to wake up sweating, longing to feel their smoothness one more time." He captured first one tip with his warm mouth, sucking and nipping at it, then transferred his attention to the other, drawing it deeper into his mouth until Beth thought she would surely go insane with desire. She ground her hips into the mattress begging for him to end this erotic torture.

Her hands glided across his back, reveling in the dramatic play of muscles. Then she purposely moved them lower, caressing him. His buttocks were as firm and warm as the rest of his body.

Her body was a piece of art, and he was awed by its beauty and her reactions to his loving. He shifted and moved between her legs. Kissing her, he groaned as she arched and cried out his name. Again and again he kissed the delicate nub that throbbed like a heartbeat against his mouth, his tongue.

Finally he covered her once again, and they flowed together like wine—heady, tart, mysterious. Rocking together, their destinies mingled as surely as their bodies. They balanced on the edge of the precipice for precious seconds, intoxicated in the swirl of sensations, emotions. With a final thrust, Beth was hurtled to fulfillment. Grant luxuriated in her pleasure, kissed her throat, her ear. Then he, too, plunged over the edge.

Hours later they awakened. Grant was still buried in Beth's warmth. As they stirred, he grew hard inside her.

Both came fully awake, staring in each other's eyes, awed by the responses of their bodies.

"I can't get enough of you," he whispered.

She wrapped herself around him. "Thank goodness." She smiled and held on tight as they loved each other again.

"Your headache seems to be much better," Beth observed as they dressed.

"Yeah, I know a miracle cure." He grinned at her. "It may not get rid of your headache, but you'll die happy."

She threw a pillow at him, but he ducked out of the way.

Suddenly serious, Beth asked, "What will happen after this mess with the counterfeiter and the killer is cleared up?" She watched him closely as he finished buckling his belt.

He came to her and pulled her hard against him. "We'll work it out when this is over. And I swear that we will, but for now I have to focus on getting you to a safe place." He kissed her quickly. "Let's have a nice supper and then I'll call in and find out the exact location of the safe house."

After a pleasant dinner in a small Mom and Pop family-style restaurant, Grant drove to a gas station and made his call to his office from there.

When he got back in the truck, his face was a mask of nonchalance. It didn't fool Beth.

"Okay, out with it. What is it this time?"

He was backing the truck, but at her words braked and looked her directly in the eyes. "We're in more trouble than I thought. We can't go to Houston. We're on our own for right now."

Chapter 13

"What exactly does 'on our own' mean?" Beth asked.

Grant eased the truck into traffic before he answered. "The safe house's been violated."

"How could anyone have found out the location of the safe house?" Beth asked.

"I don't know for sure." Grant's eyes scanned the rearview mirror constantly as he drove. "The people who want me killed are very powerful. Money can open a lot of doors and leak a lot of information."

"Where are we going?"

"We're picking up a new vehicle."

"How? Where?"

Grant glanced at Beth. Her voice was becoming strident, revealing her stress. "One of my men dropped off a car—they were just waiting to tell me."

"It's all more than I can take in," Beth commented as she blinked her eyes in the bright sunlight. "How will we know which car is the one we're supposed to get?"

"I'll know." Grant downshifted at a light. "The service gets very ordinary cars and then puts powerful engines in them so they'll be able to chase anything on wheels and win."

"Oh. And I suppose just like the shoe elves, an agent drove this car down from Houston and left it for us?"

"Something like that."

Beth glanced out the window as they traveled. Soon they pulled into the parking lot of a small, country grocery store. There was only one car there.

"Is that it?" She studied the station wagon sitting next to them.

"Let's see. Culpepper said he couldn't get much on such short notice." Grant got out and opened the driver's door of the station wagon. He nodded. "Yeah, this is it."

Beth got out of the truck and went around to the passenger side of the vehicle.

Grant held up a hand. "Wait. We've got to pick up some groceries. Let's do that while we're here so we won't have to leave again today. The less we're out of that room, the less risk there is." He reached into the car, pulled out the keys and locked it. "Come on."

Beth went with Grant into the small grocery store to stock up on the essentials: instant coffee, doughnuts, milk, cereal, sandwich fixings and candy. She wondered how much she should buy. Grant hadn't told her how long they were supposed to stay in this out-of-the-way place, but he'd lectured her on never walking out of the room without him, and never picking up or talking on the phone. She was glad Delores and Shorty thought they were in Houston spending an idyllic holiday. She didn't want them to worry if she didn't report in for a few days.

They passed the aisle that contained dog and cat food. She wondered for an instant how the animals on New Start

were doing. Had all the horses survived the fire? She'd
called the vet from Grant's hospital bedside and told him to
check them out. He'd reported later in the day that they were
in good shape.

Had it only been two days since the fire? It felt as if a
century had gone by—a century of watching Grant lying on
the ground, barely breathing, seeing him recoil in pain, seeing him load his gun.

"Do you want anything else?" he asked as he took her
arm and headed for the cash register. "We're not coming
here every day, so get what you need."

"Let me get some toothpaste and soap and deodorant
then." She walked to the appropriate aisle and picked up the
items. "Let's go."

Beth put her stuff on the counter and noticed for the first
time the box Grant had placed there alongside the items. She
blushed when she saw what it was. "I should've been using
them all along." His voice was low, for her ears only. "I
don't suppose you've been using anything?"

She shook her head.

"Sorry."

She was unable to respond. Since there hadn't been any
men since Grant, she'd completely forgotten about birth
control. What if there already was a baby? She used to
dream about the beautiful children Grant and she would
have. They had been careful during their marriage since they
wanted to get through college and begin their careers before starting a family. But they'd had dreams of a perfect
family.

"You folks need anything else? We've got a special on
sixteen-ounce sodas. Buy two and get the third one free."
The clerk pointed to a display behind them. Grant turned
around and picked up three bottles.

"Thanks. That's it." He paid with cash, took the sacks in his arms and followed Beth out to the car.

"What will happen to the truck?" Beth asked as they left the lot and got underway.

"It'll get back to New Start. Don't worry."

"All very neat, huh?" He made it seem as if they were just going for a nice drive instead of ditching one vehicle and picking another up that had been supplied by the Marshal Service. "This doesn't scare you at all, does it?"

Grant took his eyes off the road a second to glance at her. "What?"

"This whole running game. The car and . . . everything." Beth motioned outward, to the world beyond the windshield of the car. "You act like you do this all the time."

"Beth, this is a part of my job." He turned onto the old highway where their motel was located. "Let's talk when we get inside."

He drove the car into the closest parking space to their rooms, grabbed the groceries and directed Beth toward their cabin. After unlocking the door, he swung it open so that it banged against the door stop on the inside. "Stay in the doorway while I check things out."

"Grant, this is so silly." Beth started across the threshold but a solid arm across her middle stopped her.

"I said stay here." His tone brooked no refusal, so she stayed where she was. He set the grocery bags down on the small table in the kitchenette, then checked under the bed, under the sink, in the closet, behind the shower curtain and under the small vanity in the bathroom. At last he turned to her. "It's okay. At least there's no air-conditioner duct he can hide in. Culpepper chose this old motel with that in mind, I guess." He motioned to the air-conditioning unit mounted in the window. "Also the window in the bathroom is much too small for anyone to squeeze through." He grinned. "Help me put the groceries away."

She did what he asked, watching as he stacked the paper plates in the one cupboard. He looked at her and his grin widened. "It's not nice to stare."

"How can you just calmly put groceries away when someone is trying to kill you?"

His eyes suddenly looked wary and tired, but his tone remained patient. "Because over the years I've learned that doing the mundane, the ordinary, at times of crisis calms me. Now come here. It's time we got a few things straight."

She walked close to him and he rested his hands on her shoulders. "I'm scared. I'd be stupid not to be. This is a dangerous situation, but it's under control."

"How do you know that?" Her clear eyes searched his for reassurances.

"Because we're still breathing, and my people know where we are." He smiled and placed his hand against her cheek. "You've got to trust me. If I have to, I'm going to protect you with my life."

She gasped. "I don't want you to do that. I'm not worried about me. They don't want *me. I* don't even know who *they* are. One of them could come right up to me and slap me and I wouldn't know who he was. How can I be on the lookout for them?"

Grant let her tirade die down. He gently stroked her lips with a finger and she grew quiet. He knew she was tight, like a clock that had been overwound and was ready to break. She'd been too calm through all of this. "I don't know what they look like, either. That's the point. We've got to stay hidden until we get to a safe house. Culpepper and his people are working on it right now so it won't be long."

"How much longer?"

"A couple of days. I promise." He glanced at his watch. "Why don't I make us some coffee? Then we'll climb back into bed and have doughnuts and coffee there."

"Grant, don't treat me like a child."

"I'm not going to treat you like a child, I promise. In fact far from it." He smiled wickedly and dropped his hands. "Fix us some instant coffee? I'm going to the bathroom." He walked toward the small room but turned back for a minute. "I get the chocolate-glazed doughnut."

She stuck out her tongue at him before he dashed for the bathroom and shut the door. Laughing, she drew water from the sink in a saucepan. Setting it on the hot plate, she checked the temperature and turned back to the table to put the doughnuts on a paper plate. Not having anything else to occupy her until Grant returned, she walked to the bed and sat down on the edge.

She glanced down at her hands, noticing how ragged they looked. She made a mental note to pretty herself up once they got out of this mess. Then a funny ripping sound penetrated her senses, startling her out of her thoughts. Before she could jump off the bed and turn to see what had caused it, a stocky arm snaked around her chest, pulling her up; a hand covered her mouth.

Grant opened the door to the bathroom and froze as he reached for the gun he had tucked in his belt. Beth's face was bleached white and her eyes were huge. At her throat was a six-inch blade and holding the knife was every cop's nightmare—Louie Rogers. For a moment Grant shut his eyes. Rogers. He had attended medical school a year before the administration had figured out that he was a brilliant psycho and booted him out.

"Don't do it, Stephens. Before you even got your hands around the gun, her blood would be flying around the room.'' To illustrate his point, he pressed the blade more deeply against Beth's throat. She whimpered.

That tiny sound made Grant's gut constrict painfully, and his muscles clenched. He stood stock-still, his eyes locked on the sight of her long, lovely neck so totally exposed. ''Let her go.''

''Can't do it, Stephens. I've got my orders. Someone wants both of you.'' He pushed Beth toward the bed. ''Take the gun off and put it on the floor.''

He watched as Grant complied. ''Now kick it over here and don't try anything stupid.'' Again Grant did what he was told. He had to think rationally, not let his feelings for Beth cloud his judgment. Right now all he could do was bide his time and wait for an opening. That knife was too deadly for him to do otherwise.

''How'd you do it? How'd you get in here?'' Grant looked in disbelief at the hole in the mattress.

''It was so simple.'' Rogers chuckled. ''While you were out, I jimmied the lock, replaced this hollowed-out mattress for the one that was here, and no one was the wiser.''

Neither Grant, nor Beth said anything. Beth's eyes begged Grant to do something. He gritted his teeth in frustration. He knew this madman thrived on fear.

He watched the stocky man with his shaggy brown hair and black aviator sunglasses. His eyes were shaded by the tinted glasses, but the furrow between his brows revealed his intention. Grant wanted him away from Beth, but to make a move now would doom her.

Rogers addressed both of them. ''Don't move and don't say a word. I'm not going to hurt you unless you make me. Do you understand?''

Beth just stared with stricken eyes. He shook her hard. ''Do you understand?''

She nodded.

Rogers looked over at Grant.

"You don't expect *me* to believe you, do you?" Low and deadly, Grant's voice was unruffled.

Rogers smirked. "No, but I do expect you to nod unless you want your lover's throat cut." He emphasized his point by drawing a pinprick of blood.

"Stop!" Grant growled, and lunged forward, but pulled up short when he saw Rogers press the knife farther. "All right, *all right, damn it,* I understand."

"Good." He pulled Beth up, and shifted her so that he could grab her hands and snap handcuffs on them. Then he attached two more pairs of handcuffs on her—one cuff on each wrist. He then tied a large bandanna around her mouth. She looked down at her cuffed hands and then at Grant. Her eyes told him she was contemplating doing something, anything to get free.

"Just do what he says." His eyes pleaded with her. "You'll be okay."

"That's right, Beth. You'll be okay if you listen to me." Rogers pushed her toward Grant. "Hold your hands out, Stephens."

Grant watched him, looking for a crack in his plan. But before he could react, he had been handcuffed to Beth. Rogers roamed one hand over him, looking for other weapons.

"Now we're going to leave your little lover's nest and go somewhere more private."

Rogers held up the vicious-looking knife in front of their eyes. "It's my weapon of choice." He smiled, and his teeth glistened in the sunlight pouring in from the slit in the curtains. He lay the knife across Beth's cheek, watching Grant the whole time. "And I enjoy using it, so don't tempt me."

Without waiting for them to speak, he grabbed their cuffed hands and pulled them to the door. He peered out, looking both ways before he moved, towing the two with him to a dark green car parked directly in front of their door. He threw them into the back seat, except there was no seat. Before they even realized what he was doing, he had chained them onto a bar that was fixed to the floor of the car. They could do nothing but sit or kneel on the floor. Grant looked at the windows, hoping someone would be able to peer in and rescue them, but the windows were tinted almost black.

Rogers got into the driver's seat and took off, throwing them off balance, slamming them into the back of the front seat. He glanced back and smiled at Beth.

Grant helped Beth maneuver herself so that she sat with her back to the seat. He sat facing her and braced himself with his legs, one on each side of her. If they jerked to a stop, he could keep himself from crushing her.

Rogers spoke to them. "I've never seen this side of you, Stephens. Such a gentleman."

Grant glared at him, his eyes full of cold fury. "Let me take the gag out of her mouth. She won't scream."

"No, although I don't care if she does scream." He took a corner too fast, causing them to slide toward the left. "I just like the way a woman looks with her mouth gagged. Gives me a rush, you know? That's why I gagged her and not you, too." He laughed, a lifeless, sick sound.

"I'll kill you for this, Rogers," Grant promised, his voice deadly soft.

"I don't think so. You'll be dead before you can touch me. And if you make me angry, I'll cut her up, *before* I kill you, and you don't want that."

They turned off the main road. The ride was bumpy, forcing Beth to concentrate on keeping herself upright and out of Grant's lap. She felt his legs tighten and brace her as they took the turns.

She stared into his eyes. They begged her to be calm and trust that he would get them out of this situation. His lips were a tight slash in his face and tiny worry lines crevassed around his eyes. She knew him well enough to know that he considered this killer to be extremely dangerous, and that their predicament could not be worse.

Just a few short hours ago, she'd found fulfillment beyond measure in Grant's arms. She'd begun to dream about a life they could share. She might even now be carrying his baby. Was it all to end in the hands of a lunatic?

"We're here," their abductor informed them. He got out of the car and then opened the back door. "Hope the ride wasn't too rough. I don't want you injured . . . yet."

Rogers smiled as he leaned in and unlocked them from the metal bar. He grabbed Beth, using her as leverage to force Grant from the car. "You're going to continue to be a good little girl, now aren't you?" He pushed her, sticking the knife against her spine for emphasis.

Grant pushed himself against Rogers, grinding out from between clenched teeth, "Don't touch her with that thing again."

"Your orders don't work around here, *Marshal* Stephens. Just walk."

Once inside, he shoved them over to a bed. A length of chain about a foot long was attached to the iron headboard. On the end of the chain was a large loop of metal with two handcuffs attached to it. Working quickly, Rogers snapped the free side of each handcuff to first Grant's and then Beth's handcuffs. He then positioned them so they lay facing each other, with their hands stretched above their heads.

"I'm going to do just as you suggested and take her gag off, even though she looks lovely with it on." Rogers leaned

over Beth and smiled. "You can even scream if you want.
It'll give me an excuse to get rough with you."

With that warning, he sliced in half the bandanna covering her mouth. She spit it out, looking at him with what she
hoped was defiance. She was terrified, but she wasn't going
to give him the satisfaction of knowing that.

Rogers frowned, straightened and walked away from the
bedside.

"Are you okay?" Grant whispered.

She nodded her head. Grant's back was to Rogers, but she
could see him as he wandered around the cabin. Transfixed, she couldn't make her eyes look away.

The cabin was made up of one room. There was a kitchen
in the corner with a small table. A fireplace almost covered
one wall, with a couch in front of it, making a cozy, romantic alcove. The bed was against another wall. Incon-
gruously, the place looked as if it were designed for lovers.

It was obvious they weren't there for a romantic hide-
away. Her eyes sliced back to the kitchen table. There were
guns and knives of every imaginable size—handguns, ri-
fles, shotguns, kitchen knives, hunting knives—and what
looked like a walkie-talkie was next to the guns. She was sure
Grant's Smith & Wesson .357 Magnum was among the
group of weaponry.

"Beth." Grant's voice, while low, compelled her to look
at him. "Where is he?"

"He's over by the kitchen table." She whispered, trying
to keep her voice steady. "It's full of weapons."

The statement was hardly out of Beth's mouth when
Rogers said, "I'm checking one of my guns, Stephens."

He cocked a gun and aimed it at the back of Grant's head.
Beth screamed.

"Don't, Beth." Grant's voice was still low but very dis-
tinct and filled with deadly intention.

Behind them, Rogers laughed in a high-pitched tone. "Don't worry. It's not time yet. And when it is, it won't be with a gun, anyway." He walked over to the bed and pulled a chair to the foot of it, angling it so both of his prisoners could see him. Rogers addressed Beth. "I've been after your man for some time. I've never been able to get him—until now." He chuckled. "And I'm even getting paid for it. Everyone has a weakness. If you wait long enough, listen long enough and follow up on every little clue, you discover it." He took off the aviator glasses and looked with a gray hollowness into her eyes. "I always like to make the end interesting. And knowing my victim's weakness makes it that way."

Beth knew she was in the middle of hell, even as she felt Grant's hands crushing hers. This man, Rogers, would use her to torture Grant. She didn't know how she knew, but the certainty was a cold knot in her stomach. Grant knew it, as well.

Rogers kept eyeing her, as if measuring her for something. Panic became a tangible thing. It crowded the oxygen in the room and threatened to suffocate her. She gasped, trying to gain control, taking in measured gulps of air.

Grant felt her shaking and knew she was headed for shock. "Beth. Beth, look at me," he coaxed her.

He closed his eyes momentarily when he saw the raw fear in hers. "We'll get out of this. I promise." He spoke loud enough for Rogers to hear.

"No, you won't." Rogers leaned over and grabbed the iron bedstead. "I'm enjoying this little scene, Stephens. It's really quite touching," he said, walking over to the side of the bed where Grant lay.

Grant clenched his jaw. "Look, Rogers, you haven't hurt either of us yet. If you take the cuffs off now, you'll only spend a little time in jail for threatening a federal officer. I promise I'll testify to no more than that. But you've got to make that decision now, because my people are looking for me even as we speak, and once they get here, I won't be able to help you."

"You can't bluff me, Stephens. Think about it. Don't you wonder how I found you, how I knew exactly when you'd be gone from that cheap motel room?" He laughed, malicious delight evident in the high-pitched tone. "I'm going to carve Beth's name on your back before I kill you." Rogers smiled, insanity shining in his eyes. "A fitting tribute to your lady love. Something you can carry to eternity with you."

"What do you want to know?" Beth spoke in desperation. "I'll tell you anything you want to know." She pulled, helpless against the chain that imprisoned her.

Grant's voice was soft, yet terse. "Don't. You're giving him exactly what he wants."

"But I'm scared," she whispered.

"I know. But trying to reason with him will only egg him on."

Rogers reached for Grant's shirt and slit it from bottom to top, wielding the knife with an easy grace. Beth, startled, screamed again.

"Yes, scream," Rogers crooned, leaning forward and studying her face. He made a small movement with his hand. Grant winced, unconsciously tightening his hold on Beth's hand, telegraphing his pain to her as Rogers drew first blood. "Let me get my scalpel. I can carve in a more delicate pattern with it."

He moved across the room to get the instrument.

"Look at me, Beth," Grant commanded, urgency in his tone. He had to make her understand before that psycho came back. "Ignore him. Don't give him the opportunity to feed off your fear." Fiercely he looked into her eyes demanding that she stay with him on this. "Pretend to faint the next time he cuts me."

Her eyes were huge and her face very pale, but she acknowledged his words with a minute movement of her head. She swallowed convulsively as Rogers shuffled back beside Grant. "Now, now I can produce a work of art," he said cheerfully as he held the scalpel up to the light. The reflection of the metal instrument glittered in her eyes. She watched, tormented, as he bent over Grant's back.

Her body trembling violently, Beth winced when she saw Grant's eyes glaze in pain, though he was grimly silent. Suddenly unable to take it any longer, she lunged at Rogers. "You bastard," she yelled.

Turning to her with a snarl, Rogers slapped her with the back of his hand. At that exact instant, Grant jerked around, scissor-kicking his legs. The scalpel flew out of Rogers' hand and across the room. Wasting no time, Grant caught Rogers' head between his thighs. With one mighty twist, Rogers' limp body fell to the floor.

Seconds ticked by in silence, with only the pair's heavy breathing filling the air. Finally Grant spoke, his voice hoarse. "Are you all right?"

"Yes. And you?" She scanned his body, but could detect no wounds from this angle. "God, Grant, did you kill him?"

"No, I just knocked him out for a few minutes. He'll be coming around soon, so we've got to work fast to get these cuffs unlocked." His voice was strained as he still held Rogers' head trapped between his legs. "I'm going to try to drag his body up on the bed and position him. You're going to have to stretch out and get the key."

Swearing silently, Grant concentrated, using every ounce of his lower body's strength to maneuver his and Rogers' body so that the other was sprawled on the middle of the bed.

"If we have any luck at all," he bit out, breathing heavily from the exertion, "the key will be in the pocket closest to your hand. See if you can find it."

Straining to reach Rogers, Beth searched the man's jeans' pocket and was rewarded when her hand touched metal. Hands trembling, she uncuffed Grant, watching dazedly as he took the restraints off her, then turned Rogers and cuffed him to the headboard. Rogers began to stir and flailed his arms, knocking the keys from Grant's fingers.

Suddenly the sound of a car door slamming outside echoed in the cabin.

"Quick, Beth, get one of the guns off the table."

She jumped up and was halfway across the room when the door banged open. A man crouched in the doorway with his gun, ready to fire.

"Culpepper," Grant greeted him, "am I glad to see you."

Chapter 14

Culpepper stepped inside the cabin, taking in the scene with one swift glance. "I can see I got here just in time."

"It was pretty tense for a few minutes, but it's over now." Grant twisted his body to see just how much damage Rogers' knife work had done. "You want to take charge of this guy now?" He cocked a thumb at Rogers, then picked up the scalpel from the wooden floor, straightening up.

Culpepper walked over to the bed, looked down at Rogers, then slowly pointed the barrel of his weapon at Grant's head. "Can't do it. Drop the knife."

"What the hell?" Grant's eyes narrowed and he grew still.

"I said drop the knife, or I'm going to blow your brains out right here." Culpepper's voice, nervous and clipped, reverberated through the cabin.

Grant, a black scowl coloring his face, stared at Culpepper. *Great.* Culpepper was the inside man, the bastard who'd sold out the entire team.

"Maybe you didn't hear me, Stephens. Drop the knife and give me the keys to the handcuffs." With a barely noticeable tremble, Culpepper placed both hands around the butt of the gun and spaced his legs apart, bracing for a confrontation.

Grant didn't move.

"The girl—shoot the girl." Rogers' insidious whisper filled the room.

Culpepper looked over at a white-faced Beth, leaning against the table. Assessing the situation, he backed away so that both Grant and Beth were in his line of vision. Ominously, the barrel of the gun shifted, making her his target.

Cursing inwardly, Grant dropped the knife and moved away from the bed. "Okay."

Culpepper smiled. "Good." He pointed to the handcuffs on Rogers. "Uncuff him."

"Can't do that." Grant spoke slowly, his mind clicking through every means of escape. When they'd come into the cabin he'd automatically taken in every detail of the entire room. There was another door beside the one Culpepper had just come through, near Beth, in the kitchen. If he could just get closer to Beth, he could divert Culpepper's gunfire toward himself while she escaped.

"Don't play with me, Stephens. I don't have the time." Culpepper's eyes narrowed. He took a step toward Beth. "Don't make me lose my temper." His voice rose and fell unevenly, betraying the fact that he was upset.

"I dropped the key when Rogers and I went at it. They got kicked across the room. You'll have to find them."

"He's telling you the truth." Rogers hissed, yanking at the bedstead and rattling the handcuffs. "Just shoot them off. It'll save time."

Culpepper didn't move, but Grant didn't trust the situation. The way criminal minds worked, Culpepper might well decide to kill Rogers, too.

Edging closer to the table with the guns, he started talking, hoping to distract Culpepper and buy precious seconds. "What are you doing with this scum?" he asked with contempt, inclining his head toward Rogers.

"Getting rich."

"So rich that you can forget all your years in the service? All the men you worked with, side by side, the ones you're betraying right now?"

"I gave it lots of thought, Stephens." Culpepper's face was red but the lines of determination around his mouth hadn't softened. "There're plenty of things I want to do and places I want to see. I couldn't do it on a federal marshal's pay."

"Yeah, but once your payoff on this job is gone, you'll have to do another dirty job. What's that going to get you but a lifetime of looking over your shoulder." Steadily, keeping his eyes on Culpepper, Grant inched toward Beth and the table loaded with weapons. Inwardly he thanked the powers that be that Rogers, from his position on the bed, couldn't see what he was doing. Just a little bit more...

"I've got it all planned." Culpepper warmed to the subject. "I'm gonna buy a cabin in Canada and use it as a retreat, between travel and jobs, of course. It'll work. I'll make it work."

"Nope." Grant smiled only with his lips. "You'll be dead or in jail in a matter of hours if you kill me or Mrs. Stephens."

"Mrs. Stephens." Culpepper's attention suddenly swung back to Beth, who had stood, without moving, during the entire exchange.

The brief lapse in attention gave Grant all the opening he needed. Diving for the table, he yelled at Beth, "Get down!"

A shot echoed through the cabin and something inside of Beth snapped, releasing her from the panic-stricken inertia. She lunged for the table and sent it sprawling, guns and knives flying everywhere.

As if from a surrealistic distance, she saw a blossom of red stain the shoulder of Grant's tattered shirt and the next thing she knew, her hand curled around a black revolver that lay on the floor. In the next instant she whirled around, standing up and pointing it at Culpepper, who was stalking toward her. He stopped.

"Drop the gun." He glanced over at Rogers, who lay immobile on the bed. "I'll shoot you before you can even get off a shot."

Beth just stared at him, a curious numbness coming over her. This was the man who had shot Grant. She watched emotionlessly as his mouth moved, but she couldn't hear the words. Her hand tightened around the gun and she took careful aim. It was clear to her now. The man with the creased, weathered face was supposed to be their rescuer, but was, instead, their enemy. She tilted her head curiously, studying him, memorizing him.

"You won't kill me." Culpepper's voice bordered on soothing. His lips quirked as he continued. "I know all about you. You save animals for a living, and as a human being I'm more important than they are. Now put the gun down, and I'll let you stop Grant's bleeding."

He's lying, she thought. *He's going to kill me, too.*

At that moment, Grant's voice, loud and firm, called out, "Culpepper."

Culpepper turned his gun on Grant. Beth reacted. Her fingers squeezed the trigger, the resulting blast ripping through her hand, up her arm and through her entire body. Ears ringing as the sound of the shot seemed to multiply in the small room, she watched, horrified as Culpepper staggered toward her. She screamed as his body toppled onto hers.

She waited on the floor for him to shoot her. Strangely, she was calm, almost peaceful. She wanted to tell Grant that she loved him, tell him to take care of New Start, tell him she had always loved him. But it was too late. She knew she wouldn't be able to now.

What must have been seconds but seemed like hours crept by. Beth realized Culpepper wasn't moving. She gingerly pushed his shoulder, and he flopped away from her. She stared at him and knew he was dead. There was blood everywhere, on him, on her, on Grant.

Grant! She crawled over to Grant's still body on the floor. "Grant?"

"He's dead." Rogers smiled slyly from where he was still chained to the bed. "You need to let me go so I can help you."

Dismissing Rogers from her mind, she touched Grant. Pushing the hair away from his face, she tried to clean the blood off with the tips of her fingers. His eyes fluttered open.

"Oh, Grant." She slid his head onto her lap and just held him. "You're alive."

He groaned and shook his head slowly. "Beth?"

"I'm here." Tears slid down her cheeks. She brushed them aside impatiently. "You're all right."

Grant pulled himself up to a sitting position and glanced around. He saw Culpepper's body lying beside her, and then looked at the gun.

"What happened?" He looked into Beth's dazed face and frowned. "Beth, are you okay?" He noticed the blood covering her. "Where are you hurt?" He ran his hands over her body, looking for a wound. She took his hands and brought them to her cheeks and pressed them there. "Beth?"

"Grant, I thought you were dead. You were so still. So still." She kept repeating those words, holding tightly to his hands.

His jaw clenched. She was in shock. He closed his eyes for a minute and breathed deeply, searching for a way to ease her out of this emotional trauma. He'd brought so much turmoil into her life. Now, more than ever, the truth was inescapable. This federal marshal business and Beth didn't mix.

He opened his eyes. This is what he'd done to her, his Beth. Culpepper's blood covered her, and she sat, repeating the words *so still* in a singsong voice. Gently he withdrew his hands from hers.

"Looks like your lady's gone over the edge." Rogers' voice cut into his thoughts.

Grant's head swiveled to coldly meet that one's eyes. "Shut up." He lifted himself up and looked around the floor, strewn with guns and knives. Spotting the two-way radio, he picked it up. Keeping his eyes on Rogers, he called for backup, his ears filled with Beth's soft voice still murmuring . . . his heart bleeding.

Within twenty minutes the cabin was swarming with lawmen of all kinds—the local police, the highway patrol and more federal marshals. Rogers was in custody, demanding his attorney, and Culpepper was zipped into a body bag.

Beth sat quietly, staring at Grant. She had stopped chanting. Her eyes were focused on the crude bandage someone had wrapped around his shoulder to help stop the bleeding.

He ordered the officers around the small cabin, directed the cleanup, demanded explanations and gave his statement. This was Grant in his element, the thrill of the capture, the adrenaline of victory evident in his movements and voice.

Grant studied her surreptitiously while he gave his statement, frowning when he saw her eyes close. She still looked far too exhausted and dazed.

"I've got to get the woman's statement before we can get out of here." Timmons indicated Beth, where she sat on the floor, leaning against the wall.

"It can wait," Grant said tersely, using his influence without a shred of guilt to curtail Beth's ordeal. "I'll bring her in tomorrow and she can give you a statement then."

Timmons nodded, shut his notebook and spoke before he left them. "I'll probably be at the station all night, so I'll be waiting for you."

Grant barely heard him. He turned to Beth. "It's time for us to go."

Beth showed no signs that she understood. Grant cursed under his breath. "Beth." He spoke softly. "You need to come with me. I'm taking you home."

"Home?" She faced Grant, tilting her head, questioning.

"Yes, home."

Grant got her there with no words exchanged between them. She huddled on her side of the car, staring sightlessly out the window. He found a classical music station on the radio, hoping the soothing strains of the violin would erase or at least dim the terror still alive within her.

Tearful hugs and whispered greetings welcomed them home to New Start. Martin Channing, Delores and Shorty listened as Grant, holding Beth in his arms, gave an abbreviated version of what had happened. A scant half hour later, all three left, demanding to know the full details the next day.

The moment the front door closed, Grant turned to Beth. "I need a drink. Do you want one?" He made his way to the corner bar. "How does brandy sound to you?"

"Fine."

He handed her the drink and guided her to the sofa. Sitting down next to her, he encouraged her to sip the brandy.

After a few minutes, he took the drink from her hand and set it on the table next to them. "Beth, I want you to tell me exactly what happened."

She closed her eyes and shook her head.

"It's time, Beth. You need to tell me."

Beth's eyes opened slowly and the blue of her irises stood out startlingly against the whiteness of her skin. She glanced at him, shuddering. "I don't want to talk about it."

Unable to control himself, his heart aching, he pulled her into his arms and just held her, giving her his comfort and strength. He waited until he felt her relax and then coaxed her. She had to talk about it or it would fester within her. "Just start with what happened when we returned to the motel."

Beth recounted her memory of the events in a clear voice until she got to the part about Culpepper. She stumbled over her explanation and stopped when she got to the part of Culpepper falling on her. Grant held her tighter and then whispered, "Who shot him?"

Beth leaned back and looked at him questioningly. "What?"

Grant pressed. "Beth, who shot him?" He anchored her with his arms, hoping his presence would break through the veil of unreality she'd cloaked herself in.

"I don't know." Her voice, shaky and unstable, cracked.

He shook his head, wishing he could spare her this, but knowing he couldn't. If nothing else, she would have to give a statement soon, in front of many others. She had to be prepared. "I was on the floor, Beth. What happened next?"

"You moved. I saw you move. Then he came toward me and..."

Grant urged her on. "And what, Beth?"

She talked quickly. "I shot him to keep him from hurting you."

He hugged her to him and rocked her. "Think back for a minute. Can you see what I did?"

"You?" Her eyes were glassy but then they sharpened. "You had a gun, too... you shot Culpepper, too."

"That's it. *I* killed him, Beth, not you. We found the bullet from your handgun in the wall on the other side of the motel room. *You didn't kill anyone.*"

She seemed satisfied for a moment and then her eyes fogged over again. "But I would have to protect you."

Grant swallowed his rage, keeping it from her. He had done this to her and he knew it would take a long time for her to get beyond this trauma.

"It's all right," he said rocking her gently. "You're safe now. You won't ever have to do that again."

Beth stayed sheltered in his arms, her head pressed into his shoulder. She didn't cry; she just shook. Grant soothed her, rubbing her back with a slow, circular motion and murmuring reassuring words into her ear.

He continued holding her until the tremors of her body stopped and she could take a deep breath. When he felt her relax, he took her face in his hands and looked deeply into her eyes.

"Forgive me for doing this to you," he whispered. Tenderly he kissed her eyelids and cheekbones, and gently brushed her lips. "And thank you for saving my life— again."

Beth sighed. "Oh, Grant, it was my fault you were in danger in the first place."

"Shhh." He picked up her drink. "Here, finish this. After that, you need to take a bath and go to bed."

Her eyes were huge as he tilted the glass to her lips and made her drink.

"Come on," he said as he set the glass down.

He took her arm and propelled her up the stairs and into her bathroom. Before she could get her bearings, he had turned on the jets of water and put her directly under them. In another minute, he'd stripped off her clothing and let the streams of warm water massage her body while he took off his clothes, too.

When they were both naked, he turned to her and gently washed her entire body. His touch wasn't sexual, but comforting, consoling. His fingertips glided over the slick texture of her skin, and Beth leaned into him, allowing him to wash away her tension.

Then she held out her hand. He only hesitated a second before giving her the soap. She performed the same chore for him, running soapy hands over his body, making him moan from the pleasure of it. Her touch was whisper-soft as she cleaned around the bandages on his shoulder and back, careful to keep her body between his and the direct spray of the water so the cloth would remain dry.

Grant couldn't hide his arousal from her, but remained silent. He didn't want to frighten her or have her think he was a jerk for taking advantage at a vulnerable moment. The simple truth was he couldn't be near her without wanting her.

"Hand me the shampoo and I'll wash your hair, too," he said hoarsely.

She smiled innocently, trustingly, into his eyes and stood quietly as he gently washed and rinsed her hair. He shampooed his own hair after he'd finished, inwardly reciting the multiplication table.

Shutting off the faucet, he stepped out onto the plush rug and grabbed a large towel from the rack. Taking Beth's hand, he helped her step out of the shower and then proceeded to rub the fluffy towel firmly against her skin, hoping to warm her in this way, too. Next he wrapped a terrycloth robe around her and set her in front of her vanity, brushing out her honey-toned hair. Fastening a towel at his waist, he then led her to the bed. After tucking her between the smooth sheets, he went downstairs and retrieved two fresh snifters of brandy.

"Here. Drink this. It'll make you sleep."

Beth sipped the strong liquor before looking up at him. "Will you sleep with me?"

Grant smiled. "I've been waiting for that invitation." He took a sip from his glass and then set the drink on the nightstand. "I don't own any pajamas. Does Red have some I can wear?"

"You don't need anything," she said. Sitting, she peeled off her robe, shifted to get it off and then let it fall to the floor.

"Beth—"

"It's all right. I just want to fall asleep curled in your arms. I don't want to ask for anything from you." Her eyes suddenly filled with tears.

"Beth," he whispered.

Pausing only to whip off the towel, Grant slid between the sheets and gathered her close. She laid her head on his chest and let the crying wrack her slender frame. Grant held her tightly and kissed the top of her head and smelled the fragrance of her shampoo, rich in his nostrils. Crying was probably the best thing she could do right now. She hadn't shown any emotion in this entire frightening scenario. He hoped each teardrop washed clean a different area of her emotional storehouse.

He spoke softly to her, murmuring words of encouragement and understanding. Finally the torrent subsided and nothing was left of her cathartic cry but great hiccuping gulps of air. Grant relaxed his hold on her and moved one hand to splay across the curve of her buttocks, the other slowly tracing a circle on the smooth expanse of her back. In moments, the evenness of her breathing told him she was asleep.

Unable to stop the path of his thoughts, he worried what would have happened to her if Louie Rogers had gotten to her with his knife. What would have happened if Culpepper hadn't hesitated to shoot her? His body tensed and, almost in answer, she stirred in her slumber.

His arms tightened around her as he thought what would happen after he testified at the trial. Now Beth might well be dragged into the whole thing. He swore out loud. He had tried to work it so she wouldn't have to appear in court, after all, he'd been an eyewitness to everything she'd seen. Her sworn statement would have to be enough.

He was kidding himself. Yes, he was worried about her testifying, but that wasn't the problem. She could handle the trial as well as he could. No, what was really making his belly feel like it was filled with hot coals was the decision he'd made about their future. When the trial was over, he wouldn't come back to New Start.

There was no way in hell he would put her through another episode like the one they'd just been through. And in his life, he was all too aware that it could happen again.

He loved her. Yes, he loved her with every fiber of his being... and so he'd made up his mind.

To keep her safe, he would leave her.

Chapter 15

He'd rather be anywhere but here. Grant grimaced at the words, remembering he'd thought the same thing the day the will had been read. Only this time it was different. This time he wanted to be anywhere else but the present locale because he was going in to tell Beth that after the trial they would never see each other again. And it was for her own good.

He wouldn't be here at all if Beth hadn't demanded it. She'd told the federal marshals charged with her welfare that she would march out of this safe house in Joplin, Missouri, unless he came to see her. So he was here.

Grant admitted to himself he'd rather face a thousand Culpeppers or Louie Rogers than face the woman he loved. Yes he loved her, had always loved her and would always love her. That didn't change the facts, though. And the facts said they couldn't make a life together because he couldn't guarantee what had happened to her this time wouldn't happen to her again. He would rather live in his own personal private hell than put her in jeopardy again.

Slowly he walked up to the door of the house, feeling like a man going to his own funeral.

"Just the card I needed."

The young deputy, John Parker, smiled at Beth and picked up the jack of clubs she'd just discarded.

In the past few weeks, Beth had quizzed him about the trial and everything surrounding it. Her mind was healing every day, the trauma and turmoil it had been through disappearing slowly but surely.

"You're too good to me." Beth smiled back at Parker. He was a cheerful presence in the boring, sterile world where she'd been hidden for weeks. But even as she smiled at him, he glanced up at the door behind her and his expression sobered. Fearful, Beth turned to find Grant's body filling the doorway.

At a quick nod from Grant, John threw down his cards and told Beth, "I need to check with the fellows outside." He hurried past Grant.

For several seconds no one spoke. Grant's eyes burned into hers, and Beth had the feeling Grant was memorizing every detail about her. The thought left her with a sinking feeling in her stomach.

"It's over." His voice was flat.

"Over?"

"You won't have to testify at the trial. Anderson copped a plea. He's agreed to blow the whistle on his bosses in exchange for a reduced sentence."

She nodded and the silence stretched taut between them.

Finally Beth stood up and moved toward him. He stopped her with his raised hand. "As soon as we clear up a bit of paperwork, you'll be free to go back to New Start."

When she remained silent, he turned to go.

"Grant...what about us?"

Shrugging his shoulders, he remained with his back to her. "There is no 'us.' You'll go back to New Start, and I'll go back to my life."

Beth took a step back, hurt by his coldness, his unfeeling attitude. "So I'll lose New Start?"

Grant turned then and faced her, his words abrupt and to the point. "No. Shorty and I have talked. I can establish residency and meet the terms of the will. You'll get New Start."

Her eyebrows raised. "If it was that easy, why didn't we do it before?"

"It wasn't easy, but the terms of the will can be bent, if not broken, if there are life-threatening circumstances. With my job and...what's happened with Rogers, Shorty was able to work out everything."

"So you and Shorty worked everything out without consulting me, is that right?" Beth's voice shook.

"Beth." He stepped forward, but this time she was the one to retreat. "I wanted to make sure it would work before I told you."

She took a deep breath and raised her chin. "Are you so anxious to be away from me?"

He shook his head and she read a sadness deep in his eyes. "It can't work between us, Beth."

"Anything can work if two people love each other." She turned away from him. "And I love you."

Grant closed his eyes, hoping it would seal his ears, as well. He'd known it in his soul, in his heart. *She loved him.* Now that it was out, he couldn't pretend anymore. He fought saying the words, knowing they would solve nothing, that they would only hurt her more when he left.

"I can't put you into danger again. My life is always like this—the guns, the danger. Rogers is the type of person I

deal with all the time. I won't put you in the path of someone like that again. You'd always be a target."

"Shouldn't I have some say in this?"

He grimaced, hardening his features. "No. I've already
decided. I can't live with the constant worry that something
could happen to you." He turned to the door. "Go back to
New Start. It's where you belong."

"Grant." Her voice was a breathless plea.

He turned back and hesitated for a moment before grab-
bing her and crushing his lips against hers. He took; she
gave. She took; he gave. Passion, hurt and love mixed together to rob them of their sense of reason. As quickly as it
had begun, though, it ended. Grant released her and spun
on his heel. The door banged closed behind him with
frightening finality.

Two weeks later, Beth stood talking to Shorty Bonds in
her study. "I don't understand. What are you trying to tell
me, Shorty?" she asked, staring at her lawyer.

"I've discovered who the anonymous donor is—the person who's been so generous the last two months." Shorty
ran a finger around his collar and wiped his brow with a
freshly laundered handkerchief.

"Is it Grant?" she asked hopefully.

Shorty sighed. "No."

"Who then?"

"Your father."

"I don't believe you."

"Look." He pointed to the spreadsheet on the blue screen
of the computer. "I traced it down, for tax purposes, and
frankly, because I thought it might be Grant, too." He indicated several deposit entries under the name Central Texas
Savings. Beth recognized the name of one of her father's
businesses. "It really is your father."

"I'll be damned."

"Now, Beth, don't go off and have a fit. We really need the money. It's enabled us to do a lot of things we couldn't have done otherwise."

"I'm not going to have a fit." She chuckled. "I'm going to thank him."

"What?"

"I'm not a young, naive girl anymore, Shorty. The last few months have changed that. I want New Start to be a success. Red and I started it, now it's mine, and I *will* make smart business decisions to keep it running. If my father wants to donate money, so be it. I'm going to take every opportunity life hands me, because a person doesn't always get what she wants."

She drove to her father's office, parked her truck and tiptoed past his secretary with her fingers to her lips. She entered his room without warning.

"Beth, why didn't you tell me you were coming?" Her father stood behind his desk. "I would have canceled a lunch date to eat with you."

He came around the corner of his desk and hugged her.

"I found out something today I needed to share with you." She looked him straight in the eye. "I know you're the one who's been giving the money to New Start."

Her father's movements stilled. "Now, Beth, I know you didn't want any of my money—I've tried often enough to give you some, and you wouldn't accept it—but when I watched you on that place with those animals, I knew you belonged there. I tried every other way I could to help, but you wanted to be independent so badly, you refused. You were going to lose New Start."

Beth gazed solemnly at her father.

"You can be angry at me if you want, but I did it because I love you, and I want you to be happy." He laid his hands on her arms. "And, honestly, ever since the trial, you've been so sad. I just didn't want you to lose your dream.''

She stared at him, his words ringing in her ears. He was right. The past two months, she'd been existing in a haze. Oh, she worked, she joined friends for dinner, she made polite conversation, but she no longer felt as if she were a part of the world. She'd tried to contact Grant twice, but both times his answering machine had been on and he hadn't returned the calls.

"Daddy, I'm not here to give your money back or to fuss at you, I'm here to thank you for helping make my dream come true. With your money, New Start is operating in the black.'' She smiled at him. "We won't need any more of your money, though. We're going to make it.'' She moved into the circle of his arms and hugged him. "Thank you.''

"And another thing, honey.''

She looked up expectantly.

"I'm so damn proud of you.''

They both laughed and hugged each other again. Then Martin Channing held her at arm's length. "What about Grant?''

She lowered her eyes. "What about him?''

"Have you talked to him since you got back from Missouri?''

"No.'' She turned away. "I don't want to talk about him. He's a part of the past.''

Her father moved over to the window behind his desk, staring out for several minutes. Then the corners of his mouth quirked in a self-derisive smile. "I can't believe I'm saying this, but I think you should go see him.''

She flopped down in the extra red leather chair in front of his desk. "Daddy, Grant made it perfectly clear he didn't want to see me ever again.''

"Since when do you listen to stubborn men?''

She smiled. "I don't know.''

Her father sighed and situated himself in the big chair behind his desk. "This isn't easy for me, but I have to make a confession."

Beth raised her eyebrows but kept silent.

"I promised your mother that I would always make the right choices for you, but what I didn't understand was that as you grew up, you didn't need me to make your decisions." He rubbed his temples with the tips of his fingers. "As you know, I never liked Grant, never thought he would amount to anything. I just couldn't see you living life with a small-town sheriff."

"I know all of this, Daddy. It's okay now. It's history."

Martin stared at his only child for long minutes. "You were always naive, baby. There's more to this than you think." He took a deep breath. "Remember when you came to me at the end of your first year of marriage to Grant and asked for money?"

Beth lowered her eyes. "Yes," she whispered. "It was the most foolish thing I've ever done. That broke up my marriage to Grant."

"Not really."

Beth's eyes flew to her father's. "What?"

"Oh, sure, he was angry when he found out, but then you started to work things out. You told me that you and Grant loved each other enough to make your marriage work, and that you wouldn't ask for my help again."

"That's right, but soon after that Grant became more difficult and obstinate than ever, refusing to listen to me or try to work on our marriage. He... left town as soon as he graduated, and had me served with the divorce papers." Her brows drew together as she puzzled over the swiftness of the events.

"I'm not proud of this, Beth, but I want you to remember that I loved you and wanted you to get what you deserved out of life. I still do." He looked her in the eye. "Ten

years ago, I called Grant to this office after you told me that
your marriage was going to work, and...told him that you'd
come to me for money more than just that once. As I recall," he continued with brutal honesty and self-directed
contempt, "I told him you'd come to me many times."

Beth inhaled sharply.

"This isn't a pretty story, but I have a reason for telling it
now. I...told him that you asked for huge amounts of
money each time. I convinced him that if he really loved
you, he would let you go to find someone who could take
care of you in the style you deserved." He closed his eyes.
"I can be very persuasive."

"I can't believe you did that to me—to Grant."

"I thought you would never be truly happy with him,
sweetheart, but I was wrong. I never dreamed you'd never
forget him, never marry again. I'm sorry I did it, but I'm
trying to set the record straight now."

"Oh, Daddy, we've wasted a lot of years." She closed her
eyes and rubbed her suddenly aching temples with her fingers.

She opened them again and studied her father through
pain-filled eyes. "How could you have done such a cruel
thing?"

"As I said, I thought it was the best thing for you, but I
realize now that I never had a clue what was right for you."

"This was the undercurrent I felt when you and Grant
met again at New Start, wasn't it?" she asked dully, knowing the answer already. She studied her hands as she thought
about what her father had done. He'd always been in the
background, supporting her, even though his help was often misguided. Now he was setting the record straight and
she could only respect...and love him for it. After all these
years he hadn't had to tell her the truth. She raised her eyes
to meet his. "I love you, Daddy."

"Good." Martin looked relieved. "Now what about Grant? Do you love him?"

Beth's eyes wavered from his an instant before she answered. "Yes."

Martin came around and sat on the edge of his desk. "And does he know that?"

She threw her hands in the air in frustration. "Of course he does, but Grant won't let me into his life because he's afraid for me."

"And you're going to accept that?" Martin's voice was colored with incredulity.

"What can I do?" Beth reached out to grasp her father's hands.

"Fight. Fight for him the way you fought for New Start. The way you fought me when you thought I was treating you as if you were a baby."

Beth looked up at her father, considering what he was saying.

"Honey, you're a different person with Grant—all sunshine. Don't let him get away. Go after him."

She jumped up, hugged her father tightly and smiled. "I'll think about it."

Beth stood watching the horses in the corral. She'd made it part of her routine to be there every morning. She enjoyed watching them say hello to the day and frolic with each other.

This morning she was thinking about what her father had said. Fight for Grant? Did she have the strength to go to him, to stand there and let him flay her with his objections, with his logical reasons on why they should be separated? The past months had taught her that she could survive without him, but she couldn't really live without him. Did she want to accept the grayness of her world, or should she go for the sunshine that only Grant could give her? Sure of her decision to seek him out, she turned to go back into the house only to run into the very solid wall of a man's chest.

"Beth." Grant's arms enfolded her and he kissed her, telling her with his body how much he wanted her.

She struggled away from him. "What are you doing here?"

He released her and backed away, looking at her closely. She held her breath as she saw something lurking in the depths of his eyes. Dare she hope it was what she'd been wanting to see for days, months, years? She frowned, afraid to believe.

His voice was edged with roughness and—hurt? "I thought you would be glad to see me. But I see I was mistaken."

Beth grabbed his arm. "No, you weren't mistaken. I'm very glad to see you, Grant. But, but...it hurts me to see you." He closed his eyes then, so she couldn't read any messages there. His voice as he spoke again was low, full of some emotion she couldn't identify.

"You know I've never wanted to hurt you." He was talking slowly, as if he were having trouble finding just the right words. "I know I was the one that said we couldn't build a good relationship and we probably can't, bu—"

She gasped and jumped into the conversation. "Damn you. Don't you come here if all you want is to tell me all over again we can't make it."

"Beth—"

"Shut up and listen. I'm not some toy you can play with when you want to and then just leave behind."

"Beth—"

"And to think I was getting ready to come after you."

"What were you going to do when you came after me?"

She put her hands on her hips and continued in her most dignified voice. "I was going to do whatever it took to make you come around to my way of thinking."

"Anything?" He sucked in air, hoping his heart wouldn't explode with the need that pierced him with her words. His life had been a nightmare since he'd left her. No other woman could make him forget his job, forget his duties, forget who he was like Beth could. He loved her and it gnawed at him every second. He loved her for the person she was, newfound independence and all.

She planted herself more firmly in front of him, challenging him with her answer, "Yes, anything."

God, she was beautiful. Her honey-gold hair was loose and curling around her shoulders, her eyes were clear as the Caribbean, and that bottom lip—it begged for his mouth. He grabbed her and said, "Even if that means marrying me?"

"What?" She narrowed her eyes and studied him.

"Hey, you said anything. I thought you were serious."

"I am." Tilting her head to the side, she asked, "Are you?"

"Yes, ma'am." His face was somber, and he watched her closely.

"Then . . . yes," she answered simply.

Grant's face beamed and he lifted her up, spinning her around.

"Hey, put me down. I've still got some questions for you."

"All the answers are 'yes.'" He set her down but didn't stop grinning.

"Grant, I'm serious. Why will this work *now* and not before?"

"Before you so rudely interrupted me about sixty seconds ago, I was trying to tell you that I don't know for sure if it will work, but that I'm going to give it a helluva try." His voice dropped. "What if I told you I'd quit my job?" His eyes were unreadable now.

A jet of hope shot through her breast. "What?"

"I've turned in my resignation. After this month, I won't be a federal marshal anymore."

"But, Grant, you've always wanted to be in law enforcement. You're at the top, now. You'll miss it." She searched his face, trying to judge his true feelings. "Why didn't you tell me this when you first arrived?"

"If you'll recall, Mrs. Stephens, you've been doing most of the talking." His grin widened wickedly. "You've said some very interesting things, too."

She blushed as she studied the rugged planes of his face. "Will you miss the life of a marshal?"

"Yeah, I'll miss it for a while, but I won't miss getting shot at, beat up or worrying about other people." His gaze traveled the length of her body.

Hope continued to burgeon in her. "What will you do?"

"I don't know." His eyelashes swept down to partially cover his eyes. "Do you have any suggestions?"

She glanced at her fingernails. "We could always use some help at New Start."

"Really. Can't handle Studmuffin?"

"Grant?"

He opened his arms. "Come here." She went to him. "God, you feel so good." He tightened his arms around her.

She leaned her head back to look up into his face. "Are you sure about this?"

"I may be a hardheaded bastard and like to do things my own way, but I've figured out how much I love you and that I can't live without you. So, yes, I'm damned sure."

She laughed throatily and squeezed him tightly. "I just so happen to love hardheaded bastards. They're my favorite kind of man." Then her smile faded. "My father told me what happened years ago, Grant. How he convinced you to divorce me. He's not proud of this, but he lied to you. I only went to him that once, Grant."

She felt his body tense. Before he could respond, she rushed on. "He loves me. He thought he was doing what was best for me." She ran her fingertips over the frown lines on his forehead, smoothing them. "The two of you need to get together soon and put this to rest."

Grant nodded slowly. Somehow he'd known Beth couldn't have had such little faith in him, that she'd turn to her father and not to him. His own insecurities had blinded him, though. As for Martin Channing—somehow he couldn't really blame him for what he'd done. He'd been protecting the woman they both loved. Putting it all behind him, he fastened his arms around Beth and picked her up so that her face was level with his. "You're all I ever wanted. I love you, Beth, and I'll always need you."

She wove her fingers through his hair and pulled him close. "I love you."

They smiled at each other before they kissed, sealing their love for eternity.

*   *   *   *   *

For all those readers who've been looking for something a little bit different, a little bit spooky, let Silhouette Books take you on a journey to the dark side of love with

If you like your romance mixed with a hint of danger, a taste of something eerie and wild, you'll love Shadows. This new line will send a shiver down your spine and make your heart beat faster. It's full of romance and more—and some of your favorite authors will be featured right from the start. Look for our four launch titles wherever books are sold, because you won't want to miss a single one.

THE LAST CAVALIER—Heather Graham Pozzessere
WHO IS DEBORAH?—Elise Title
STRANGER IN THE MIST—Lee Karr
SWAMP SECRETS—Carla Cassidy

After that, look for two books every month, and prepare to tremble with fear—and passion.

SILHOUETTE SHADOWS, coming your way in March.

SHAD1

Take 4 bestselling love stories FREE
Plus get a FREE surprise gift!

INTIMATE MOMENTS®

Silhouette®

CONARD COUNTY CONTINUES...

Come back to Conard County, Wyoming, where you'll meet men and women whose lives are as dramatic as the landscape around them. Join author Rachel Lee for the third book in her fabulous series, MISS EMMALINE AND THE ARCHANGEL (IM #482). Meet Emmaline Conard, "Miss Emma," a woman who was cruelly tormented years ago and now is being victimized again. But this time sheriff's investigator Gage Dalton—the man they call hell's own archangel—is there to protect her. But who will protect Gage from his feelings for Emma? Look for their story in March, only from Silhouette Intimate Moments.

To order your copy of MISS EMMALINE AND THE ARCHANGEL, or the first two Conard County titles, EXILE'S END (IM #449) and CHEROKEE THUNDER (IM #463), please send your name, address, zip or postal code, along with a check or money order (do not send cash) for $3.39 for each book ordered, plus 75¢ postage and handling ($1.00 in Canada), payable to Silhouette Books, to:

In the U.S.

Silhouette Books
3010 Walden Avenue
P.O. Box 1396
Buffalo, NY 14269-1396

In Canada

Silhouette Books
P.O. Box 609
Fort Erie, Ontario
L2A 5X3

Please specify book title(s) with your order.
Canadian residents add applicable federal and provincial taxes.

CON3